Thursday, December 8, 1960

Nick and Carter are jetting across the Atlantic to the island of Capri for the funeral of the Dowager Duchess of Boston. On the way, they're dropping off Marnie and her husband, Alex, so the two can spend a relaxing few days in Paris.

When they arrive in Europe, Nick and Carter receive a distressing message. Paul Vermaut, their good friend from the Congo, is sick with a mysterious disease that has the doctors baffled. He's been on the run from the Congolese civil war, traveling thousands of miles over land, and is now hospitalized in Salisbury, the capital of Southern Rhodesia.

Right after the funeral, Nick and Carter fly south to get Paul and bring him back to the States and, hopefully, back to health.

Once they land in Salisbury, they discover Paul is dying and his lover from the Congo, Freddie Nyemba, has likely been arrested by the police for being on the grounds of the hospital illegally in an area reserved for Europeans without a pass, something required for all Africans in the British colony.

Nick and Carter have to come up with a plan to sneak Freddie out of Southern Rhodesia and into the U.S. without getting caught.

If they fail, he'll be deported to a land he loves but thrust back into the middle of a civil war he wants no part of...

The Roving Refugee

Nick Williams Mysteries

The Unexpected Heiress

The Amorous Attorney

The Sartorial Senator

The Laconic Lumberjack

The Perplexed Pumpkin

The Savage Son

The Mangled Mobster

The Iniquitous Investigator

The Voluptuous Vixen

The Timid Traitor

The Sodden Sailor

The Excluded Exile

The Paradoxical Parent

The Pitiful Player

The Childish Churl

The Rotten Rancher

A Happy Holiday

The Adroit Alien

The Leaping Lord

The Constant Caprese

The Shameless Sodomite

The Harried Husband

The Stymied Star

The Roving Refugee

Nick & Carter Stories

An Enchanted Beginning

Golden Gate Love Stories

The One He Waited For

Their Own Hidden Island

The Roving Refugee

A Nick Williams Mystery

Book 24

By Frank W. Butterfield

Published With Delight

By The Author

MMXVIII

The Roving Refugee

Copyright © 2018 by Frank W. Butterfield.

All rights reserved.

ISBN-10: 1723736600
ISBN-13: 978-1723736605

First publication: September 2018

No part of this book shall be reproduced, stored in a retrieval system, or transmitted by any means–electronic, mechanical, photocopying, recording, or otherwise–without written permission from the publisher.

Brief excerpts for the purpose of review are permitted.

This book contains explicit language and suggestive situations.

This is a work of fiction that refers to historical figures, locales, and events, along with many completely fictional ones. The primary characters are utterly fictional and do not resemble anyone that I have ever met or known of.

Be the first to know about new releases:

frankwbutterfield.com

NW23-B-20180915

Contents

Chapter 1..1

Chapter 2..13

Chapter 3..27

Chapter 4..41

Chapter 5..53

Chapter 6..65

Chapter 7..75

Chapter 8..93

Chapter 9..101

Chapter 10..111

Chapter 11..115

Chapter 12..125

Chapter 13...135

Chapter 14...141

Chapter 15...145

Chapter 16...155

Chapter 17...163

Chapter 18...171

Chapter 19...181

Chapter 20...187

Chapter 21...193

Chapter 22...215

Chapter 23...229

Chapter 24...237

Epilogue..243

Author's Note..261

Acknowledgments....................................262

Historical Notes..265

Credits..271

More Information.....................................273

Roving

\\'rō-viŋ\

1. a. Not restricted as to location or area of concern.
   b. Capable of being shifted from place to place.
2. Inclined to ramble or stray.

Refugee

\ˌre-fyu̇-ˈjē , ˈre-fyu̇-ˌjē\

1. A person who flees to a foreign country or power to escape danger or persecution.

Chapter 1

Idlewild Airport
Queens, N.Y.
Thursday, December 8, 1960
A few minutes before 6 in the evening

"Mr. Williams?"

I looked up and saw a young man of about 30 who was dressed in a nice brown suit with a blue overcoat and fur-trimmed collar. He was holding a brown briefcase in his left hand and peering at me through thick black glasses.

I stopped and asked, "Yeah?"

He smiled earnestly and raised his eyebrows. "Mr. Nicholas Williams of San Francisco?"

I nodded. "Yeah." We had just arrived in New York on T.W.A. flight 42 from San Francisco and were on our way to the private terminal to catch our next flight which was on a Comet jet I owned.

He offered his hand, which I shook, and said, "My

name is Terrence Myers and I'm so glad I caught you."

"What's going on, Nick?" That was Carter Jones, my tall, muscled ex-fireman of a husband. He walked up and, putting his hand on my neck, guided me out of the flow of traffic and next to a window that looked out over the tarmac. The kid followed us.

Offering his hand, he asked, "Mr. Jones?"

Carter nodded and shook. "And you are?"

The man swallowed hard and said, "I'm Terrence Myers and I'm from the Treasury Department and I need to talk to Mr. Williams. It won't take long."

"Nick?" That was Marnie LeBeau, my stepsister and the best secretary a guy could ever want. She walked up next to me and looked at Mr. Myers with a frown on her face.

He grinned at her. "Mrs. LeBeau?"

"Yes?"

He offered his hand to her. "I'm Terrence Myers and they told me you would be here."

"Who told you?"

"Mr. Young at Bank of America."

She nodded and then glanced over at Alex, her husband, who walked up and frowned. He asked, "What's all this about?"

Mr. Myers looked around. Using his briefcase, he pointed to a small cocktail lounge. "I just need ten minutes of Mr. Williams's time. Could we go in there?"

I said, "Sure," and led the way.

. . .

Once the five of us were settled at a table in the back, Alex asked, "Who wants what?"

Marnie said, "Beer."

Carter nodded. "Me too."

I grinned. "Me three."

"Mr. Myers?" asked Alex.

"No, thanks, I'm technically on the clock."

"Coke? Coffee?" asked Alex.

Mr. Myers looked up. "Any kind of soda pop would be fine. Thanks."

Alex nodded and headed over to the bar.

Marnie jumped right in and asked, "What's this all about?"

Mr. Myers reached into his inner coat pocket and pulled out a small wallet. He opened it up and showed it to me. "First things, first. This is my official identification."

I looked at it. The picture was him all right. His name was Terrence Alan Myers and he worked for the Department of the Treasury in Washington, D.C.

I nodded. "OK. How can I help you?"

He grinned. "You really can, as a matter of fact. You can help the whole country, to be honest." He sat on that last sentence expectantly as if he'd just handed me a big juicy steak and was waiting for me to tell him how delicious it was.

Having no idea what he was talking about, I asked, "How so?"

His face took on a serious expression. "I'm sure you're aware of the gold crisis we're having right now."

I shrugged. "I read something about it. Why?"

"Well, Mr. Williams, my boss was given the job of reaching out to every American citizen who can help us keep gold from leaving the country. After the big surge in prices in the last couple of months, our gold reserves are hitting the limit."

"What does that mean?" asked Carter.

"Well, it means that more gold is leaving the country than we can sustain. I explained this all to Mr. Young and he suggested I could catch you here at Idlewild before you leave for Europe so I took the train up and I'm sure glad I made it in time."

I was confused. "But we're not taking any gold out of the country with us."

The kid pursed his lips for a moment. "But you are, Mr. Williams, and you probably don't realize it. That's why I'm here."

Carter held up his hand. "Wait. Why were you talking to Nick's trust manager at Bank of America?"

Mr. Myers grinned. "Because that's where the leak, so to speak, is happening. You see, every month, Mr. Young transfers five hundred thousand dollars to the *Credit Suisse* in Zurich. The bank in Zurich converts the dollars to Swiss francs and, when they do that, another half a million worth of gold has to be set aside by us to credit the Swiss. Make sense?"

Her eyes wide, Marnie looked at me. "Are you really doing that?"

I nodded. "I've been doing that since '55 or so."

Her eyes widened even more. "There must be a lot of money in that account."

"Yeah," I said without saying more. I had no idea how much was there.

Carter asked, "Are you saying, Mr. Myers, that this is illegal?"

The kid shook his head amiably. "Oh, no. It's all quite legal. We get a little report from the Bank of America every month." He looked at me. "Of course, we can't ask you to repatriate the funds, although that would be best."

"What does that mean?" asked Marnie.

"Bring the money back into the United States," replied Mr. Myers. He frowned. "It would be taxed again." I knew that. Mr. Young had explained it to me when I'd first started moving the money.

Marnie looked at me. "I don't understand why you're doing this."

Right then, Alex arrived with the drinks. Once those were passed out, Marnie turned to him and explained, "This man is from the Treasury Department. We're talking about the half million that Nick moves to Switzerland every month. It has something to do with gold."

Alex was in mid-sip when Marnie mentioned the amount. He stopped and looked at me for a long moment. I couldn't tell if he was jealous, confused, or upset that I was probably ruining the banking system.

I said, "I was just about to explain to Marnie why."

Alex said, "Probably in case you have to leave the country. Like you did five years ago."

I nodded. "You got it in one."

Mr. Myers leaned forward and whispered, "Is it because you're a homosexual, Mr. Williams?"

As soon as he said that, several things happened at once. Carter, who was taking a gulp of his beer right then, spewed it, hitting Marnie in the face. She squealed and Alex jumped up. As he did so, he knocked over the table which meant all our drinks went crashing to the tile floor with every one of the glasses breaking amid the loud gasps from the other patrons.

...

Once we were cleaned up, I looked at Mr. Myers and said, "To answer your question, yes, that's why. You probably know that Mr. Hoover doesn't like me very much."

He sighed and looked at his briefcase which was on his lap. "Yes, I know. That's why I'm here, in fact."

Carter asked, "Because of J. Edgar Hoover?"

"Oh, no! I'm here because..." He lowered his voice. "I'm a homosexual and I wanted to meet you both so I asked my boss to send me here today."

Right then, Marnie returned from the ladies room. We all stood, carefully, as she took a seat. I asked, "All better, doll?"

She grinned at me and then made a show of pretending to slap Carter on the arm. "I'm fine. I came armed with all the make-up I could need so it's all OK."

Carter frowned slightly. "I'm sorry, Marnie."

She shrugged. "It's fine, Carter. You might have to buy me a new dress in Paris, though."

Mr. Myers cleared his throat. "It would be nice if you folks wouldn't spend too much money in Europe. Every dollar spent abroad is more gold we lose."

Carter cleared his throat and, somehow, managed not to roll his eyes. "I promise to use the francs we already have in our bank in France."

The kid nodded with a grin. "Oh, that would be swell, Mr. Jones."

Marnie looked at her watch and then at me. "The plane is supposed to leave in an hour. Gustav must be wondering where we are." Gustav was our butler and valet. Once our flight had landed, he and Ferdinand, our gardener and ersatz chauffeur, had dashed ahead of us to take care of getting the luggage transferred to the Comet jet that would be flying us to Paris overnight and then on to Naples.

Mr. Myers nodded. "Sorry about taking so much of your valuable time. I was just hoping you could help us."

"In what way?" asked Carter.

The kid frowned for a moment and then giggled. "Oh! I'm so sorry! If you could stop transferring money out of the country, that would be a big help."

I was still confused. "That's fine. We have plenty to live on if we need to but why talk to me?"

"Mr. Young said he needed your permission to stop the transfers."

I nodded. "Yeah, OK, I get that." I looked around the lounge. "But why come to me about this? I'm sure there are other people and companies who do the same thing."

Mr. Myers shook his head earnestly. "No, Mr. Williams. According to our reports, you're the individual who's taking the most money out of the country right now. You're at the top of the list. So, if you could hold off for a while, until this all gets straightened out, that would be great."

I nodded, feeling slightly embarrassed, and said, "OK, I will."

. . .

"Well, what do you think?" That was me. We were about half an hour out of New York. I'd plopped down next to Alex while Marnie was a couple of rows back talking to Gustav. I knew Alex had wanted to fly on the Comet. When I'd invited him and Marnie to go with us on the trip, he'd specifically asked me whether we would be taking the jet and had been excited when I'd told him we would.

He grinned. "It's amazing. The T.W.A. 707 was great but, somehow, this is quieter."

"Do you want to go up and see the cockpit?"

His eyes widened like a kid being handed the keys to his first car. "Could I?"

"I'll check with Captain Clement and let you know."

"Thanks, Nick."

I smiled and stood. "You're welcome. I'm glad you two came with us. Did they give you any hassle at work for taking the time off?"

Alex's smile faded. He leaned forward and asked, "Can we talk in private?"

"Sure. The bedroom cabin behind the galley is for you and Marnie, if you want to use it. How about we go in there?"

Alex rubbed his hands together nervously. "OK." He stood and I backed up to let him out.

I followed him as he moved aft down the aisle. When we passed Marnie and Gustav, she glanced at him and then at me. She was obviously worried. I wondered what that was about.

...

"I have a problem and Marnie doesn't really want me to talk to you about it and I'm not sure I want to but I'm going to even though I know what you're gonna do but I don't want you to do it." He was standing by one of the windows and looking out at the blinking light at the end of the wing. He kept rubbing his hands together.

I stood by the door and watched and waited.

A few seconds passed before he spoke again. "Nick, I need a job."

I cautiously replied, "OK."

Alex exploded. "See! I knew you would say that!" His eyes were red and his face was flushed. I'd never seen him get angry before.

I tried not to laugh. Running my hand over my mouth to erase any trace of a smile, I said, "What's going on?"

He plopped down on the edge of the bed. "They fired me."

"Why?"

He looked up at me and then down at the floor again. "Because you're my brother-in-law."

I sighed and crossed my arms. "I'm sorry to hear that, Alex. I really am." Alex had been in the public relations business although he rarely talked about his work.

He nodded and stretched his legs out. As I watched and waited, he seemed to be trying to make up his mind about something. Finally, he said, "You know, the last time Marnie and I went to Paris, we flew on a prop plane and had to stop in Canada and Ireland before we got to Paris. Isn't that something?"

I nodded and replied, "The first time we flew this jet, we had to do the same thing. But now we have the newest Rolls-Royce engines and we can make it in two hops. We have to stop in Ireland first before we get to Paris."

He looked out one of the windows.

After nearly a minute, he turned and looked up at me. "Did you really have a crush on me back at St. Ignatius?" That was the high school we'd both attended. He had been on the swim team and was a kind of "big man on campus." I'd dropped out before graduating. I'd finally gotten my equivalency certificate at the beginning of November.

I grinned at him. "Yeah, but what's really on your mind, Alex?"

He looked out the window again and rubbed his hands on his trousers for a long moment. He then sighed and asked, "Do you have a job for me somewhere?" He added hopefully, "I could do public relations for your hotels."

I nodded. "You'd be welcome to work anywhere you want, Alex. Like I've said before, you're family. But I have a better idea."

He frowned and said, "I don't think I'd make a good private investigator."

I laughed. "You might be surprised but that wasn't my idea. What if I staked you to your own public relations firm?"

His eyes widened in surprise. "I, uh, well..."

"You're not doing a very good job at your own P.R. right now, Alex."

That made him laugh and relax. He stood and stretched. "I guess I'm nervous about talking to you about personal stuff, Nick." He leaned against the wall and crossed his arms. "I feel like I'm interviewing for a job in my underwear."

I smiled. "You got the job, Alex." I suddenly had a thought. "Although you don't need one, do you?"

He started and looked at me, his eyes narrowing slightly. "What do you mean?"

"I mean that you have the money my father settled on you and Marnie."

He frowned. "Sure, but that's for the future. I try to never touch that money."

I nodded. "I'm not trying to tell you what to do but maybe you should spend a little of it."

He paled. "I, well, that is to say, Marnie agrees with you."

I grinned. "Good. Then the brother-in-law part of the conversation is over. Back to business. All we need to do is figure out the best way to move forward. What about your own firm?"

He frowned. "But it wouldn't be my own firm, would it? You'd be in the mix somehow."

I was always a little worried with Alex that I was somehow crossing a line with him. I didn't know him very well although I loved the guy a whole heck of a lot because Marnie loved him. Right then I wondered if I shouldn't have brought up the money. Back in '55, my father had named Marnie as his sole heir since I certainly would never need more cash once he passed. At the time, he'd settled half a million on them. I'd always wondered if they'd managed to spend any of it. Now that I knew the answer, I was worried about having asked in the first place. It was possible that I'd made Alex even more upset. But I had no idea and decided to push right on and tell him everything he wanted to know.

I nodded. "You're right. I'm a silent partner in Henry Wilson's engineering and architecture firm. I have the same arrangement with Universal Construction as well."

"That's the company owned by that gal who used to be your neighbor, right?"

I nodded. "Pam Spaulding."

"What about Monumental Studios? Aren't you a silent partner there?"

I shook my head. "Nope. I bought out Ben White a few months ago. He works for me but I don't manage anything. He runs the place."

Alex grinned slightly. "Is it true you're getting into TV? I saw something about a deal for a western for NBC. That so?"

"Yeah. My gut says TV is the future."

Alex chuckled. "Poor Nick. You hate TV. Will you ever watch your own shows?"

I shrugged. "Probably not. I'm sticking to *Perry Mason* for right now. One show a week is plenty."

Alex nodded and turned to look out the window.

"So, we could start off as a partners," I said. "I'll put up the money and take 49 percent ownership. You'll be majority owner and we'll write something into the contract about when you can buy me out and how."

Alex nodded, still looking out the window. "I wouldn't, though. I've seen how everything you touch turns to gold. A 51/49 split is fine by me." He turned to offer his hand.

I shook and, as I did, I noticed he had tears in his eyes. "You OK, Alex?"

He laughed and pulled out his handkerchief. Wiping his eyes, he said, "You know, Marnie once told me about the night you all started Consolidated. She said how she looked out the window on Hartford and couldn't stop crying even though she didn't know why. Now I think I understand."

Chapter 2

Le Bourget Airport
Le Bourget, France
Friday, December 9, 1960
Half past 10 in the morning

After a delay of two hours at the Shannon airport in Ireland because of fog, we finally landed in Paris at just after 10. Marnie, Alex, Gustav, and Ferdinand were getting off there. Marnie and Alex were going to the George V hotel for their vacation. Gustav and Ferdinand were going to check on our house. Marnie had wanted to stay there, but it had been closed up for a while, so I'd suggested they stay at the George V. I didn't tell her, but I wanted to give Gustav and Ferdinand some time off to themselves.

As soon as the French immigration official left, I walked over to Marnie, who was putting on her thick wool coat and pushed a check into her hand.

"What's this?" she asked as she looked at it.

"Walking around money. It's in francs. Take it to any Credit Lyonnaise." I mispronounced the name, of course. "And you can cash it there."

She frowned and then said, "I need to talk to you."

I nodded and followed her to the bedroom she and Alex had shared during the flight. As we walked by Carter, he looked at me. I shrugged and he winked in reply.

Once inside, she closed the door and then handed the check back to me. "You're only making it worse when you do this."

"Making what worse?"

"Alex believes that if we touch any of that money your father settled on us that we'll be eating out of trash cans by the time we're in our 70s."

I laughed. "Marnie, I—"

She narrowed her eyes. "It's no laughing matter, Nick. Alex is cheap and I'm having a hard time with it. But he doesn't seem to mind taking your money."

"But, Marnie—"

She crossed her arms. "Oh, he told me about your plan to set him up in his own P.R. firm. I told him to forget the whole thing. We have plenty of dough for him to work for free for two years or more. You can *hire* his firm, Nick. But I don't want you giving him any more money."

I stepped back. I hadn't seen Marnie that angry since the previous summer when Carter and I had returned to San Francisco without telling anyone we were on our way home. I took a deep breath. "Are you sure?"

She nodded. "And Mother agrees with me and so does your father. And..." She took a deep breath. "So do Alex's parents. But don't tell him they know."

I was pretty sure my eyes were as wide as they could get because Marnie suddenly grinned at me. I held out the check. "But you have to take this."

Her grin faded. "No, I don't."

"Yes, you do. You heard Mr. Myers. Every dollar you spend in France means we owe them more gold."

She snorted and pressed her lips together. Taking the check, she slipped it in her coat pocket. "Fine, but we'll pay you back when we get home."

I nodded. "And I already told the George V to bill my account. They'll do that in francs."

She rolled her eyes. "I suppose I have to let you do that because it's my patriotic duty?"

I grinned at her. "That's right, doll."

She sighed. "Gee, I'm sorry, Nick, but I'm so fed up with Alex right now."

"Well, whatever you two need to work out can wait until we get back to San Francisco. Now you're in Paris and the whole city will be at your feet. Try and have some fun while you're here."

She gave me a hug and whispered, "I'll try. I don't know about Alex."

. . .

"Have fun!" That was Carter. We were both standing at the top of the portable stairs and waving at the four of them as they piled into two taxis. As they drove off, I saw a middle-aged woman emerge from the private terminal building and make her way towards us. A man in a uniform was pushing a small cart that consisted of a suitcase and two small valises.

Carter said, "There's Mrs. Dewey." He and I both dashed down the stairs to greet her.

Mrs. Violet Dewey had been working for us for a little over five years. We'd hired her at the request of Lord Gerald Whitcombe, a real English lord who also ran a secret British intelligence agency we'd never heard the name of. We were on our way to Naples where we would be getting on a boat that would carry us over to the island of Capri. Lord Gerald's mother, the Dowager Duchess of Boston, had died a few days earlier and he'd asked us to attend the funeral.

A couple of days earlier, Mike Robertson, my first lover and best friend who also ran Consolidated Security, the company we owned, had stopped by my office and asked if we could pick up Mrs. Dewey in Paris and take her with us to the funeral and then bring her back to San Francisco.

A lot of the work Mrs. Dewey did for us involved requests that Lord Gerald had made. They mostly involved her checking on things for him in Canada, where Mrs. Dewey had lived for 30 years before her husband died. She did other jobs for us, particularly where a solid middle-aged woman was the best operative, and Mike had been very happy with her work.

As we met halfway between the plane and the terminal, she broke into a smile and offered her hand. I shook and said, "Good to see you, Mrs. Dewey. How are you?"

"Fine, just fine, thank you Mr. Williams. So looking forward to a bit more warmth. I hear it's almost balmy on Capri right now."

Carter offered his hand, which she shook, and then his arm, which she took. As the three of us walked side-by-side, Carter asked, "Did you ever meet the dowager duchess?"

"Oh my, yes. A number of times since I've been working for you, Mr. Jones."

Right then, we arrived at the stairs. Carter said to me, "I'll take care of the luggage."

I nodded and said to Mrs. Dewey, "A very smart lady once told me that a gentleman always goes first on stairs. Is that right?"

Mrs. Dewey laughed. "I'm sure it is, for all I know." She motioned for me to go ahead, so I did. "But, to tell the truth, I was in service when I was young and then met my husband while working in a restaurant in London. Then it was off to the farm in Manitoba so what I know about ladies and gentlemen, I've only learnt in these past few years."

By that time, we were in the cabin of the plane. Juliette, our stewardess, offered to take Mrs. Dewey's coat and asked her if she wanted something to drink.

Mrs. Dewey looked around the plane and took it all in with a single glance. "Thank you, my dear, I'd love a cup of tea, plain if you don't mind."

Juliette smiled and replied, "But, of course, *madame*." She took Mrs. Dewey's coat and hung it up before heading towards the galley.

I asked, "Have you been on this plane before?"

Mrs. Dewey nodded. "Oh, yes. Twice, I believe. But that was when it was all regular seating."

"We had two bedrooms installed a few months ago, added a dining room that can also be an office, and expanded the galley. Now there's only three rows of seats up front. We also took out the front compartment where two rows faced each other." I motioned in that direction and Mrs. Dewey moved forward. "We sit up front for take-off and then move around once we're in flight," I added.

Right then, I heard the cargo hold doors close in the belly of the plane.

Mrs. Dewey asked, "How about this seat for myself?" She was standing next to the second row on the starboard side.

I said, "That's fine. Can I help you with anything?"

She smiled in reply as she took the window seat. "I'm quite fine, Mr. Williams."

"Well, if you'll excuse me, I want to check in with the pilot."

She smoothed out her skirt and nodded. "Of course. When we're aloft, I have a very important message for you."

I nodded and wondered what it could be.

. . .

"As you requested, I have an early lunch set for you at the table, *Monsieur* Williams." That was Juliette. We were about 15 minutes out of Paris. The plane had leveled off and we were on our way to Naples.

I smiled up at her and said, "Thanks. We'll be there in just a minute."

Carter and I both unbuckled our seat belts and stood as she moved to the rear of the plane. Carter stopped by Mrs. Dewey's seat and said, "Nick thought we should go ahead and eat something now. We'll land in Naples in a little over an hour."

Mrs. Dewey stood. "It is just about time for elevenses, so I could stand to have a bite to eat."

Carter led the way with Mrs. Dewey between us. We turned right into the first compartment we came to, which was the room we'd set up with a big round table and six chairs bolted to the floor.

Juliette had laid out three plates on linen place mats. Two other plates piled with half sandwiches of all sorts stood in the middle of the table. Once we were all seated, Juliette walked in and asked about drinks.

Mrs. Dewey put in for another cup of tea, plain, while Carter and I asked for Burgie, our local beer in San Francisco that all of our planes were always stocked with.

"Aren't these all quite lovely?" exclaimed Mrs. Dewey. Reaching out with a gloved hand, she took two sandwiches and put them on her plate.

I said, "I thought we should eat now. When we get to Naples, we'll be met by a couple of cars that will take us to the port where we'll get on our boat and head over to Capri. I wasn't sure if there would be any food between the airport and the island."

Mrs. Dewey smiled. "Will that be the little yacht your Captain O'Reilly has been piloting all over the Med. for the last few years?"

I laughed. "Well, it's really a sailboat, but yeah." Captain Dan O'Reilly and his first mate and lover, John Murphy, had been living on the sailboat for the last three or so years. They'd shuttled tourists around the Mediterranean and had done other little odd jobs for us and Lord Gerald, as well. They had known each other for nearly 40 years but had only been together for the last five.

Carter added, "This is actually the second sailboat. And we've just sold it so this trip back and forth to Capri is the last one. Captain O'Reilly and his first mate will be going home with us when we leave Naples on Monday."

I said, "And, did anyone tell you we'll be spending a few days in Paris before going back home?"

Mrs. Dewey nodded. "Yes, Mr. Robertson briefed me night before last."

I asked, "Where are you coming from?"

She reached for another sandwich. "I've had a nice long month in London." She grinned at me. "I must say that living in London with an expense account is quite an improvement over sharing a bedroom with my sister in what you would call a boarding house."

Carter asked, "Did your sister move to Canada, too?"

"Oh, my. That's been such a long time ago but, sadly, no. I met Mr. Dewey in London and we were married. That was in 1925. We left for Manitoba not long after and had only been there for a year when my sister was murdered."

"I'm sorry," offered Carter.

She nodded. "Thank you, Mr. Jones. It was quite a shock. That was when I first met Lord Gerald. He discovered the murderer and was able to prove how it was done. It was a queer and twisted series of shocking events." She paused and took a deep breath. "Our mother never got over it. I brought her back to Manitoba with me and she lived another two years. I expect it was the winters. We grew up near Christchurch, you see." She glanced at me. "That's on the south coast of England. And, as winters go, it was quite balmy compared to the prairie. Mother and I didn't always see eye-to-eye but I'd just had my second, my Tim, when she passed and it was rather awful, if you don't mind me saying so."

I asked, "How many children do you have?"

"Just the two." She smiled wanly. "My Susan lives in Toronto with her Pete and they have two little ones, both of them just as rambunctious as you can imagine." She wiped her mouth with her napkin. "Susan reminds me so much of my sister, Daisy. They could easily have been twins. She's all Gregory, that's my maiden name, you see, and was never a drop of Dewey. Even my husband thought so." As Mrs. Dewey talked, I could hear her accent becoming more English and less Canadian by the word.

"What about Tim?" asked Carter, helping himself to his fourth or fifth sandwich.

"Ah, well, I'd like to have a talk with you both about Tim." She frowned slightly. "I always thought that the shock of his being born so close to my own mother's dying had a bad effect on him. He's always been so moody." She sniffed. "He's all Dewey. My husband was the happiest of his family and never went a day without telling a joke and laughing long and loud but the rest of the family were just as sour as you could imagine. That's how Tim is."

"Where does he live?" I asked.

"He was in Winnipeg for a while. There was a girl he fancied, or so he said. Then she chucked him over and he moved to Toronto as his sister was there. He's a good uncle, Susan says, and is always happy to help out with her little ones. But she says he's quite unhappy and has no interest in the *opposite sex*." She looked at me with a piercing stare.

"Do you think he might be one of us?" I asked.

"Pardon?"

Carter said, "What Nick's asking is whether you think he's a homosexual."

Mrs. Dewey looked down at her plate for a long moment and didn't reply. Finally, she looked up. "Now, of course, I know who's who and what's what. Lord Gerald gave me your story before asking me to work for you. And I've always been open-minded about these things. Each to his own and so on. But it's different when it's your own child."

Neither of us said anything for a beat or two. Finally, I asked, "Would you like to talk to Carter's mother about this?"

Leaning forward, my husband nodded. "I think she'd be the perfect person."

Mrs. Dewey frowned slightly. "I wouldn't want to intrude into private family matters."

Carter shook his head. "You wouldn't be. When we get back to San Francisco, I'll ask her to take you to lunch. If you'd like, I can ask Lettie, Nick's stepmother, to be there too. You met both of them when my mother got married in 1955."

Mrs. Dewey smiled. "Yes. Such a beautiful wedding it was, too. Thank you for asking me. It made me feel right at home."

"We were glad to have you there," said Carter.

I reached over and touched Mrs. Dewey's arm. "You have to say yes to us. We're both stubborn and, well, Carter's mother is even more stubborn than us." I paused and looked around the table. "Or is it we? More than we?"

Mrs. Dewey laughed. "Us, Mr. Williams. And thank you very much. That's a tremendous relief."

. . .

Once Juliette had cleared away the plates and brought more tea and beer, Mrs. Dewey leaned forward and said, "As I mentioned earlier, Mr. Williams, I have a message for you and it might change your plans."

I nodded and waited.

"I can't say how I know, but we've heard through a contact in Salisbury that Paul Vermaut is in hospital there and quite ill. He's indigent and, until recently, was being cared for in the charity ward."

I blinked a couple of times and then looked at Carter. He was frowning. I asked, "When was the last time you heard from Paul?"

He swallowed hard. "It's been a while. I got a short letter from him from Léopoldville in August, maybe. I've sent him several letters since then but haven't heard back. None of them have been returned, either."

I nodded, feeling a knot forming in my stomach. Paul was a friend of ours. He'd owned a men's clothing store in Léopoldville and went to Carter's gym almost every day. After the rebellion in the Congo following independence, he and Freddie Nyemba, a Congolese man who'd worked for Carter, had taken off upriver to meet

Freddie's family. They were in love and had hoped to be able to hide out from the capital when the rebellion flared up. "Was Freddie still with him?" I asked Carter.

He nodded. "Freddie's family bought the story that they were just friends. But Paul said he wanted to go salvage what he could from his store and his house. Freddie went back to Léopoldville with him to protect him."

Mrs. Dewey said, "I've read the natives were quite vicious with the whites."

I took a deep breath and tried not to get angry. We had missed the rebellion by a few days but we had lived there long enough to know that one was coming and that it would be bad. The Belgians had mistreated the Congolese for a long time and were betting that the transition to independence would be painless. It hadn't been and that came as no surprise to Carter or me.

However, from reading the stories in magazines and newspapers, you would have thought that it was open season on every white man, woman, and child in the Congo. Carter had, on more than one occasion, said the reporting reminded him of the papers in his home state of Georgia and how, when he was growing up there, they had always justified every lynching as being necessary and every perceived attack by Negroes on whites as being something close to the end of the world.

Before I could say anything, Carter jumped in and said, "The situation there is very complex, Mrs. Dewey."

She took the hint, nodded, and subtly changed the subject. "In any event, Mr. Vermaut is in hospital in Salisbury and very ill."

I sighed. "Do we know what it is?"

She shook her head. "From what I could gather, the doctors are mystified. They had him under quarantine for a few days but released him back to the general population when it became obvious he was not contagious."

Carter asked, "How do you know all this?"

"Well I can't tell you how I first found out but I was able to phone the hospital and talk to a doctor." She grimaced. "A most unpleasant man. In order to get him to tell me the details of the case, I told him I was from the Canadian side of the family, his mother's side."

I snorted. "We met his mother and she was definitely not Canadian."

Carter added, "She was very Belgian."

Mrs. Dewey asked, "What makes one Belgian as opposed to French?"

We both laughed. Carter replied, "In the Congo, Belgian just meant white in the same way you'd use that word in the South."

Mrs. Dewey nodded thoughtfully. "I see. Well, I suspect that Dr. Thomas is *English* in the same way your friend's mother was *Belgian*. He was quite disagreeable. I would have hung up on the man if I hadn't needed the information and known it would take another six hours to get a line into Salisbury again."

"How so?" I asked.

"I take it your friend was traveling with a native?"

I nodded. "Freddie Nyemba. He's Congolese."

"Ah, right. Well, apparently your friend's friend—"

"Mr. Nyemba," prompted Carter. "He used to manage my gym in Léopoldville."

Mrs. Dewey nodded. "Mr. Nyemba was trying to get into the hospital grounds to see Mr. Vermaut and that is quite forbidden in Salisbury. Southern Rhodesia is very much like South Africa in that way. A very well-enforced segregation all the way around."

Carter asked, "Do you know how they ended up in Salisbury?"

"According to Dr. Thomas, Mr. Vermaut and Mr. Nyemba left Léopoldville for Elizabethville on the border of North Rhodesia."

Carter said, "That's the capital of Katanga, the province that's broken away from the rest of the Congo."

Mrs. Dewey nodded. "In spite of himself, the doctor was quite impressed with their ability to make the journey. It's a war-zone in the Congo, of course."

Carter asked, "So they crossed Northern Rhodesia and then made it to Salisbury?"

"Yes. And, about two weeks ago, Mr. Vermaut developed a fever that wouldn't break. He went to Central Hospital in Salisbury. At first, they thought it was Dengue fever but he never developed the tell-tale rash. His fever is still high. He can't easily take food but he is drinking water. Doctor says he's lost weight but doesn't know how much."

I nodded, feeling a range of emotions, sadness most of all. "How do we get there and get him out?"

Mrs. Dewey reached over and put her hand on my arm. "Mr. Robertson wants you to call him later this afternoon. I believe he is working on a plan. On his suggestion, I wired two hundred pounds to Mr. Vermaut care of Central Hospital, Salisbury. We thought it best to maintain the fiction that I am his aunt."

I nodded as the tears finally came. "Thank you, Mrs. Dewey."

Carter nodded but couldn't speak. His eyes were red and there were tears pooled in them.

She pulled out her handkerchief and waved it at me. "I'm so sorry. I can't tell you how much."

Chapter 3

Aboard the San Nicola
Bay of Naples, Italy
Friday, December 9, 1960
Just before 3 in the afternoon

"It's like I told you when I found her, the name said everything. It's rare to find a boat with a man's name much less one that's named for my favorite boss." That was Captain Dan O'Reilly. He'd been working for us since the summer of '53 when we'd met him in Newport, California, after buying our first yacht. Carter and I were sitting just behind him and watching as he piloted the boat away from Naples and towards Capri.

Carter laughed. "Shouldn't the boat be called 'he' if it has a man's name?"

Captain O'Reilly kept his eyes facing forward and replied, "A boat is always a 'she', Mr. Jones."

Carter looked at me with a grin and then sat back.

The day was beautiful. Mrs. Dewey, who was sitting

aft and chatting with John Murphy, had been right. It was around 70 with a bright, warm sun. I couldn't help worrying about Paul, but it did feel good to sit in the sun and feel the Mediterranean air wrap its arms around me.

Captain O'Reilly said, "I thought this funeral was to have been on Thursday."

I replied, "It was. But we got a telegram from Lord Gerald on Monday telling us it had to be moved to Saturday. Apparently the English priest couldn't be here on Thursday."

"Ah," said O'Reilly.

After a few minutes of listening to the wind in the sails and the boat cutting through the water, Carter said, "Captain, we're not going straight home after we leave here."

I had been leaning against Carter but sat up after he said that.

"That so?" asked the captain.

Carter replied, "Yep. We need to head down to Salisbury in Southern Rhodesia to pick up a couple of friends who are in trouble."

"What kind of trouble?"

Carter briefed him on what we'd heard from Mrs. Dewey.

Captain O'Reilly said, "You're good friends, you are." He took a deep breath. "But I don't like Rhodesia any more than I like South Africa. T'ain't fair and t'ain't right what they do with the blacks."

"I know how you feel, Captain. That's why I never go home to Georgia if I can help it."

The captain turned and looked at Carter with a somber nod. "Aye."

. . .

While Captain O'Reilly and John Murphy tied the boat up to the dock at the marina, I looked around. Capri looked pretty much the same as it had in '57, the last time we were there. The crooked road that led up the side of the hill seemed to be less busy but that could have been because we were there in the off-season. As I continued to take everything in, I realized there weren't any tourists.

"What ho?" asked an English voice off in the distance.

I turned and saw Lord Gerald. He was getting out of the cab of a small truck with half a grin on his face. He was dressed in a dark suit and looked a lot older than he had the last time I'd seen him.

Mrs. Dewey met him first. They shook and spoke quietly. He nodded and quickly glanced at me. She then appeared to launch into a lengthy conversation. I thought I heard her say, "Salisbury," but I wasn't sure.

As I was standing with one foot on the gunwale of the boat, Carter put his hand on my shoulder. "Whatcha doin' there, son?"

"Trying to eavesdrop on Mrs. Dewey and Lord Gerald," I replied in a whisper.

He squeezed my shoulder and said, "Let's go and break it up."

I laughed as I followed him aft to the little gangway that John Murphy had set up.

. . .

"I'm sorry about your mother." That was Carter as he was shaking Lord Gerald's hand.

"That's quite kind of you to say, Mr. Jones."

I offered my hand and said, "Thanks for inviting us to be here. Your mother was one of my favorite people."

29

Lord Gerald nodded with half a smile. "I think the feeling was mutual. You seemed to have made quite an impression." He looked up at Carter. "You both did. I think it did the mater good to see the two of you together. She was always quite broad-minded, as you know, but seeing how you were no different than Charlotte and myself was a true eye-opener for her."

Carter asked, "Where is Lady Gerald?" That was the formal name for Lord Gerald's wife, Charlotte.

"She's at the hotel with my brother and his wife and dear Amelda and her husband, Timothy." Amelda was the Dowager Duchess's grand-niece. Lord Gerald looked around me. "I see your good captain has your luggage ready to go. These two men from the hotel"—he motioned to two Italian men in their late 30s—"will load the luggage in the lorry here and we'll be on our way." He smiled at me. "I'm afraid we'll have to squeeze into this Fiat." The car he was pointing to was just about as small a sedan as I'd ever seen. Looking up at Carter, he said, "Perhaps you might want to ride in the lorry with Carlo? More head room, what?"

. . .

As we made our way up the side of the hill in the little Fiat, Lord Gerald said, "As you may remember, Mr. Williams, I mentioned we would be staying at the *Villa Ercole*." That was a villa on the island, about five miles from the center of town, that his father had given us when he'd died back in September of '57. For the last three years, we'd been trying to give it to Danilo Carfaro who lived there. The red tape had been thick and hard to cut through so the villa still belonged to us.

"Yeah," I replied as I held onto the strap as we bounced along.

"Well, I'm afraid my brother really put his foot in it. Again." Lord Gerald sighed. "Even after everything that happened around my father's death in 1957, Peter got it in his head, once again, that the villa is his by rights and he made certain to say so to *Signor Carfaro* in no uncertain terms last night and right at the man's dining table. We were all ordered out and I can hardly blame the man." Lord Gerald chuckled to himself. "Peter, of course, is only playing Lord of the Manor because he doesn't know what else to do. Just wait until he discovers the priest coming over from Naples tomorrow is American. An Episcopalian, no less."

Mrs. Dewey clicked her tongue and said, "Oh, my!"

I asked, "Is that bad?"

"Quite," replied Lord Gerald in an amused voice. "But, back to the point of all this. Fortunately, we're practically the only tourists on the island at the moment so the Hotel la Palma is quite empty and happy to have our trade, if you'll pardon that turn of phrase. I asked them to hold a suite for yourself and Mr. Jones, and comfortable rooms for Mrs. Dewey, Captain O'Reilly, and Mr. Murphy, although not all together, of course."

Mrs. Dewey laughed at that.

I was in the front seat and trying to hold on as the driver zoomed around every hair-pin curve on the road up the hill. I wondered what we could do, if anything, about Danilo but that thought was crowded out by my worrying about Paul.

As if reading my mind, Lord Gerald said, "Mrs. Dewey has fully briefed me on the situation in Salisbury." By that point, we'd made it to the top of the hill and the car was headed towards the hotel.

I turned in my seat and looked at Lord Gerald. He was frowning and appeared to be as worried as I was.

"If you don't mind my butting into your affairs, Mr. Williams, might I suggest you head back to Naples tomorrow right after the funeral so you can get to Salisbury as fast as possible?"

I nodded. "Thank you, Lord Gerald."

He grinned slightly. "My pleasure. If mater were here, she'd have bundled you back onto the boat already and have told everyone else to go to blazes if they didn't agree."

I smiled as much as I could. "I think you're right about that."

"Have you thought about who should go with you?"

I sighed. "Not really. I'm still in shock."

"At a minimum, you'll want his dear Aunt Violet, from the Canadian side of the relations, doncha know, on the case." Lord Gerald looked at Mrs. Dewey who smiled at me and nodded. "Was he a close friend?"

I thought for a moment. "We'd only known him for about 18 months before we left. But he's been on my mind since we left." I sighed deeply. "Everyone we knew there has been."

Lord Gerald looked out the window. "I don't know how I'd feel if I'd lived in Léopoldville all that time and couldn't be there to care for kith and kin, as it were. It was a middlin' paradise for the Belgians and a kind of lower purgatory for the Congolese. Now it's hell for everyone."

I nodded. In my opinion, that was the best way to describe things.

...

"This is New York. Go ahead San Francisco." That was an efficient female voice that sounded clearer than I thought I'd ever heard on an international call. Carter and I were squeezed together in a phone booth at the end of the lobby so he could listen in. For some reason, the hotel operator was able to get a line within ten minutes of my asking to make a call.

Another female voice said, "Your call is ready, sir." Her voice was a little more wavy but still clear.

I heard Mike say, "Nick?" That was followed by several clicks as all the operators on the line disconnected.

"Yeah. How are you, Mike?"

"Fine. I just got up." I looked at my watch. It was 4:10 where we were which meant it was 7:10 in the morning at home. "How was the flight?" he asked.

"Not bad," I replied. "Helps when you have your own bed. I wanna talk to you about Salisbury."

"When can you leave?"

"We can be at the Naples airport by 4 tomorrow afternoon."

"Good. I'll tell Robert." That was Robert Evans. He managed all my real estate, including the planes. "He's waiting to hear from me. He said you can take the Comet all the way down."

"We can?"

"He said that B.O.A.C. flies Comets down there every day of the week. You fly from Naples to Khartoum to Salisbury. It's five hours on the first leg and about six hours on the second."

"Where's Khartoum?"

"It's in the Sudan, just south of Egypt. Are you OK?"

I leaned into Carter as much as I could. I did feel better knowing we were leaving sooner rather than later. "Getting better, thanks to you and Robert."

"Good. Is Mrs. Dewey going with you? She told me all about being Paul's Canadian aunt."

"Yeah."

"Watch your back down there. I don't think it's as bad as it was in Léopoldville right at the end, but you and Carter better get separate hotel rooms. Everyone Robert's talked to says it's like going to Georgia. They don't like queers and they don't like darkies and they don't mind telling you right to your face."

"OK."

"Also, Robert says to take as much cash as you can. Did you take your usual briefcase?"

"Yeah but most of it's in dollars."

"So?"

"Well, a very nice man from the Treasury Department stopped us in New York and asked me to stop sending so much money out of the country."

"This about the gold problem?"

"Yeah."

"Somehow I doubt the balance of payments between the U.S. and Southern Rhodesia is as big of a deal as it is with France and West Germany."

I chuckled. "Well aren't you smart all of a sudden?"

Carter laughed at that as Mike said, "You're not too big for me to take you over my lap, Nick Williams."

Carter grabbed the receiver out of my hand and said, "I'll take care of that later, Mike." He paused and then said, "Give Greg our love and we'll see you as soon as we can." He put the receiver back on the hook and whispered something very suggestive in my ear.

. . .

"Knock, knock and all that." That was Lord Gerald at the door of our suite.

I walked down the short hallway and pulled it open. "Come in. Dinner just arrived." I offered my hand. "Good to see you, again, Lady Gerald."

She smiled wanly. "I wish it was under better circumstances."

I nodded. "Me too. Carter is in the dining room making sure the kitchen cooked his steak right."

Lord Gerald chuckled. "Still to shoe leather, what?"

I followed the two of them as we walked into the sitting room. "Yeah. I doubt that'll ever change."

The waiter smiled as he made his way past us and out the door. He said, "Call when finish, *signore*," but didn't wait for my reply.

Lord Gerald looked around the room. "I think they've modernized since we were here last."

Carter nodded. "All the furniture in this suite is new, as far as we can tell."

I said, "We thought we'd have a couple of bottles of the house red wine. Will that be OK?"

Lord Gerald replied, "Oh, rather. House wine in Italy is like champagne in France. You'll likely never find better."

Carter pulled out a chair for Lady Gerald. As she sat, he said, "I ordered a couple of bottles of beer for myself. And we have port for after dinner."

Lord Gerald sat across from his wife at the medium-sized round dining table while Carter and I did the same. He looked across and asked, "My dear, would you care to serve or shall I?"

"Do let me. Serving is half the fun."

I sat back and suddenly felt grateful that it was just the four of us. I asked, "What happened to Mrs. Dewey?"

"Ah," said Lord Gerald. "I think she sensed my desire—"

"Our desire, dear duck," interrupted his wife.

He grinned at her as she put a mound of steamed green vegetables I'd never seen before on her plate. "Yes, indeed. I think she sensed our desire to spend time alone with the two of you and claimed a headache and a desire to curl up with a good book." He looked around. "And what about your good captain and his first mate?"

Carter said, "When we told them about our plan to leave tomorrow, they decided to sleep on the sailboat tonight. In fact, I think they were planning on taking it to some cove that you can only get to by boat." He exchanged his empty plate with the one offered by Lady Gerald. "Something like that."

"Capri is simply brimming with spots like that. But why the boat instead of the big feather beds of the hotel?"

I replied, "Because we sold the boat and when we tie it up in the marina tomorrow, we're leaving it there for the new owners. Captain O'Reilly and John Murphy have decided they're ready to come back to San Francisco for a while."

Lady Gerald looked at me with raised eyebrows. I exchanged plates with her. As she put a piece of fish on the new one, she asked, "And have you bought a sailboat for the San Francisco Bay now that your captain will be there?"

I shook my head. "Not yet. But I think Captain O'Reilly is already in touch with a couple of sellers."

Carter added, "We've really missed sailing on the bay and under the bridge since we've been home."

"Yeah," I said. "When are you two coming to visit us? We'll have to go out. Sailing under the Golden Gate Bridge is something else."

Lord Gerald sighed. "Duty still calls although I'm slowly disentangling myself from some of the dirtier jobs."

His wife looked at him for a moment and then said, "To be honest, dear duck, I'm quite ready for you to chuck the whole thing."

No one said anything for a moment. Finally, Carter asked, "Is that possible?"

"No," said Lord Gerald at the same time Lady Gerald said, "Yes."

We all laughed at that.

"I shouldn't talk like this, Jerry, I know. But we're not going to live forever and I, for one, would like to sail under the Golden Gate Bridge sooner than later."

Lord Gerald looked at his wife for a long moment. "And you shall, my dear, you shall."

. . .

"What's really happened, as I'm sure you both know much better than I, is that the so-called 'Congolese Bet' simply didn't pay off." That was Lord Gerald. We were just about done with the pasta course which consisted of shells stuffed with cheese and sausage.

Carter said, "From almost the minute we got there, we could see how the Belgians were treating the Congolese like slow children."

Lady Gerald tilted her head. "How so?"

"Well, for one, they wouldn't let hardly any of them get an education until the very end. Very few were allowed to have jobs better than a waiter in a restaurant."

"But what about the president and his prime minister? They seem very educated."

Carter nodded as he took a sip of his beer. "There was a small group that was sent to college in Belgium. But compared to the amount of smart men and women we met wherever we went, the Belgians were only letting a handful get a real education."

I added, "We hired as many Congolese as we could. It just made sense."

"It got us in a little trouble, here and there, but nothing bad," said Carter.

"Considering how much you had been model residents," said Lord Gerald, "I thought it was shocking how they treated you at the end."

Carter grinned ruefully. "There's always that one thing that gets us in the end."

Lord Gerald nodded. "Of course," he said with a serious tone. "You're much too tall and much too handsome."

We all laughed at that as Carter blushed which made Lady Gerald laugh even harder and turn red herself.

As I poured myself another half-glass of wine, I asked, "How have you both been since we last saw you?"

Lady Gerald smiled. "Jerry has been quite busy saving the nation and the world while I've been busy in my studio. After my father-in-law's death and all that took place here, I realized how much I wanted to be more dedicated to my art, as it were."

I watched Lord Gerald just about burst with pride. After a long moment he said, "Her work is the best it's ever been and an old friend is working on staging a show in London."

Carter said, "Be sure to let us know when it happens."

I added, "Maybe we can sneak in the country." We couldn't go to England since we were in trouble over an incident that took place in Hong Kong a few years earlier.

Lord Gerald turned to me and said, "Ah, yes. That." He cleared his throat and took a sip of wine. His lower lip was quivering just a little.

His wife whispered, "Jerry's the perfect Englishman. He rarely cries. And not ever in mixed company. But I think he's afraid he's about to do so now." She sat up in her chair and, in a normal voice, continued, "So, I'll speak for him." She looked at him and he gratefully nodded. "Right." Leaning forward, she said, "One of my mother-in-law's final acts was to get a private members' bill pushed through the House of Commons that, essentially, clears you both—"

"And Captain O'Reilly and Mr. Murphy," added Lord Gerald in a croaky voice.

Lady Gerald smiled. "Yes. The bill clears the four of you from all suspicion and instructs the Home Secretary to grant you visas, should you wish to apply for them."

Carter and I sat back. He looked shocked. I was confused.

Lord Gerald said, "Mater cashed in every last favor she ever held in Commons to do this. When I asked her about it, she said it was what my father would have done if he could." He nodded. "And I think she was quite right on that score."

I said, "I don't understand."

Lady Gerald put her hand on mine and said with a warm smile, "It's quite simple. You're welcome to come visit us at any time."

I looked over at Carter who said, "And the dowager duchess did that?"

Lord Gerald nodded. "She worked on it for almost two years. She was quite adamant."

I lifted my wine glass and said, "She was quite a gal."

Lord and Lady Gerald both smiled at that as Carter lifted his beer glass and added, "She sure was."

Chapter 4

Protestant Cemetery
Island of Capri
Saturday, December 10, 1960
A quarter past 1 in the afternoon

"*Unto Almighty God we commend the soul of our sister departed, and we commit her body to the ground; earth to earth, ashes to ashes, dust to dust; in sure and certain hope of the Resurrection unto eternal life, through our Lord Jesus Christ, at whose coming in glorious majesty to judge the world, the earth and the sea shall give up their dead; and the corruptible bodies of those who sleep in him shall be changed, and made like unto his own glorious body; according to the mighty working whereby he is able to subdue all things unto himself.*" That was Dr. Miller, the English priest who had sailed over from Naples earlier that morning and had a late breakfast at the hotel with the Duke and Duchess, Lord and Lady Gerald, and Amelda and her husband. He was reading from a small book as he conducted the burial service.

Carter and I were standing in the thick grass on the side of the hill above the family. The Protestant cemetery was overgrown everywhere. It looked like no one took care of the place.

As soon as Dr. Miller finished reading, the duke and Lord Gerald respectfully tossed small handfuls of dirt on the polished brown coffin with brass handles which had been lowered into the ground a few minutes earlier. The dowager duchess was being buried next to her husband whose grave had a small tombstone to mark the spot.

As the priest continued the service, I looked out over the Mediterranean and sighed. Carter and I had slept in later than usual after a long night of lovemaking. It had reminded me of other times in the past when one or both of us was under some type of stress and we would go at it as hard as either of us could with as much tenderness as we would allow ourselves.

We got up around 9 and had some coffee and pastries sent up to the suite. At half past 10, right when Dr. Miller arrived, we'd taken a cab to the villa to see if we could talk to Danilo. The driver dropped us at the bottom of the long, marble staircase, and drove off as we slowly walked up. When we got to the top, we found Danilo sitting on the steps of the marble porch in front of the villa. It was if he was waiting for us.

When he saw us, he stood and motioned for us to follow him without saying anything. He led us to the wall at the cliff's edge that overlooked the sea and crossed his arms. After a few moments, he said, "I fucking hate the English," and didn't say anything else.

After five or so minutes of standing there, the three of us looking out at Naples in the distance, Carter said, "We love you, *Danilo*."

The man nodded but didn't reply.

I reached over and kissed him on the cheek. He smiled and kissed me on the lips without lingering. Finally, he shoved his hands into his trouser pockets and said, "Go. Go to the funeral of the wife of the only man I ever truly loved."

Somehow neither of us had anything to say in reply so we turned and walked back towards the villa, down the marble steps, and made our way to the hotel by foot. In the end, we were gone all of an hour.

...

"How was it?" That was Captain O'Reilly. We were back on the *San Nicola* and headed towards Naples. We were in the same places we'd been the day before. Carter and I were watching O'Reilly pilot the boat. Mrs. Dewey was aft with John Murphy. We'd left Lord and Lady Gerald along with Amelda and her husband at the marina. They all seemed resigned to whatever was next. We'd never said anything to the duke and duchess, which was fine by me. It was obvious they didn't want us there.

Carter said, "It was English, I guess. No one cried."

"Of course not, the poor bastards," replied the captain. "They never do."

None of us said anything for a few minutes. Finally, the captain spoke up without turning. "John Murphy reminded me that we might have a time of it in Rhodesia."

"Why's that?" I asked.

"Because of all that mess in Hong Kong. Rhodesia is a British colony, after all."

Carter said, "The duchess took care of that."

"Did she now?"

"Something to do with parliament and a private members' bill."

Holding his hand firmly on the wheel, the captain turned and looked at Carter. His eyes were wide with surprise. "That so? From what I know those are almost impossible to get through. How'd she do it?"

Carter shrugged. "Lord Gerald told us she worked on it for two years and that she called in every favor she had."

The captain nodded and then winked at me. He pointed to the sky. "Good to know we've all got at least one angel in heaven lookin' after us."

I smiled. "If she's in heaven, then I hope St. Peter is ready."

Carter laughed and put his arm around my shoulder. "I have a feeling they were ready for her when she got there."

I leaned against him as Captain O'Reilly turned face forward. "You're probably right about that."

...

"Monsieur Williams?" That was Captain Clement. He was the chief pilot of the Comet. About five minutes earlier, he'd turned the engines on. But, before we'd begun to taxi for take-off from Naples, he'd shut the engines down without any announcement over the loudspeaker. Carter had looked out the window on the port side, where we were seated, and couldn't see a reason. Mrs. Dewey, on the starboard side, had reported the same.

I looked up. "Is there a problem, Captain?"

He smiled briefly and shook his head. "We had a message from the tower. Madame LeBeau is just arriving on a flight from Paris. She will arrive to the plane in 15 minutes, or so they say."

"Mrs. LeBeau?" I asked.

"Yes, *monsieur*."

Carter asked, "Not Mr. and Mrs.?"

The captain shook his head. "No, *monsieur*. I did ask since they were both with us from New York to Paris. They say it is just she, no more."

I could feel a knot forming in my stomach. But all we could do was wait, so I asked, "Have you flown this way before?"

"To Salisbury?"

I nodded.

"No, *monsieur*, but I have a colleague who works for B.O.A.C. and he said it is very easy. He say it is easier for us since we do not stop in *Léopoldville* as they do although not always since the airport is not always open, as you know."

Carter asked, "Do they fly from London direct to Khartoum?"

"No, *monsieur*. Their *route* is London to Rome and then to Khartoum."

Carter nodded. "Thanks, Captain."

He tipped his cap to both of us and then said, "*Pardon*. I return now to the cockpit."

. . .

"So, what happened, doll?" That was me talking to Marnie by the galley. We were about 20 minutes out of Naples and over the Mediterranean. Juliette was pouring Marnie a cup of coffee.

"We had a big fight last night and then again this morning." She took the offered cup from Juliette. "Thanks."

I led her to the front bedroom cabin. Once we were inside and the door was closed, I asked, "Wanna tell me about it?"

She shrugged. "What's to tell? I tore up your check and he got mad."

"How did he know you even had it?"

"When we checked into the hotel, I asked the gal at the front desk where the closest branch of that whatever French bank was and she told me." She sipped her coffee, sat on the edge of the bed, and sighed.

"Why'd you tear up the check?"

"Because Alex went on and on about how we need all the money we can get and we don't, Nick. So, to prove my point, I tore up the check and threw it in his face." She screwed up her mouth. "That made him kinda sore."

I skipped over that and asked, "What are you gonna do?"

"I'm going with you to Rhodesia and then, when we get home, hopefully Alex will have cooled off." She took another sip. "Maybe his parents can talk to him. I've done as much as I can."

"How did you even know where we were going?"

She gave me half a smile. "I called that Robert Evans last night and he told me the whole thing. Then, this morning, when Alex was going on and on about how careful we have to be with money, I told him I was going to Africa with you and Carter to do something useful and, boy, did he blow his top at that." She rolled her eyes.

I tried not to smile as I said, "I bet. How'd you buy the ticket?"

"It's amazing what that American Express card will buy."

I frowned. "But I thought you could only get one in Alex's name?"

She shrugged. "So? I'm still Mrs. LeBeau, ain't I?"

I nodded. "Yeah."

She smoothed her skirt with her free hand. "By the way, I don't have any clothes. I only brought a small case with my make-up and a change of undies."

46

I grinned. "I'm sure they'll have clothes in Salisbury."

She sighed. "I sure hope so."

. . .

"How is she?" That was Carter. We were stretched out on our bed in the cabin all the way aft.

"She's mad," I said.

"She looks like she's having fun." He was right. Over dinner, Captain O'Reilly got on a roll with bawdy jokes and Marnie had laughed longer and harder than anyone. She'd also added a few of her own which had really tickled Mrs. Dewey who'd been both amused and appalled by the captain's jokes.

"Yeah." I didn't know how much I should say about what I knew.

"Are you going to tell me?" asked Carter as he slowly unbuttoned my shirt.

"It's not really my story to tell."

Carter held up his right hand and flexed his fingers. "You know, I have my ways."

I laughed. "Do your best but I'll never tell."

Carter looked at me. "Fine. I guess I'll have to just resort to kissing you and a few other things."

"Like what?" I asked with a grin.

He listed them in great detail.

. . .

I suddenly sat up. It was dark outside and, from what I could tell, we were flying over the Nile because I could see a string of lights below curving to the left with darkness everywhere else. Captain Clement had mentioned that was the route we would take. I was thrilled to be able to see it from above. I wondered what the people below thought of a jet flying overhead in the darkness until I remembered that B.O.A.C. made the same trip every day of the week.

"How are you, son?" asked Carter with a sleepy voice.

"Good. I'm watching the Nile below."

He sat up and moved over to my side of the bed. Plopping down, he ran his hand over his face and yawned. Leaning forward, he nodded. "There it is. Isn't that amazing?"

"Yeah." I leaned against him and reached my hand under his arm. We were both in our BVDs and t-shirts. Normally, we slept in the nude but we'd recently made it a habit to wear clothes when we were sleeping on one of our planes in case something happened and we had to move fast.

He squeezed my hand. "Did I tell you that I talked to John Taylor on Wednesday afternoon while I was at the office?" Taylor was a new friend who'd been arrested for murdering his lover down in L.A. a few days earlier. We'd found evidence that got him released but it seemed likely would charge him with sodomy, so we'd invited to move up to San Francisco to get out of harm's way. He'd decided to go visit his sister in Santa Barbara before coming up to San Francisco.

"When's he coming?" I asked.

"Not for a while. He said he wanted to go to Mexico to get away from everything for a while. He was thinking about Acapulco but I suggested he go stay at my house on Kauai and I told him to stay as long as he wanted." Carter had bought a place there back in '54. It was a great spot on a cliff overlooking the ocean with a beach down below.

I nodded. "Good idea. What about his house in L.A.?"

"He said his sister was going to go take care of it. I told him to contact Robert to make all the travel arrangements. He should be there by now. I also told him that if he wanted to, Robert could arrange to sell his house or set it up as a rental."

"What'd he say about that?"

Carter sighed. "I don't think he's ready to do anything like that. He believes that all this will blow over and he can go back to L.A. in a few months."

"I wish he was right."

Carter turned, pushed me down on the bed, and leaned down to kiss me on the lips. "Me too."

. . .

"I am sorry. You do not have the yellow permit." That was the Sudanese passport official. We were at the Khartoum airport and the night air coming through the open cabin door was warm and dry. The man was tall and dressed in a khaki uniform with a green cap. He'd performed an inspection of the plane and had slowly, very slowly, gone through our passports and written down our names. Just when it seemed like everything was in order, he began to talk about the yellow permit. That was the fourth time he'd repeated himself.

Captain Clement nodded slowly. "Yes. We do not have the yellow permit. Where can we obtain the yellow permit?"

"It is too late to obtain the yellow permit."

Mrs. Dewey stepped forward. "My good man," she said, sounding very English and not at all Canadian, "do you have a superior officer?"

He nodded to her respectfully and then proudly replied, "I am the only official awake at this time." That wasn't surprising. We'd arrived at around 11 in the evening. It had taken an hour and a half to get the fuel truck out and on the job. From what I could tell, they only serviced B.O.A.C. jets and had been taken by surprise that we wanted fuel so the men on duty had to make a couple of calls to get permission. Then, they wouldn't take any checks from any country and demanded cash so we'd paid in dollars. That was one of the reasons we always traveled with several thousand dollars in cash in a briefcase. Once that was taken care of, it took another 30 minutes before the passport official arrived and, because he'd moved so slowly, it was nearly 3 in the morning.

I looked at Captain Clement. "Maybe we should stay here tonight? That way your crew could get some sleep."

He shook his head. "We're rotating duties and everyone is rested well enough."

The immigration official looked at me. "You will need the blue permit to disembark but you may stay in the plane if you wish to sleep overnight."

I heard Marnie mutter, "The blue permit. Jeez."

Captain O'Reilly gave it a shot. "How much does the yellow permit cost?"

The immigration official smiled and replied, "Ten pounds sterling."

We all breathed a collective sigh of relief. I asked, "How about if we give you 40 American dollars?" That was a bit more but not much more.

The man shook his head slowly. "I am sorry, but the fee for the yellow permit is ten pounds sterling."

I looked around the plane. "Does anyone have pounds? We don't."

Before anyone could reply, Mrs. Dewey, who had her pocketbook in the crook of her arm, snapped it open. She removed her change purse and, looking at me, said, "I was saving all this to give to the grandchildren in Toronto but I believe it's more useful here." She walked over to the galley and began to count out bank notes and coins on the counter. "Here's a fiver. And here are three quid rolled up together. That makes eight pounds. Let's see. Here are two... Wait! There are four here. Four half-crowns. That brings us to eight and ten." She looked in her change purse. "Oh! Here are two ten-bob notes all the way at the bottom. That brings us to nine and ten." She looked again. "Here are some pennies and half-pennies but I think I have florins somewhere." She kept digging. Finally, and with a triumphant smile, she pulled out a handful of silver coins and counted them out. "And here they are: one, two, three, four, and five florins." She grinned up at the patient immigration official. "That brings us to ten pounds even."

The immigration official began to count. "Five pounds and three. That is indeed eight, miss. Eight and ten with ten bob. Nine with another ten bob. And, yes, miss, ten in total with five florins and four half-crowns." He picked all of it off the counter and carefully put the cash and coins in a special zipper bag, tipped his cap at Mrs. Dewey, and bowed. "Thank you, miss."

Chapter 5

Salisbury Airport
Salisbury
Southern Rhodesia
Sunday, December 11, 1960
Just before 11 in the morning

"Good morning. My name is Captain John R. Quincy and I'm the duty chief today for immigration control here at Salisbury Airport." That was a short, dark man in a crisp khaki uniform with a green cap tucked under his arm along with a clipboard. His black hair was close cut and he sported a bushy mustache. His voice was friendly but his dark brown eyes were wary. The six of us, seven counting the captain, were gathered in the cabin with the big round table. The crew were waiting in the forward section of the plane.

Just as we'd planned on the flight down, Mrs. Dewey stepped forward and offered her gloved hand. In her flattest Canadian accent, she said, "Good morning, Captain. My name is Mrs. Violet Dewey and I am here only long enough to retrieve my nephew Paul who is currently ill and in hospital."

The captain nodded and looked around. "And who are these other folks?"

Mrs. Dewey looked first at Captain O'Reilly and said, "This is Mr. Daniel O'Reilly and Mr. John Murphy. They're both friends of the family from many years ago who are accompanying me on this trip." The two men, who were both wearing their best suits, nodded. She then pointed to me. "And this is our benefactor, Mr. Nicholas Williams from America. This is his jet and, through a mutual acquaintance, he has offered his assistance."

The captain stared hard at me as I nodded but didn't say anything.

"He's traveling with two business associates from America, Mr. Carter Jones and Mrs. Marnie LeBeau."

The captain took them both in and then turned to Mrs. Dewey. "May I see your passport, please?"

She offered up her Canadian passport. She had permission to work for us in San Francisco and was still working on obtaining American citizenship.

The captain looked at her passport and then put his hat down on the table. He looked at Mrs. Dewey. "May I have a seat?"

"Of course, Captain. Would you like some coffee?"

He smiled tightly as he sat and pulled out a ball-point pen. While he began to make notes on his clipboard, he said, "No, thank you, madame."

...

Once he was done writing down our names and passport numbers, Captain Quincy stood and asked, "In which hospital is your nephew at the moment?"

Mrs. Dewey replied, "Central."

The captain nodded. "You say you're only here long enough to retrieve him, correct?"

"Yes, Captain."

Looking at me, the captain asked, "And how did you come to be involved in this trip if I may ask, Mr. Williams?"

I smiled. "Mrs. Dewey and I have a mutual friend in England. When he found out that she needed some help, I volunteered."

"Salisbury isn't exactly between Canada and San Francisco."

Mrs. Dewey impatiently jumped in. "Of course, not. Mr. Williams is a man of great resources and he happened to be in Italy when our mutual friend contacted him. I flew down from London, where I had been staying for a month, with my friends Mr. O'Reilly and Mr. Murphy, and he was kind enough to bring the three of us down on a moment's notice." She looked at her watch. "I do hope we're in time. Doctor doesn't know what's the matter with dear Paul and I hope we're not too late."

The captain frowned slightly and crossed his arms. "Of course. Now, I assume you will be staying overnight."

Mrs. Dewey nodded. "One night at least. It all depends on how soon we can move my nephew."

"Well then, if you don't mind, may I suggest staying at The Ambassador Hotel on Union Avenue? It's our newest hotel." That sounded good to me.

Mrs. Dewey smiled. "Thank you, Captain. We none of us have been here before and that's a great help."

He nodded and stared at me for a long moment before saying, "Now, if you'll excuse me, I'll check the passports of the crew and then I'll be on my way. Have a pleasant stay in Salisbury." And with that, he took his hat and clipboard and stepped out of the cabin.

. . .

"Welcome to Salisbury Motor Rental, my name is Suzanne. Have you a car reserved with us?" That was the gal at the car rental desk. Normally, I would have used Hertz but they hadn't made it to Rhodesia yet, from the look of things.

Mrs. Dewey stepped forward and, back to her British accent, said, "Oh no, my dear. We are a small party and came completely unprepared. I do so hope you can help us."

Suzanne, who was blonde and about 25 with freckles, smiled and said, "Of course. How many cars will you require?"

"Three, my dear."

"Oh," said Suzanne, momentarily taken aback. She looked at a piece of paper on the counter and then looked up. "Well, I happen to have two matching Ford Anglias, both blue and one yellow Ford Consul Estate. Will that be sufficient?"

"Oh, quite, my dear." She turned and looked at me. "A Consul Estate is a station wagon. Plenty of room for luggage and such."

I nodded with a grin and didn't say anything.

Mrs. Dewey turned back to Suzanne and continued, "Now, our other predicament is that we simply do not have any Rhodesian currency. Not a pound, shilling, or penny."

Suzanne was eager to help. She said, "We understand. We do take traveler's checks in almost any currency in deposit for the rental. We also accept charge cards."

"American Express?" asked Mrs. Dewey. I'd given her a list of my cards while we were planning everything.

"I'm sorry, no, but we do take the Diners' Club. Will that be acceptable?"

Mrs. Dewey smiled. "Quite, my dear, quite."

...

"Welcome to the Ambassador Hotel." That was Carl. I knew that because it was on his name tag. He was six foot even, had thin blond hair, and light blue eyes. I pegged him at around 35 and immediately knew he was one of us. While Carter and John Murphy took care of the luggage outside, Mrs. Dewey and I had walked up to the front desk. Captain O'Reilly and Marnie were hovering in the background.

Firmly in her British accent, Mrs. Dewey said, "Good afternoon. My name is Mrs. Violet Dewey. I'm here in Salisbury for a day or two with a small party and we require rooms. I hope you can accommodate us."

Carl gave her a tight smile. "How many rooms do you require?"

"Ten. All singles." We'd decided it would be better if everyone had their own room.

Carl paused for a moment and then nodded. "Very good, madame." He thought and then added, "I'm afraid we have no floor with ten singles together so I may have to scatter your party across the hotel but I will try to keep the rooms in close proximity."

"Thank you."

"My pleasure. Give me one moment while I consult our available rooms. Shall I check for one night or two?"

"Two, I should think."

"Very good. Excuse me." With that, he walked over to a man who appeared to be a manager and began to talk to him.

Mrs. Dewey turned and looked around the lobby. "Not too busy, it seems. And it's remarkably modern, isn't it?"

I nodded. It was a little too modern for my taste. I liked furniture to be comfortable. The lobby was full of Danish Modern knock-offs. I figured the rooms were probably the same.

"And it's hard to believe that we're in the middle of Africa, isn't it? As we drove into town, I felt as if we could be anywhere in Canada, to be quite honest."

"Except for driving on the wrong side of the road and the weather."

She laughed. "For me, this is the *right* side of the road even though I've now lived most of my life in Canada and the U.S. I always feel slightly more relaxed when I'm in a country where the motor cars are all on the left side. And, as for the weather, it can be just like this in Toronto or Montreal in the summer."

Carl was back by then and said, "I'm able to secure rooms for five of your party on the tenth floor. I have an additional three rooms on the eleventh floor and two rooms on the twelfth floor. That was the best I could do."

"That's quite alright," said Mrs. Dewey. "Thank you for the effort."

Carl smiled. "If you could, I'll need passports for each member of your party. They'll be ready later this afternoon." Carl suddenly seemed to realize I was with Mrs. Dewey. He looked at me and frowned slightly. I smiled in reply.

Mrs. Dewey said, "Now, four of our party are still at the airport but should be arriving soon."

Carl, still frowning at me, didn't reply immediately. He came to himself with a start and smiled at Mrs. Dewey. "That's no worry, madame. If you will give me their names, I shall take care of checking them in when they do arrive. In the meantime, if I could get passports for those who are here now." He quickly glanced at me again.

Mrs. Dewey nodded and turned in my direction. "Nicholas, would you take care of that for me, dear?"

I winked at her and began to make my way over to where Carter was sitting with Marnie. Captain O'Reilly and John Murphy were standing nearby. As I did, I heard Mrs. Dewey ask, "Now, my good man, can you exchange American dollars for Rhodesian pounds?" I'd given her five hundred bucks before we'd landed.

"Of course, madame," replied Carl. "How many do you need?"

. . .

"Well, the rooms are small but modern. I like that." That was Marnie. The six of us were sitting at a round table in the back of the Bird and Bottle, the hotel's main restaurant. We'd put in our orders and were sipping drinks while waiting for our food.

"So, Mr. Hotelier," said John Murphy with a grin. "What's your verdict on Salisbury's most modern hotel?"

I shrugged. "It's too modern for me but you already knew that, Mr. Murphy."

He laughed and had a drink of his beer. "Aye, 'tis true. I remember how you spoke of that one hotel in Tripoli that was just as modern and fancy as this one here."

"What was the name of that place?" asked Captain O'Reilly.

"The Al-Waddan," replied Carter. "I seem to remember you liked the casino, particularly the craps table."

The captain smiled and nodded but didn't reply.

Carter looked at me. "I agree with Nick." He then turned to Marnie. "The outside of that hotel looked like something out of the Arabian nights but they had just finished remodeling the inside and we could have been in New York or L.A. It was kind of disappointing but the service was good."

Right then, our waiter arrived with the food. Once it was all passed out, and we were all tucked in, I said, "Once we're done here, I want to head over to the hospital with Mrs. Dewey."

She looked up from her large tomato stuffed with chicken salad and said, "Yes. I think the sooner the better. I'm quite worried about your friend."

I nodded. "Me too."

Carter, who was sawing into his steak, said, "I'm going with you."

Mrs. Dewey shook her head. "I haven't quite figured how to fit Mr. Williams into the story that will let him in and I can't imagine how to explain the presence of you both."

Carter shrugged. "Fine. I'll drive and wait in the car. But I'm going. Paul is my friend and I want to see him and we also need to find Freddie."

John Murphy piped up. "Why not say he, meaning Paul, works for Nick there? That should have some weight."

Mrs. Dewey nodded thoughtfully. "That's a good thought, Mr. Murphy."

Marnie, who was eating a stuffed tomato as well, said, "I'm going to the hospital as well. I can't just sit around here and wait for something to happen."

Carter laughed and said, "Well, since you *do* work for Nick, you can add some truth to the story."

I said, "Mrs. Dewey works for me and I think four people storming the gates at once is two too many."

Captain O'Reilly said, "Beggin' your pardon, Mrs. Dewey, but shouldn't you go in first, all alone, and assess the situation before anyone else does anything?"

Smiling at him, Mrs. Dewey said, "Quite right, Captain. Sound thinking."

I looked at Marnie. "Did you bring a deck of cards with you, doll? I guess the three of us will be stuck playing penny poker in the car."

John Murphy said, "And on the Lord's day, no less." As everyone laughed, he shook his head and took a big drink of his beer.

. . .

"What about the two of you?" That was Carter. We were almost finished with our lunch.

John Murphy glanced over at the captain and, in a quiet voice, said, "I was thinkin' we should probably do some lookin' around the town. To be able to help find your friend, Freddie, we'll need to see how the races mix here." He looked around at all the black waiters. "I doubt these fine fellas can help us. I'm thinking more of those who do deliveries and know the area real well like. I seem to remember that the town is divided into sections and we're in the heart of the white part. I suspect there are edges where folks mix. That's where I think we'll be able to get help."

I nodded. "That's how it was in Léopoldville. I think the policing of the sections is more enforced here than it was there. Legally, there was no segregation. It was all done by the business owners."

Carter added, "Which we didn't do and that's one of the reasons we got in trouble."

Captain O'Reilly leaned forward. "I think me Johnny here is right. While you are on your errand, we'll snoop around and see what we find."

After wiping her mouth, Mrs. Dewey added, "Something else that might be helpful—Lord Gerald said he thought there are likely small informal refugee areas for blacks coming from the Congo. The Belgians have been put up by the government but he doubted the Congolese have been given the same accommodation. He also said that any who make it this far by foot, and that's the only way an African could get here, will be well-known among the local worthies, particularly the native chiefs who hold a lot of sway."

John Murphy nodded. "They do. Or so I heard. But that's more in the bush, I think, and not so close to town. I imagine we'll find something closer to party bosses, or the equal of that, instead of chiefs around here."

"A very good point, Mr. Murphy."

Looking at the first mate, I said, "Before you leave, let me give you some dollars so you can change them for Rhodesian pounds. How many do you think you'll need?"

Mrs. Dewey interrupted quickly. "The hotel will only exchange 50 pounds per person per day. I bought 140. That took up the allotment of three of us."

"How much is that in dollars?" I asked.

She frowned slightly. "They do have a very rapacious service charge, so those hundred and forty pounds cost quite nearly the whole of the five hundred dollars you gave me. It was close to a hundred and eighty dollars for fifty pounds."

John Murphy whistled. "I thought the Rhodesian pound was equal to the British pound."

"Oh, it is, Mr. Murphy. It is. As I said, it was the service charge that did us in."

I looked at John Murphy. "Well, I'll get you four hundred dollars upstairs so you can pick up another hundred pounds today and then we'll go to the bank tomorrow if we're still here and need more."

Marnie looked around the table, her mouth half-open in surprise, and asked, "What on Earth do you need nearly a thousand dollars for on a Sunday afternoon?"

Mrs. Dewey patted her hand and said, "Bribes, my dear."

"And buying rounds of beer at the local pub," added John Murphy.

I threw in, "Don't forget tips."

Everyone laughed at that.

Chapter 6

Central Hospital
North Avenue and Mazoe Street
Sunday, December 11, 1960
Half past 3 in the afternoon

"Full house. Kings over threes." That was Marnie from the back seat.

I threw my cards on the pile of coins between Carter and me. "I only had a pair of aces."

Carter waved his cards in the air. "Sorry, Marnie. I have four of a kind. All sixes."

Marnie dropped her cards over the seat back and then threw herself against the backseat cushion and crossed her arms with a disgusted sigh.

As Carter gathered all the coins in the middle, I said, "Well, I'm done." Looking through the foggy windshield, I asked, "Is it gonna drizzle all day?"

Marnie waved her face with her hand. "I just wish it was less muggy and less hot. This is ridiculous."

"I wonder how Mrs. Dewey is doing in there?" asked Carter.

"Yeah," I added. Every time I thought of her or Paul, the knot in my stomach got tighter.

Carter turned around and looked over the seat back. "OK, Marnie. Nick won't tell me anything. As much as I'm always glad to see you, why are you here?"

I turned to see Marnie's response. She didn't reply. Instead she rolled down the window and took in a deep breath while feeling the drizzle on her hand. "I can't believe I'm really in Africa." She paused. "Even if it does look a lot like Sacramento."

I waited to see if she would reply. After a moment, Carter said, "I'm going to give it a stab."

Marnie sighed and kept looking out the window.

Carter continued, "I think you're mad that Alex took Nick up on his offer to set him up in his own company and I think it's because Alex doesn't like spending the money Dr. Williams settled on the two of you. You two probably had a big fight on Friday night and, knowing we weren't going home yet, you flew down to meet us in Naples, more to get away from Alex than anything else even though you love him a lot and love being with him in Paris. How's that?" I was impressed. I had only told him about the offer I'd made to Alex. When he'd asked me why Marnie had suddenly showed up in Naples, I'd told him it wasn't my story to tell. I didn't do that very often, but it felt right at the time.

Marnie snorted. "Are you sure Nick didn't talk to you?"

"He told me it was none of my business."

I said, "Cross my heart, doll."

For some reason, Marnie relaxed after hearing that. After a long moment, she looked at Carter and said, "That's about it."

"Does Alex have any money of his own?"

She nodded. "Of course. What's in the bank is his."

"But part of that is yours, right?"

She shrugged. "Sure."

"I know you make a lot more than most secretaries."

I frowned at Carter and started to say something. Before I could, Carter held up his hand. "Which I fully agree with."

I sat back and sighed. The metallic pitter-patter of the drizzle on the roof of the car was about to drive me nuts.

"Yeah, that's right. I make about the same as Alex."

"And who did Dr. Williams give the money to?"

I looked over at Marnie. She was making an "O" with her mouth and frowning. After a moment, she said, "It's all in my name."

"So, in other words," said Carter, "Alex doesn't want to spend *your* money."

Marnie put her hand to her mouth and nodded. "But it's his, legally."

"Yes, and all of Nick's money is mine, legally, because of all the complex documents we drew up but do you think anyone ever says, 'Well, Mr. Jones, how does it feel to be a multi-millionaire?'"

I looked out the windshield. I'd never thought about that. In my mind, it was settled. Carter was as much a multi-millionaire as I was.

Marnie echoed my sentiments. "I just assumed he knew it was as much his as it was mine. He's never said anything about it."

Carter glanced over at me before turning more fully in his seat. "And he never will."

"Just like you never will," I added, swallowing hard with a sudden and intense emotion. I reached over and took his right hand.

He squeezed in reply as Marnie said, "Oh, gosh! I've made a terrible mistake." She looked around desperately as if a telephone might appear out of anywhere.

Carter let go of my hand so he could reach over the seat and touch Marnie's arm. "You can send a telegram when we get back to the hotel."

"What should I say?"

He grinned. "Just tell him you're sorry and that you love him." He looked at me and winked. "Works for me every time."

I grinned at him.

...

"Well, my dears, I have good news and not-so-good news." That was Mrs. Dewey as she got in the car behind me. She took the handkerchief that Carter offered her over the seat and dried off her face with it. "This weather is simply beastly. It'd be winter in England if it were forty degrees cooler." She sighed and then dotted her hair a little. Since we'd picked her up in Paris, the only time she'd worn a hat was the black one she sported at the dowager duchess's funeral. Otherwise she kept her brown and gray hair pinned in place off her face and neck.

"What's the good news?" I asked.

"Paul is now in a private room with a view and has a nurse specifically assigned to him. Lord Gerald's idea of wiring money to the hospital was spot on. And I hear that Mr. Robertson sent more and it arrived yesterday. So, all in all, he's now receiving the best care possible."

"What's the other news?" asked Carter.

Mrs. Dewey sighed. "He's not well. That, of course, is no surprise. He's been unconscious for three days. They still have no clear idea the origin of the fever. Since the money arrived, they gave him an ice bath twice. It helped somewhat but the fever came back a few hours later both times. He's running around 103 most of the time. That's not good."

I looked out the windshield and sighed.

Carter took my hand in his and asked, "Can Nick see him?"

"Oh, yes! Money may not be able to cure him, poor boy, but, in the private wards, visitors are welcome day and night. We can all go up right now, if you wish."

...

Paul's room was on the third floor. It overlooked a green park. The floor was a light brown tile and the walls were painted a cheery yellow. There was a painting of a zebra on the wall opposite his bed. A radio sat on a small table. It was turned off.

Carter and I stood next to the side of the bed furthest from the window. Marnie and Mrs. Dewey were out in the hall, talking with the nurse, and the windowless door to the room was closed.

Paul looked smaller, somehow, as if he'd shrunk. All his muscles were gone. He'd spent hours and hours at Carter's gym working on them until they stood out as much as they could.

Looking at him in the bed, he was just skin and bones and not much of either. His chestnut hair had streaks of gray in it and his cheeks were so sunken that he reminded me of some of the people who'd been liberated from the concentration camps after the war.

A rubber tube was plugged into his arm with a needle held in place by a big piece of gauze and tape. The tube was connected to a glass jar hanging from a metal pole next to the bed. A thin white sheet covered him up to the chest. It was efficiently tucked in on either side of the bed. A thin blue blanket covered his legs.

As we watched, he sighed, moved around a bit, and began to talk to himself. I leaned down and tried to listen. I'd heard it often enough in Léopoldville to recognize the rolled R's of Dutch, the language he'd been raised on even though he was also fluent in French and English. I put my hand on his cheek and then quickly pulled it back. He was burning up.

Carter gently pulled me back and said, "Let's find the doctor."

I nodded and then turned into his chest. As he pulled me in close, he ran his hand over my head while I cried for a while.

. . .

"We're quite stumped." That was Dr. Bernard Thomas. When he introduced himself, he told us he was originally from South Africa, had attended medical school in England, and had been in Rhodesia since right after the war. He was somewhere close to 50, about 5'9", a little pudgy but not much, had dark hair and brown eyes, and sported a bushy mustache. He was dressed in a lightweight tan suit with a blue tie and a stethoscope around his neck. I was surprised he wasn't wearing a white coat.

"I explained much of this to Mrs. Dewey but, she being a woman and all, it likely went right over head." He grinned at me.

I didn't do the same.

"When your employee first presented himself, he was partially malnourished." He pointed to the rubber tube attached to Paul's arm. "We've stabilized that condition somewhat by feeding him intravenously. But he continues to lose weight regardless how many calories we give him per day. We're watching his kidneys closely. So far, so good. His fever is curious. There's no apparent cause for it. He doesn't test for any of the usual diseases of the bush. When he told me he'd traveled on foot from the Congo, I assumed that was the trouble." The doctor sighed and crossed his arms. "But not so, from what we can tell. Last Wednesday, I sent a number of cables to London, Paris, and New York for any assistance in diagnosing his case. A doctor in Paris referred the matter to his colleague in Brussels who sent me a lengthy wire yesterday. Apparently, there is a high-fever illness that appears, from time-to-time, out of the bush of the Congo. Usually the patient dies. Sometimes the fever does him in. However, the disease, whatever it is, suppresses the immune system and the patient can die of a mild case of influenza, or a simple pneumonia, or any number of routine infections. All things that most healthy men easily survive."

The man shook his head. "The man in Brussels asked that I collect blood samples and send them to him. Apparently, he's been interested in this disease for some time. His theory is that it may have come from some other animal, a chimp, perhaps, or an ape. I find that theory highly suspect although I'm not a specialist in bush diseases. I believe he worked in Léopoldville before the recent troubles."

The doctor looked directly at me and frowned. "He also asked if I would confirm that the patient was a *kafir*. Do you know if he might be colored? I believe in the States, he would be called high yellow. Is that right?"

I looked at Carter who began to rub his jaw, which wasn't a good sign.

The doctor instinctively backed up. "I'm not calling your employee a nigger, but I wondered if he might have some mixed blood in him."

Neither of us said anything for a tense moment. I couldn't decide what to say and was secretly hoping

Carter would slug the man. Finally, I felt calm enough to talk and said, "As far as I know, Paul is Belgian." I suddenly remembered the backstory Mrs. Dewey had come up with and quickly added, "And Canadian, meaning English, of course."

The doctor nodded thoughtfully. "But I take it he was raised as a Flemish Belgian since he speaks Dutch from time to time. I understand some of it since Afrikaans is my second language and it's closely related to Dutch."

In a tight voice, Carter said, "That's what he told us."

The doctor frowned slightly. "And you are?"

"He's another employee of mine, Doctor," I said.

The man tilted his head. "You both look familiar but I can't quite place you."

Carter quickly said, "Mr. Vermaut was traveling with a Congolese man by the name of Freddie Nyemba. Do you know where he is?"

The doctor smiled and shrugged. "I expect he's just outside of Mabvuku. That's just off the Umtali Road, although I wouldn't suggest you go there without a police escort. I hear there's a makeshift camp of *kafirs* from the Congo who've made a home somewhere around there." He looked at me. "We had quite a scene down in the public ward when he tried to get in to see your employee a few days ago. The police were called and he was expelled from hospital grounds. This area is restricted to Europeans."

Carter was rubbing his chin again. I quickly asked, "What's that word you keep using?"

"*Kafir*?" asked the doctor with a smile.

"Yeah. What does that mean?"

In a cheery voice, he replied, "Oh, in the States you would say nigger."

Carter turned, grabbed the man by the lapels, pulled him close, and quietly said, "No, doctor, we wouldn't."

He quickly let go and then stormed out of the room.

Dr. Thomas straightened his coat and looked at me. "I take it your employee is a communist of some sort?"

I shook my head. "Nope. He almost voted Republican in November."

The man frowned in confusion.

Taking a deep breath, I said, "We want to take Paul back to the U.S. with us. When can we do that?"

Dr. Thomas shook his head. "I'm afraid that's out of the question, Mr. Williams. I couldn't allow the patient to travel. In his condition, it's much too dangerous. The best we can do is make him comfortable. I expect Mr. Vermaut has a week to live, at best."

...

"So, what do we do?" That was Marnie. We were all standing around the bed. After the doctor left, she and Mrs. Dewey came back into the room with Carter and I explained what the doctor had said.

Mrs. Dewey looked down at Paul and very gently touched his cheek. "Well, I don't know about the rest of you, but I plan to stay here. This boy shall not be alone one more minute, as far as I'm concerned."

Marnie took out her handkerchief and dabbed her eyes. "That's good," she said. "We'll take shifts." She looked up at me. "I'll come back after dinner and stay with him tonight. I had plenty of sleep on the plane."

I nodded, unable to speak.

Mrs. Dewey patted her hand. "Good girl. I brought a book with me for just this purpose. It's a copy of *Tales of the Arabian Nights* I found in a shop in London on Wednesday. My Tim loved it so much when he was a child and I suspect Tim and Paul have much in common."

Carter wiped his eyes with his own handkerchief and then blew his nose. "Thank you, both." He let out a big sigh. "And now that we know where to maybe find Freddie, that's what I want to do." He looked at me expectantly.

I nodded and surveyed the room. I could easily see the love and care in everyone's faces. I was so grateful to each of them for being there and for the fact that we could be there and help our friend, who was looking so small in the bed, even if it was just to be right next to him until the end.

For a brief moment, I had a strong feeling we'd all done the same thing before somewhere. But that was ridiculous since our only other friends who'd passed away were Mack and Evelyn. Mack had died in Korea, so that couldn't be what it was. I thought about the feeling, the almost haunted sense of having done very similar, as I looked outside at the rain and the green park below. I decided that what felt familiar was probably the time in Hawaii with Evelyn, right before she died, and the fact I'd sat by the bed and read a book out loud to her. That was probably it. Reading a book was the connection...

However, something in the back of my head said it wasn't. We had all—Carter, Marnie, Mrs. Dewey, and myself—played out a bedside scene before. At some point. I just didn't remember when, for whatever reason.

Chapter 7

Police Station
Donnybrook Road
Mabvuku
Sunday, December 11, 1960
Just before 6 in the evening

"Do you think this is a good idea?" That was Carter. He'd just pulled the Ford into the gravel parking lot in front of the local police station.

I shrugged. "Let's start here and see what happens." As we got out of the car, a strong stench hit my nose. "What is that?"

Carter shook his head. "Smells like raw sewage."

We were obviously in the part of town that, back home, would have been called, "the wrong side of the tracks." When Carter had made a left off Umtali Road, following a tattered sign to Mabvuku, the paved road quickly became a muddy gravel-covered one with big holes in it. Carter had slowed down to keep from breaking an axle by falling into one of the holes. The police station was the first building we'd come to and I'd suggested we stop there first. Beyond that, I could see a larger cluster of buildings that was less like Sacramento and more like some of the poorer parts of Salinas, down by Monterey. There were a lot of cement-block buildings with peeling paint and a few older houses that needed new roofs.

As we walked across the muddy parking lot towards the cement-block police station, it continued to rain.

Carter pulled the door open and he followed me inside. The first thing I noticed was how quiet everything got as soon as we walked in. The next thing I noticed was that the sewage smell was replaced by a mix of strong body odor, antiseptic cleaning liquid of some sort, and a faint trace of vomit.

Everyone in the room was African. Three men were seated on a bench, just to the left of the door. One had a broken nose and a big bruise under his left eye. His shirt was torn down the front, revealing a couple of nasty scars on his chest. The second one had dirty and bloody gauze wrapped around his right fist. He was holding it in his left hand as if it hurt. The third man had a grin on his face and a toothpick in his mouth. He was sitting in such a way to make it clear he wasn't with the first two men. His clothes were cleaner, newer, and neatly pressed. He was tapping his right foot impatiently.

A policeman in a light green uniform seated behind a metal desk stood as quickly as he saw us. He took off his brown cap and held it under his arm. With an official smile, he looked at Carter and, in a mild accent, said, "Yes? May I help you, sir?"

Carter smiled and nodded. "My name is Carter Jones and I'm an American. We're trying to find a friend of ours who we heard might be around here. He's Congolese and—"

One of the men on the bench, I wasn't sure which, muttered something.

The cop looked around me and snapped his fingers at the men on the bench. He then bowed slightly and said to Carter, "I beg your pardon, sir. Do go on."

Carter nodded. "Anyway, he's Congolese and is a refugee and we heard there might be a camp around here where we might find him."

The policeman slowly nodded and ran his right hand over his chin. "May I ask you to wait, sir? I wish to inquire with my lieutenant." He pronounced the word in the English way, so it sounded like he said, "leftenant."

Carter smiled. "Of course. Thank you."

"My pleasure, sir." The policeman moved over to a closed door and quickly knocked on it. As he did that, another policeman from in the back put down his pen and stood. He walked towards the front of the room, where we were standing, and crossed his arms as he watched the three men on the bench. He nodded at me and smiled officially. "Good evening, sir."

I nodded. "Good evening. Does it rain like this all the time?"

One of the men behind me made a sound like a snort.

The policeman snapped his fingers in that direction and then replied to me, "My apologies, sir, for the rudeness." He smiled at me officially again. "In this time of year, it can rain for days and days."

I nodded. "Does it get very hot in the summer?"

"Yes, sir. I should think so."

I nodded again. No one in the room said anything. After what seemed like about two or three minutes, the first policeman emerged from the office and closed the door behind him. As he did, the second policeman tipped his cap at me and then returned to his desk.

The first policeman walked back to his desk and

looked at Carter. "My apologies for the delay, sir. May I ask, what is the name of this Congolese man?"

"Freddie Nyemba," replied Carter.

The policeman nodded. I expected him to make a note of the name or something like that, but he didn't. Instead, he said, "I'm sorry, sir. We do not know of anyone by that name, sir, although it is certainly a common name for a Congolese person."

Carter asked, "Is there a camp?"

The policeman looked down. "There is, but we do not suggest that Europeans, particularly from America, go there. If you would like, however, Constable Gwelo, will accompany you to the temporary camp. Perhaps you will find your friend there."

...

Constable Gwelo turned out to be the second policeman. When we got to the car, he was reluctant to sit in the front seat, so he sat behind me and gave Carter directions.

He pointed out the windshield towards the road on the other side of the police station. "This road is Mabvuku, sir. Make left here." As Carter did just that, the constable continued, "We follow this through Tafara. When we come to a river, there will be the camp."

I turned around in the seat and looked at the man. He looked away from me and kept his eyes on the road. I asked, "How long have you been a constable?"

"Since 1954, sir," he replied without looking at me.

"Do you like the work?"

"It is not unpleasant, sir."

As we slowly moved over a pothole, I asked, "Are you from around here?"

He shook his head without taking his eyes off the road. "I live in Ruwa, sir, seven miles down the Umtali Road."

I felt like I was being rude, so I smiled and turned around in my seat.

Because of the muddy potholes, Carter was driving slowly. The few people out and about were openly staring at us.

From the backseat, Constable Gwelo said, "We are now in Tafara, sir. It is not far."

Carter looked in the rear-view mirror and smiled. "Thanks."

"Yes, sir."

After another five minutes, with the rain coming down a little bit more than earlier, we came to a bridge. The sewage smell was stronger there than it had been at the police station. Off to the left, I could see a ramshackle collection of tents and lean-to tar-paper shacks. No one was outside in the rain but I could see a couple of makeshift stovepipes with wisps of smoke curling out of them.

Carter pulled the Ford off to the side of the road and the three of us piled out. Constable Gwelo led the way along a narrow path and, when we got to the edge of the riverbank, he stopped and called out, "Police! Present yourselves!"

I could hear several people talking and muttering and, after a moment, some heads began to appear in the rain.

The constable called out again, "These American gentlemen are looking for a native of Congo by the name of Nyemba. Who among you is Nyemba?"

Several people looked at us in surprise. I heard a group of men close to the river, huddled together under a group of blankets, talking in what I was pretty sure was Lingala, the language most Congolese from around Léopoldville spoke. One of them looked at me and said, "Nyemba is very usual. What is the Christian name?"

I said, "Freddie."

The man looked at one of the other men in the small group. They talked among themselves for a moment. Finally, the first man looked at me and asked, "You are Williams, no? You had the *Hôtel Albert 1er*, no?"

I nodded and stepped forward.

Constable Gwelo said, "Please, sir, do not approach."

I stopped where I was and said to the man under the blanket, "That's me. Do you know where we can find Freddie Nyemba?"

The man shook his head. "No. I am sorry, no. No one here knows that name."

Carter asked, "Are all of you from Léopoldville?"

The man shook his head. "We are all from Congo. Only two of us are here from *Léopoldville*." Looking around, I figured there were about 30 people in the camp, including some kids I could hear but couldn't see.

"What do you need?" asked Carter. "What can we bring you?"

The man smiled, showing off a couple of missing teeth. "We need warm homes and jobs to work. Can you bring us these things?"

Carter looked at me. I said, "We can try." I reached for my wallet. As I did, the constable said to me, "It is forbidden for you to give these people money."

"Why?" asked Carter.

"They must be returned to Congo. That is the ruling of the government." He raised his voice and looked at the people who were watching us. "Tomorrow we will remove you from this camp. Be prepared."

He turned and walked back up towards the car without waiting for us. I quickly reached into my pocket and pulled out my wallet. I pulled out the hundred Rhodesian pounds, all in fives, I'd gotten from Mrs.

Dewey and kept five for myself. I folded the rest up, walked down the side of the bank, and handed them to the man under the blanket who quickly took them and stuffed them under his shirt.

Everyone who had been watching suddenly surged forward and surrounded me while keeping a respectful distance in a way that reminded me of the Congolese I had worked with before. They began talking, some in French, some in Lingala, and some in other languages.

The first man made a waving motion with his hand and everyone stopped talking. He looked at me in the eyes and said, "These people do not wish to return to the Congo. We are all capable. We can work on the farms here or in the mines. Can you help us?"

I didn't know what to say. I knew 95 pounds would only go so far and I didn't know what else I could do, so I said, "I don't know but I'm going to try. What's your name?"

The man smiled and offered his hand which I shook. "*Monsieur* Williams, my name is *Laurent Kabeya*." He held my hand as the rain dripped off the blanket covering his head. "Please help us."

I nodded. "I'll try. I promise."

. . .

"Where will those people go?" That was me. We were back in the car and headed towards the police station.

The constable, once again in the backseat, replied, "I do not know, sir. We are told to warn the people. I have made that same warning for several weeks since they first appeared."

Carter, still driving slowly as the rain picked up, asked, "Who can we talk to about helping them?"

"I am sorry, sir. I do not know." He thought for a moment. "Since you are Americans, perhaps you can ask the American consul to help."

I said, "Thanks for your help with this, Constable."

"You are very welcome, sir. I am sorry you were not able to find Nyemba." He paused for a moment. "As for the others, I do not know what anyone can do for these Congolese. They are Africans."

Carter said, "But this is Africa."

"Yes, sir, it is. But Rhodesia is not for Africans, sir."

Neither of us said anything as the car slowly moved down the bumpy road in the rain.

...

"This is a job for Lettie." That was Carter. We'd dropped off Constable Gwelo at the police station and were back on the nicely-paved Umtali Road heading into town. The windshield wipers were working overtime in the steady rain.

I nodded. "You're right." I thought for a moment and then added, "I wish we could call her."

"You could try," said Carter.

"Let's start with a telegram and see what she says."

Carter put his left hand on my knee and squeezed.

I said, "Maybe Captain O'Reilly and John Murphy have had better luck."

"I hope so."

We drove in silence for a minute or so.

I said, "I liked what you did with Marnie at the hospital, Chief. I guess you're the only one who really understands how Alex feels about all this. Maybe you should talk to him."

Carter looked over at me for a quick moment before turning back to the road. "Maybe. I don't think Alex knows what to do with me. He likes you. That's obvious."

"I think that's because we have a connection to St. Ignatius." I laughed. "Or he thinks we do, anyway. I remember him, particularly my first year. He seemed so tall to me. I didn't get my growth spurt until I was 16."

Carter said, "I knew you had a crush on him."

I laughed again. "Of course. He was handsome. But everyone liked Alex. It makes sense that he's in P.R. He's very likable."

"He is," said Carter.

"But?"

He shrugged. "I've never seen why he and Marnie are in love. In a lot of ways, she's smarter than he is. But she'll never be a good wife for him to show off."

"That's the kinda stuff people think about in their 20s. Alex will be 40 next year and so will Marnie. He probably doesn't care about that. Besides, with Marnie, you get what you see. She's an open book. If Alex had been worried about something like that, he wouldn't have married her in the first place."

"Do you know anything about their previous marriages, if any?"

I shook my head. "There was some guy in Marnie's past but she's never told me about him. As for Alex, I've never heard."

"I once asked Lettie about Alex," said Carter. "She said Marnie was his first wife. Then she said how glad she was they agreed about children."

"About not having any?"

"Right."

By that time, we were driving into the downtown area where the hotel was located. Carter asked, "Do you think maybe Alex is a Kinsey 4 or 5?"

I snorted. "Why? Because he was in his mid-30s before he got married?"

"Well, it makes you think."

"Not me." I tried to remember what I knew about Alex in school but nothing came to mind, one way or another. "Having worked around so many of us for so long, I doubt that Marnie would have married a man who wasn't a Kinsey 0 or 1."

"Maybe." Carter sounded doubtful as he pulled in front of the hotel.

. . .

Carl, the man at the front desk that morning, had put Carter, Captain O'Reilly, John Murphy, Captain Clement, and myself in a row of single rooms on the tenth floor. Not surprisingly, two sets of the rooms had connecting doors. So, Carter and I had our own kind of suite as did the captain and his first mate. We left the fifth room for Captain Clement who, as far as I knew, was not one of us. He wore a wedding ring and I thought I'd heard Juliette mention a wife in Paris to Marnie.

Carter and I were in rooms 1006 and 1008. Once we were back upstairs, Carter decided he wanted to put on a fresh shirt before we went down for dinner. I left him to it and walked down the hall to knock on the door of 1010 to find out if Captain O'Reilly was back yet.

"Yes?" That was the captain.

"It's Nick."

The door opened a crack. "Come in, Mr. Williams."

I pushed open the door and grinned. The windows were open and, in the twilight, the lights in the room were off. However, in the shadows, I could make out that the men were both buck naked and sitting on the unmade single bed.

John Murphy winked at me. "Well, boyo, want to go a round with us?"

I smiled and shook my head. "No, but thanks. What'd you find out?"

Captain O'Reilly stood and walked over to the desk. He grabbed a pipe and began to knock out the old tobacco over the trash can. "Well, we heard about a camp of Congolese over by some place called Maboku."

"Mabvuku," I corrected, surprising myself that I remembered the word. "We were just there and they'd never heard of Freddie."

From the bed, John Murphy said, "What we mostly heard, from the group of blacks we came across, was admiration for any Congolese who made it here. They said it was no easy journey."

"But they also said there are no jobs for those who come," added Captain O'Reilly who had begun to scoop out fresh tobacco from his pouch with the bowl of the pipe.

"One man, a white one, we talked to said he thought if Freddie had been caught on the hospital grounds, he was likely in jail. Usually they get thirty days for being caught in a European area without a pass."

I nodded. I felt better, somehow, knowing that he was in a dry cell somewhere instead of huddling under a blanket by the river. Then I remembered my own days in jail and decided I would rather be cold and hungry and outside than being somewhat warm and partially fed and unable to move around freely.

Captain O'Reilly tapped the tobacco in the bowl and then walked over to the bed, lighter in hand. "The man gave us the name of a solicitor who works on behalf of the blacks. The solicitor is a good Johnny who sounds a bit like your lawyers back in San Francisco." He handed the pipe to John Murphy and, as that man put it in his mouth, the captain worked the lighter and held it in place while his first mate puffed on the pipe to get it lit. It was a marvel to watch. "Working for the oppressed," continued Captain O'Reilly.

I nodded as John Murphy got a good draw on his pipe. He then patted the captain on the shoulder with an indulgent smile.

...

"Did you get the name?" That was Carter. We were sitting at a table for two down in the Bird and Bottle and waiting for our food. I'd just told him all about my encounter with the captain and John Murphy.

"Yeah. It's Lionel Attaborough. And his office is in this part of town. The man told them he would be easy to find."

Carter pulled a telegram form out of his coat pocket along with a pencil. "Let's write out that note for Lettie and send it tonight before we go to bed."

I nodded and took both the form and the pencil from him. After a moment, I started writing:

```
MRS. LETICIA WILLIAMS 1055 CALIFORNIA ST
SAN FRANCISCO CAL USA. DEAR LETTIE. IN
SALISBURY SO RHODESIA. HAVE FOUND SMALL
GROUP CONGOLESE REFUGEES WHO NEED HELP
CLOTHING HOUSING FOOD JOBS. ANY IDEAS
PLEASE REPLY. MARNIE WITH US BUT NOT
ALEX. LOVE YOUR SON NICHOLAS.
```

"Are you sure about that last sentence?" asked Carter as he read what I'd written. He quickly added, "Not your signature but the part before that."

I shrugged. "If I don't tell her and she doesn't know..."

He nodded. "You're right. You'd be in a hell of a lotta trouble with her if you didn't say anything."

I snorted. "You'd be in just as much trouble, fireman."

He folded the form and put it back in his coat pocket. "Who's going over to the hospital tomorrow to relieve Marnie?"

"I was going to but, after Captain O'Reilly gave me the name of the lawyer, he said the two of them would head over about 7 in the morning and stay with Paul all day."

Carter nodded. "We know some wonderful people, Nick."

I nodded and smiled at him. "We really do."

We sat there for a moment until Carter shifted in his chair and leaned forward. "Now, tell me one more time how Captain O'Reilly lit Mr. Murphy's pipe."

"Don't get any ideas about taking up pipe smoking."

"Oh, I wasn't thinking about that at all, Nick. I have something else in mind."

I laughed as our waiter arrived with our food.

. . .

As we snuggled together on the single bed in Carter's room, he said, "I've said this before and I'll say it again. I love that big bed of your grandfather's at home but I never mind sleeping double in a single bed with you, Nick."

I kissed the side of his arm and replied, "I feel the same way."

I had opened the window before going to bed and the rain was continuing to pour down outside. Even with the window open, the room was close and humid, so we were sleeping without any sheet or blanket and that was fine with me.

Neither of us said anything for a long while. I was about to doze off when Carter asked, "I wonder how Marnie is doing at the hospital with Paul?"

I shifted a little and replied, "I have a feeling she found a magazine or something else to read."

"Why's that?"

"Can you imagine her reading *Tales of the Arabian Nights*?"

Carter guffawed. "Not really. But I can imagine her reading a Nancy Drew or Hardy Boys book."

"Did you read those?"

"A couple of Hardy Boys books, if I remember. I mostly read for school. What about you?"

"I didn't read much when I was a kid."

"But you used to read a lot when we met. You know, *Moby Dick* and books like that."

I nodded. "Sure. But after the house on Hartford Street burned down, I guess I kinda lost interest."

Carter sighed. After a moment, he asked, "Did your mother read to you?"

I tried to remember. "She must have. When I think about her, what I most remember is her sitting in that big bed with her long brown hair. But that was at the end. I don't know if I said so at the time, but once we found out it was arsenic that was making her sick, I realized that was why I remember her as being so beautiful."

"What do you mean?"

"If you take arsenic slowly, it can make your skin and hair take on a kind of glow. Or that's what I read in a book once."

Carter kissed the back of my neck. "I'll keep that in mind."

I sighed. "Speaking of home, at some point we need to find a cook. Gustav makes the best grilled cheese sandwich I've ever had but cooking isn't his job."

"We could just eat at the Mark Hopkins for every meal. Like we did when we lived at the Albert in Léopoldville."

I sighed again. "Well, that's an idea."

"You could start cooking again."

"I've thought about that but, it's like the song says, when you've been to Paree how're you gonna go back down to the farm again?"

Carter laughed. "I love your lasagna. And your chicken pot pie."

I kissed his arm. "Thanks, Chief, but I'd rather have a good American cook. Someone who can make all that and do something fancy when we want that, too."

"I can tell you that when I used to lay awake at nights at home, particularly in 1939 and Henry and I had made our plan to get the hell out of Albany, Georgia, I dreamed of a lot of things but I never once thought I'd be holding a man like you in my arms and be worrying about hiring a good cook while lying in bed in the middle of Africa."

I laughed. "I bet you never thought you'd be thrown in jail, either."

"Oh, I did. Every homosexual I'd ever heard of had been arrested or thrown in jail. I wasn't surprised *that* it happened, only *the way* it happened. What did you dream about when you were a teenager?"

"Nothing, really. I was too busy dealing with life. I used to throw myself down on my bed and look at my toy soldiers. I dreamed about their lives. I couldn't always put it together but I knew they were all men in love."

"And every one of them one half of a couple, right?"

"Of course."

"Well, you got your dream, Nick. Wait..."

"What?"

"Haven't we talked about this before?"

"Maybe." I waited for Carter to continue. When he didn't, I said, "Doesn't matter. Keep talking."

He kissed my neck again, licked it once for good measure, and then said, "You got your dream. You're in charge of all these men in love. Only a few of them were ever soldiers but they all used to wear a uniform or two and most of them are in couples."

I laughed. "It's true. I would never have imagined it would have turned out this way."

Carter pulled in as tight as he could. "Somehow, I get the feeling we've only just gotten started. You know, we've only been at this for seven and a half years? I was a fireman for almost twice as long as that."

"Yeah," I said sleepily.

He kissed me on my neck a third time and said, "Sweet dreams, Nick."

"You too." I could feel myself going in and out. Before I was completely gone, I said, "I love you, Carter Jones."

By that time, he was already asleep but I didn't care because I was ready to head off to dreamland myself.

. . .

"Africa, my boy. Again." That was my Great Uncle Paul. He and I were standing inside a vast ballroom. He was in his usual tuxedo and was looking like he did at 30 or so. I was wearing my usual outfit, a tuxedo like his, right down to the shoes that squeezed my feet.

The ballroom was so large that I couldn't see the far walls. An orchestra somewhere was playing a waltz. He offered his gloved hand to me and I took it. As we made our way around the floor, I realized we were the only white couple. The other couples were all black and all men. Everyone was dressed in either black tie or white tie.

"It's very nice here, is it not?" asked Uncle Paul.

"Who are they?"

"Who, my boy?" he asked as he whisked me around the floor.

"The other men here."

"They are the men of this land. The ancestors of every man and woman you will see on the street."

I looked around. I had never seen so many black faces in one place. It seemed like the room held at least a thousand couples. I noticed that the air was filled with the aroma of a fragrance that was both sweet and earthy. Every time I got a deep breath of it, I could feel myself swoon in Uncle Paul's arms but he held me up and we kept moving, dancing to the waltz from the mysterious orchestra. "Are all of them homosexuals?"

Uncle Paul laughed. "Your affinity for that term is quite charming, my dear boy. Now you have a scale, thanks to the late Dr. Kinsey. You can assess a man, take his sexual temperature, and place him on a scale. Then, and only then, do you know who you're engaging with, am I not right?"

There was something about his tone that I didn't like, so I grudgingly said, "I suppose so. But the Kinsey scale just makes sense."

"But what of these men? They are all long dead and gone and they've never heard of such a word as 'homosexual'."

"But there have always been..." I paused. "Men like us."

"There have indeed but your modern need to clarify and classify tends to get in the way of truly watching and knowing who you're seeing. Not every man, or woman, can classify themselves. Nor should they be subjected to such classification."

I shook my head. I knew it was all a dream but sometimes Uncle Paul confused me.

He pulled me in close, so we were dancing cheek to cheek. "I don't think your Carter will mind if I hold you this way. We are family, after all, and I do have a great affection for you, Nicholas, even if you don't always share my sentiment."

I could feel myself relax in his arms. "But I do."

He kissed me on the forehead and said, "Let's go for a walk, shall we?"

Before I could reply, we were walking down a narrow path. It was suddenly very hot. I looked down and saw that I was wearing a khaki uniform like I'd seen in the movie Gunga Din. Uncle Paul was walking ahead of me and he was wearing the same outfit.

In the distance, I could see a range of mountains. The sound of insects around us was loud. I caught a whiff of the fragrance from the ballroom. I breathed it in, hoping I'd find more of it in the air.

Right then, I heard the sound of men off in the distance. I couldn't understand what they were saying, but there was something about the way they were talking that made me want to hear more.

Uncle Paul stopped and turned to look at me. He had a monocle in his left eye and he grinned. "Do you hear that?"

I nodded. "Who are they?"

"The ancestors of this land. They're inviting us to visit them. Shall we?"

I shrugged and, before I knew it, Uncle Paul and I were in the center of a very large circle of men who were dressed in ways I couldn't understand. I looked all around and saw welcoming faces but, like the language they were all speaking, I couldn't understand how they were dressed. Even as I had that thought, it didn't make sense.

As a group, they began to come closer and, as they did so, I was reminded of the Congolese men and women at the camp by the river who had surrounded me but kept a certain distance. I knew they wanted something from me but I had no idea what it was or how to give it to them.

As I stood in the rain, they all seemed to melt away and I was left by the rushing river, running by its green banks in the twilight. I looked up at the sky and realized the rain had stopped and the stars were out. I gasped as I took in the southern sky and felt the awe of it all.

Chapter 8

Office of Lionel Attaborough, Solicitor
Cheltenham House
Corner of Manica Road and First Street
Salisbury
Monday, December 12, 1960
Just past 9 in the morning

It was a beautiful morning. The rain had stopped by dawn and the air was cool and clear. Carter and I had breakfast that morning with the crew from the Comet. I told them we would be staying for a while since we couldn't take Paul back to the U.S. I asked them to decide whether they wanted to stay in Salisbury or go back to Paris. Captain Clement told me he would get back to me that afternoon with a decision.

Cheltenham House, the building where Mr. Attaborough's office was located, was about a ten-minute walk from the hotel which included a nice stroll through a park called Cecil Square. Carl at the front desk had given us the address along with another hundred

Rhodesian pounds and directions to the brand-new Barclays Bank building a couple of blocks north on First Street from Mr. Attaborough's office.

Following the sign in the lobby, we walked up to the second floor of the building and found room 6. As Carter pushed the door open, I walked in and he followed behind.

The outer office was clean and neat. A row of bookshelves and file cabinets lined the wall to the left. Behind a desk, a woman looked up, surprised, from her morning coffee and roll and smiled. "Good morning," she said as she wiped her mouth with a napkin. "May I help you gentlemen?"

I smiled. "We'd like to see Mr. Attaborough."

"Might I know the nature of your inquiry?"

"We're trying to locate a Congolese refugee who might be in jail."

She nodded and then stood. She was wearing a light orange dress that was a few years out of date but that perfectly matched her brown hair and green eyes. Motioning to a sofa and padded chairs by the front door, she said, "Please have a seat and I'll be right back."

We did as she said and waited while she slipped into an inner office and closed the door behind her.

I looked around. The walls had been recently painted. There were 20 blown-up color photographs of African wildlife and landscapes in modest frames hanging in five sets of four each. Carter stood and walked up to one of the sets.

"Come look at this, Nick."

I stood and walked over. He was looking at four different photographs of what appeared to be one hippopotamus. In one picture , the hippo was yawning. In another picture, it appeared to be looking right at the camera while partially submerged in a body of water.

In the third photograph, it was walking along a dirt road. And, in the fourth, it was standing with another, slightly pinker, hippo.

"Do you think those are all the same animal?" asked Carter.

Before I could answer, from behind us a man replied, "They are indeed. I call him Henry."

Carter and I turned. The man was 6'1", about 45, and trim and tan with weather-beaten skin. He had thinning brown hair, light brown eyes, and a generous mouth that was grinning. He was wearing a heather green suit with a matching vest and a brown tie. He continued, "He's Henry the Hippopotamus and Henry lives in the Zambezi. I took those photographs last summer in Mozambique."

The woman sat down at her desk and went back to her roll and coffee while the man put his hands on his hips.

"My name is Lionel Attaborough and, unless I'm very much mistaken, you are Nick Williams and Carter Jones here in my little office all the way from San Francisco, U.S.A."

The woman looked over at me when he said that and stared for a moment before turning her attention to a folded-over newspaper.

I grinned. "Right in one."

He bowed slightly and stood back from his office door. "Please, gentlemen, do come in and have a seat."

We did as he asked. As we did, he said, "Miss Harroway, I'll be busy until further notice."

As Carter and I sat in the green leather chairs across from his desk, I heard her quietly ask, "Is it really them?"

Attaborough replied but I couldn't hear what he said. She giggled in return as he closed the door.

"Now, what brings you here all the way to Salisbury and to my office?" Attaborough made his way around to his desk and plopped down unceremoniously.

Behind him, I could see a small garden and another office building behind that. All the windows were open and I could hear the traffic from the busy intersection nearby.

Carter said, "We're looking for a friend of ours. His name is Freddie Nyemba. He's from Léopoldville and we think he might have been arrested for trying to get into Central Hospital."

Attaborough leaned back in his chair and nodded. "Quite likely. I take it by his name that he is Congolese and not Belgian?"

Carter nodded.

"Well, I can inquire with the police and find out soon enough. The penalty for being in a European area without a pass is usually 30 days in jail. If they have him, he's in Salisbury Central jail." He thought for a moment. "I don't suppose you would know if he had a Belgian passport."

Carter said, "I don't know but I doubt it. I don't think the Belgians were in the habit of giving passports to most Congolese."

"That's sadly true. Has he an education?"

Carter replied in an irritated tone. "He's very smart but no, I don't think so."

Attaborough held up his hands. "Please don't be offended. I ask only to find out if he was in the colony with papers or without and it would appear to be the case of the latter." He looked at Carter with an expression that was a cross between sympathy and worry. "I'm quite familiar with how the Belgians managed things in the Congo. The government hasn't done much better here so it's rather awful all around, isn't it?"

Carter and I nodded. I asked, "What happens if Freddie doesn't have papers?"

"Well, he'll be deported back to the Congo at the end of his term of incarceration, won't he?"

"Is there any way we can take him to the U.S.?"

Attaborough looked up at the ceiling. "I frankly don't know. I'd say you should head over to the American consulate and ask there. That's rather outside of my scope. While I check with the police you could pop in over there and then we could meet for lunch."

"Where is the consulate?" I asked.

"It's on Rhodes Avenue near Milton. Ask any taxi driver. They'll know."

I nodded and then asked, "How'd you know who we were?"

Attaborough smiled and laughed. "What? You're the most famous homosexual couple in the world! How could I not know who you are?" He blushed suddenly under his tan. "If there were a Nick Williams enthusiasts club, I'd be the chair of the Salisbury branch."

"Do you have a boyfriend?" asked Carter, daringly.

Attaborough shook his head ruefully. "No. I had one once. He was African. Manica Shona, to be precise. We lived together for a few years until the pressure was too great on him and he returned home to Umatli and was married by custom."

"What was his name?" asked Carter.

The lawyer smiled. "He called himself Tavaka but that isn't a real Manica name. In Shona it means, 'I build,' and I think he gave himself that name when he moved to Salisbury so he could blend in. He was a carpenter, so it makes sense. Among our friends, I called him Tavvy."

Right then, there was an apologetic knock on the door. Attaborough said, "Yes?"

The door opened and I heard Miss Harroway say, "Mr. Chuma's cousins are here. They just arrived on the overnight train from Bulawayo."

Attaborough nodded. "Oh, of course. Please ask them to wait five more minutes and when you've done so, can you return with your receipt book?"

I heard the door close behind me.

The lawyer said, "Poor Mr. Chuma. He got into it with a white police officer. I'm hoping we can get him released on a fine instead of having him rot in Salisbury Central. It's quite awful in there. The cousins have arrived to bring what part they could of the fine." He looked at me hopefully. "I'm always looking for willing donors to the cause."

I smiled. "How much?"

"As much as you can spare, quite frankly. The fine for Mr. Chuma is a thousand quid." He paused. "Pounds, I mean. I'm sure the family could only bring fifty or a hundred at most..."

I nodded. "Before we go to the consulate, we're going to the bank. Do you think they'll give me checks?"

"Which bank?"

"Barclays."

He nodded. "Once they know who you are, they'll be happy to let you do anything you want. Only—" He frowned.

"What?" I asked.

"There was a bit in the paper today about how the Americans are trying to restrict cash transfers because of your gold crisis—"

Right then, Miss Harroway knocked and quietly slipped in. She walked over to the side of Attaborough's desk with a big ledger and a ball-point pen.

Attaborough added, "I don't know how much they'll let you bring in."

I grinned. "That's OK. I was planning on moving money from Switzerland."

"Very smart," said Attaborough with a big smile. "Everyone loves Swiss francs, don't they?" I nodded as he turned serious. "Now, as for my fees in your case..."

Pulling out my wallet, I said, "I have exactly a hundred pounds."

"Perfect," replied Attaborough. "My fee is fifty and I'll take the other fifty on account for Mr. Nyemba's fine. You'll need to bring 450 more at lunch and in cash, if you can."

I nodded and handed over a hundred in ten-pound notes. The bills were a russet brown with a lion on the left and the face of Queen Elizabeth on the right. Miss Harroway took them from me, counted them, and then walked over to a small safe on the floor and opened it. Once she had put the money in a locked drawer, she closed the safe and then made her way back to the desk. She wrote out something in the big ledger book, tore out a receipt, and handed it to me. "Here you are, Mr. Williams."

I folded it over and put it in my inner coat pocket without looking at it.

Attaborough stood as Miss Harroway closed the ledger and went back to the outer office. "Where are you staying?" he asked.

"The Ambassador," I replied.

He grinned. "All nice and modern but they forgot to install the air-conditioning, didn't they? Must have been muggy last night without a nice cross-breeze." He looked over at the windows. "This weather is a nice break today. But it will probably pour this afternoon. We'll know by noon or 1 based on how hot it gets." He clapped his hands. "Now, to the point, shall we meet for lunch at Meikles Hotel? It's rather the opposite of the Ambassador although they added a modern wing a couple of years ago. We might see the P.M. having lunch with his cronies. Half past 12, shall we say?"

Carter and I both laughed. It was obvious that Attaborough was getting all worked up and giddy about something. I had the feeling he was looking forward to being seen with us in public, something I wasn't sure was such a good idea. But his enthusiasm was infectious, so we both said, "Yes!"

Chapter 9

Barclays Bank
Corner of Stanley Avenue and First Street
Monday, December 12, 1960
A few minutes before 10 in the morning

The bank was in a brand-new building about nine or ten stories tall that looked like it was made out of red sandstone. I figured it was something more durable than that but, to my mind, the red color was right for Africa.

Carter and I had walked the couple of blocks from Attaborough's office in just under a couple of minutes. As we did, I noticed that most of the people on the street appeared to be white housewives doing their daily marketing. I'd seen a couple of department stores and what looked like a supermarket as we'd made our way up the street. The one thing that stood out, however, was the fact that, in more than one instance, it looked to me as if a black man was following a specific white housewife. As we came to an intersection and waited for the light, one housewife, dressed in yellow, wearing white gloves and a matching yellow hat, and holding her pocketbook in the crook of her arm, stood at the corner and the black man with her appeared to be standing about three steps behind carrying a couple of bags and a parcel. When she crossed the street, he followed. When she entered a shoe store, he stopped and waited a few feet from the door, bags and parcels in hand. I'd never seen anything like it and wondered if maybe I was imagining what I thought I saw.

However, as we entered the bank and walked into the cool and dry of air-conditioning, all of that faded from my mind as I tried to decide exactly how to handle the next part. The big lobby was new with a marble floor and chrome fittings.

Carter tugged on my arm, jutted out his chin, and said, "Let's go over there."

I looked where he was pointing and saw a sign that said, "New Accounts." A young girl was sitting at a desk and looked up as we approached.

She smiled. "May I help you, sir?"

"I'm an American and would like some help exchanging some dollars and opening up an account where I can wire in some money."

Her hair was styled in a way that reminded me of Jackie Kennedy, the wife of the President-elect. The girl even slightly resembled the soon-to-be first lady. Her turquoise dress was tight, up-to-date, and perfectly fit her figure. "Welcome to Barclays Bank. I'll phone Mr. Deavers and see if he is free to come down." She looked at a small row of chairs. "If you'll have a seat over there, I'm sure he'll be right with you."

Carter and I followed her directions and had a seat.

Whispering, Carter said, "Air conditioning is one of God's miracles, son."

I laughed. "It sure is."

As we waited, I watched a woman walk by with two small kids, one boy and one girl. The girl, about 6 or so, was having trouble with her skirt and insisted on stopping in the middle of the lobby to have her mother fix it. "Come along, Pauline," said her mother in an irritated tone. "I'll take care of it but not out here."

The boy, who was 9 or 10, said, "I'm glad I have me own munt house-boy to dress me, mum, since you can't ever seem to do Pauline proud." I had a feeling whatever he'd just said wasn't very nice. That feeling was confirmed when his mother swung back her gloved hand and swatted him on the behind a couple of times.

"How many times, Michael Anthony, must I tell you not to us that word?"

He smiled at her, not at all intimidated, and said, "I'll tell dad how you hit me when he gets home tonight."

His mother, holding Pauline's arm, said, "You do that and see if you don't get more where those came from. Now come along, the both of you."

Whispering, I asked, "What do you think 'munt' means?"

Carter sighed and crossed his arms. "You know exactly what it means."

I nodded.

Right then, a rangy man in thick black glasses walked up and smiled at me. "My name is Mr. Roger Deavers, I'm an officer of the bank, and I understand you wish to open an account with us. Is that correct?" He had a clipped British accent.

Carter and I stood. I shook the man's offered hand and replied, "Yes. My name is Nick Williams. I'd like to exchange some dollars for pounds, wire some money into an account, and, hopefully, get some checks I can spend locally while I'm here."

The man, who was about 40 or so, had dark hair that was slicked back, was clean-shaven, and stood about 6'3" nodded and said, "Well, I'm sure we can do all that, can't we? Will you follow me, please?"

He led us past the desk with the girl who looked like Jackie Kennedy and into an office with his name on a brown plaque just to the right of the door. He motioned to two brown leather chairs in front of a wide wooden desk that was free of clutter except for a photograph of a woman and a boy who were standing in front of a big tree in the middle of an open grassy field that was thick and green. The woman had on sunglasses and the boy was mugging for the camera.

"Have a seat, won't you?" asked Mr. Deavers. He walked around the desk and had a seat in a chair that was the same style as ours. He caught me looking at the photograph and smiled. "That's my Laura and our Joe. He's a little nipper, that one. We were on holiday last March, after the end of the rains and before the school term began. That's a thousand-year-old tree, or so they say, right about ten miles this side of Victoria Falls. Quite a beaut up there. You should visit while you're here..."

He frowned slightly. "Mr. Williams, is it?"

I nodded.

"Welsh, are you?"

"My great-grandfather left Wales to join the gold rush in San Francisco back in 1849."

"Ah," said the man. He looked at Carter expectantly.

"I'm Carter Jones. I work with Mr. Williams."

Mr. Deavers nodded but didn't offer to shake. He looked at me. "Another Welshman, what? Bet you two don't spend a dime between you." He laughed at his own joke, which I didn't get. He then grinned. "But a dime, at least, since neither of you are Scottish."

Carter and I sat there and looked at the man until he cleared his throat. "Right." He pulled out a pad of paper and a pencil from under the desk. "On to business, shall we?" He licked the pencil. "Do you have your passport with you, Mr. Williams?"

I pulled it out of my coat pocket and handed it over.

As he wrote, the man said, "Mr. Nicholas Williams, I see." He looked up. "No middle name or initial?"

I shook my head.

"Very good. What is your address at home?"

"1198 Sacramento Street. San Francisco. California."

The man scribbled. "Where are you staying while here in Salisbury?"

"The Ambassador Hotel."

"Very good. Nice and modern. Prefer the Meikels myself when friends come in." He looked up. "Your profession?"

"I own my own company."

"Of course. Name?"

"Consolidated Security, Incorporated."

"Right there in San Francisco, is it?"

"Yeah."

"What type of business?"

"Private investigation and security."

Deavers looked up at me and grinned. "Private dick, is that the right name?"

"Yeah."

"I love *The Maltese Falcon*. One of my favorite books *and* films. Filmed right there in San Francisco, from what I read."

"Yeah."

Mr. Deavers nodded, finally realizing that I didn't like him. He frowned slightly. "How many pounds do you wish to buy today?"

"However much five thousand dollars will buy."

Carter pulled out a thick envelope from his coat pocket and put it on the man's desk.

Deavers looked up. "In cash?"

I nodded.

He carefully took the envelope and looked at the bills. "All hundreds, I see. Too bad Rhodesian pounds only go up to ten." He looked at me and then made some notations on his pad. "With a small service fee, that comes out to roughly one thousand, seven-hundred, and thirty pounds. Like I say, ten is the highest note we have and I'm not sure I can give you that much cash today." The frown on his face was going deeper.

I nodded. "That's fine. Could you give me five hundred in cash today, a cashier's check for another thousand, and open an account with the balance?"

He nodded, looking relieved. "By 'cashier's check,' I presume you mean a guaranteed bank draft?"

I shrugged. "That sounds right."

"To whom shall we make it payable?" The man took his pencil and waited.

I looked at Carter, who always remembered everything. "Lionel Attaborough."

Mr. Deavers looked up at Carter. "The solicitor?"

"That's right. He has an office a couple of blocks from here."

The man squirmed in his chair. "Are you quite sure?"

I said, "Yeah. I also need to wire in some additional money."

Mr. Deavers nodded as he wrote. "Yes. How much?"

"A hundred thousand Swiss francs."

The man looked up. His frown was even deeper and his mouth was half open. "One hundred thousand?" he asked slowly.

I nodded and pulled out a piece of paper I'd written out at the hotel. "This is the bank name, the account number, and the password." I handed it to him.

He looked at it. "A numbered Swiss bank account? One hundred thousand Swiss francs?"

I nodded. "Is there a problem?"

He looked at me, picked up my passport, and looked closely at the photograph. Suddenly his eyes widened and he sat back in his chair. He dropped the passport as if it was burning and put his hand over his mouth. He quickly stood and picked up the phone on the credenza behind him. After a moment, he said, "Miss Ryverson, call the police station at once and ask for Inspector Graves to come over if he's available. Right to my office, please." He paused. "No, we don't need bank security. Just Inspector Graves. Right. Thank you." With that, he hung up.

Carter slowly stood.

Deavers held out his left hand and backed into the corner. "Now, I don't want any trouble. I simply want to make sure we're not breaking any laws here by doing business with you two..." He paused and made a face. "Buggerers."

...

"Mr. Deavers, it's quite simple. The law you're referring to is about specific acts which I see no evidence of here in your office." That was Inspector Harold Graves. He looked like he'd just come from central casting. He was wearing a brown hat, a khaki trench coat over a dark green suit, and smoking a pipe. He was about 50 or so and sported a beard of salt-and-pepper hair. He was standing by Mr. Deavers's desk and appeared to be amused by the situation. Carter and I were in the same seats we'd been in for half an hour.

"That's fine, Inspector," replied the bank officer. "I just wanted to bring your attention to the matter before we proceed."

The inspector pulled on his pipe thoughtfully. His accent was definitely English and it reminded me a little bit of Lord Gerald's. "Of course, you're free not to do business with Mr. Williams. That's your prerogative under the law."

Mr. Deavers smiled weakly. "No, no. Business is business and here at Barclays, we never get in the way of business." He turned and grabbed the telephone. "Miss Ryverson, could you telephone the head teller and ask him to bring me five hundred pounds in tens and then come into my office. I have some forms for you to fill out, if you please." Without waiting for her reply, he put the receiver down and looked at the inspector. "I apologize for taking up your valuable time this morning, Inspector."

"That's quite alright, Mr. Deavers." He puffed on his pipe and looked at me. "I'll be waiting for you in the lobby, Mr. Williams, when you're done. I'd like to have a word with you and Mr. Jones, if you don't mind."

His voice was friendly and I was pretty sure I'd heard the warning before, from other police officers in other parts of the world, so I smiled and replied, "Sure."

He tipped his hat to the bank officer and said, "Good day, Mr. Deavers."

The man nodded. "Good day, Inspector."

. . .

Carter and I headed to the lobby. In my trouser pocket, I had a folded-over check for a thousand pounds payable to Lionel Attaborough. My passport was back in my coat pocket. Carter had an envelope full of pounds in his inner coat pocket. Mr. Deavers had asked us to return the next day to sign the paperwork opening the account. He said the wire transfer would be done by then and he'd have a checkbook waiting. I had a feeling someone else would be helping us when we returned.

We found Inspector Graves waiting for us just inside the lobby door. He nodded at me and motioned towards the door. I led the way and, once we were out on the sidewalk, he said, "There's a car waiting for us right around the block. Won't you come with me to the police station?"

"Are we under arrest?" asked Carter.

The inspector laughed. "No, of course, not. We can walk over to a milk bar, if you'd like. I just thought we'd have more privacy in my office. Whichever is fine by me." I was confused for a moment until I remembered that a milk bar was a soda shop. We'd been to one outside of Sydney in Australia back in '55.

Carter looked at me. I shrugged. "Let's go to the police station."

He nodded and we followed the inspector around the corner.

. . .

"I just wanted to have a friendly chat with the two of you and lay out how it works here so you won't find yourselves in trouble." That was Inspector Graves. He'd removed his trench coat, put his hat on the rack, and was sitting behind his desk and lighting his pipe.

Carter and I were seated on two hard-back chairs across the desk from him.

Once he got a good puff, the inspector smiled and said, his pipe still in his mouth, "I'm a broad-minded kind of fellow but I'm duty-bound to warn you not to do anything that will attract attention or cause the police to be called." He leaned back in his chair. "To begin..." He reached over and tapped on his desk with two fingers. "Two hotel rooms. Single beds only."

I nodded. "What else?"

"Stay away from the settlements and African areas. I already know you were in Mabvuku yesterday, asking about some Congolese man. Leave Africa to the Africans and mind your own business."

Carter leaned forward. "What's going to happen to those people in that camp?"

The inspector grinned and looked at his pipe. "Not really any of your concern, is it Mr. Jones? That's an internal matter and will be dealt with promptly."

"How?" I asked.

"By repatriation, no doubt."

I nodded and then stood. "Anything else?"

The inspector smiled at me. It was authentically friendly but I didn't like it. I wondered if he was one of us. I didn't think so. He reminded me a lot of Carter's stepfather, Ed Richardson, who had been a deputy sheriff in Vermont before he married Carter's mother. Ed had once told me that he considered himself to be a Kinsey 0. He had no interest in men at all and that meant he wasn't threatened by other men who did. I was pretty sure the inspector would have said the same thing, if I'd had the guts to ask him. He turned towards the door. "Nothing at the moment, Mr. Williams. If I can be of any help whilst you're in Salisbury, please let me know." He put his hand to his empty forehead as if he was tipping his cap. "Good day to you both."

And, with that, we left.

Chapter 10

Consulate of the United States of America
Rhodes Avenue
Monday, December 12, 1960
Half past 11 in the morning

"Mr. Smith will be here in just a few minutes. Would you like coffee or tea?" That was a nice Rhodesian gal of about 30 in a dark blue dress with a frilly blouse. Her heels made a discreet tapping noise when she walked across the wood floor of the consulate building, which I figured dated to the turn of the century.

Carter and I were seated at a beautiful round table made of inlaid wood. It was glowing in the sunlight from the big windows that were open to an interior courtyard. Outside, some birds I'd never heard before were chattering to each other. I looked at the gal and said, "No, I'm fine."

Carter echoed the same and the gal left, closing the door behind her.

"It smells in here," was the only thing Carter had to say.

I nodded. "Wood rot, I think."

He sighed. "This has been some morning."

"Yeah."

Right then, someone knocked on the door. As it opened, a man of about 55 or so and dressed in a white suit with a light blue tie walked in. He looked at me and then at Carter. With an apologetic smile, he said, "My name is Roger Smith." He pulled up a chair to the table, sat down, and removed his hat, putting it on the table. As he removed his handkerchief from his coat pocket, he added, "The consul is over at a meeting with the prime minister." He wiped his face quickly and looked at Carter and then back at me. "Is there something I can help you with?"

I smiled. "My name is Nick Williams and this is Carter Jones."

He nodded. "Nice to meet you both. Did you register up front so we know where you are while you're here?"

We both nodded.

"Good," he said and wiped his face again.

Carter looked at me and I nodded. He leaned forward and said, "We were wondering if you could help us with a couple of things."

"Of course," replied Mr. Smith with a smile.

"There's a makeshift refugee camp of Congolese men, women, and children near Mabvuku and we want to help them."

Mr. Smith frowned. "I see. What's your interest in their situation?"

I piped up. "We used to live in Léopoldville. We left at the end of June. And that's actually why we're here."

Tilting his head at me, Mr. Smith said, "I don't follow."

Carter said, "A Belgian friend of ours, Paul Vermaut, is in Central Hospital. We flew down here on Saturday because we were hoping to take him home, to San Francisco, to get him treatment."

"What does he have?"

"The doctor doesn't know. All he knows is that Paul has a high fever and has been losing weight. They don't expect Paul to live for more than a few days."

Mr. Smith wiped his face again. "I'm so sorry." He looked at Carter and then back at me. "What does this have to do with Léopoldville?"

I smiled. "Sorry. We know Paul from there. He and a Congolese friend made their way here from Léopoldville. We were looking for Freddie, he's the friend, and that led us to the Congolese camp. Freddie wasn't there. He's probably in jail. But when we saw those people, we wanted to do something."

Mr. Smith seemed more confused than ever. We weren't doing a good job of explaining ourselves. He put his left hand on the table, looked at me, and said, "Let me see if I have this right."

I nodded.

"You flew down here on Saturday?"

I nodded again.

"From where?"

"Naples."

"I see." He thought for a moment. "You mean Rome, right?"

I shook my head. "No, Naples. We have our own jet."

Mr. Smith frowned and then began to nod. "Oh! Now I see." He smiled. "You want to take these Congolese back to Léopoldville? You have your own jet." He wiped his face one more time. "Oh, I'm sure that won't be a problem. The Southern Rhodesian government will probably give you a medal if you would take care of that problem for them. They can't seem to make up their minds what to do." He nodded. "Oh, this is quite simple. The consul will be more than happy to hear about this."

Carter put up his left hand. "Mr. Smith?"

"Yes?" he asked with a smile.

"They don't want to go back to Léopoldville. We were hoping we could bring them back to the States. We could sponsor them, put them up in houses and apartments, and get them jobs. We don't have all the details." In fact, we didn't. We hadn't heard back from Lettie by the time we left the hotel. Carter added, "But it would be something like that."

Mr. Smith was back to frowning. "I'm afraid that would be impossible. In order for these people to immigrate to the U.S., they would have to go back to the Congo first and apply at the embassy there. Regardless of the fact that you are offering to sponsor them, there is a quota of one hundred immigrants per year per country and I feel certain that limit has been reached for the Congo this year although you could certainly contact the embassy in Léopoldville to find out for certain." He shook his head and then wiped it again. "I'm sure you're both being very generous but your idea simply isn't possible." He looked at Carter, sympathetically. "Besides, these people are likely from the deep bush. Most of them are probably illiterate. They wouldn't get along well in a modern city like San Francisco."

Chapter 11

Meikles Hotel
Corner of Stanley Avenue and Third Street
Monday, December 12, 1960
A quarter before 1 in the afternoon

"Sorry we're a little late." That was Carter as the two of us sat down at Attaborough's table towards the back of the hotel restaurant, La Fontaine.

The lawyer smiled at Carter. "I just arrived myself."

A waiter appeared out of nowhere and politely asked, "Your drinks, sirs?"

Attaborough asked, "How are you, Mr. Masiyiwa?"

The man nodded quickly. "Quite fine, sir. What drinks?" I got the impression he didn't want to be seen chatting with the lawyer.

Attaborough took the hint and replied, "I'll have a coffee, black, if you would."

Carter and I both nodded. I said, "We'll have the same."

The waiter nodded and left by backing away from the table.

Attaborough sighed. "Client of mine but it doesn't do for him to be seen conversing with me." He fiddled with his spoon. "I'm not very nice to know."

I laughed. "Neither are we."

Carter added, "Seems like we're in good company."

Attaborough blushed suddenly and cleared his throat. "Well, I'm more than pleased to finally meet the two of you. I never thought I would." He squirmed in his seat again. "But on to business, I was—" A slight commotion over by the bar got his attention

Carter and I looked over in that direction. A group of four men were making their way through the dining room. One of them, sporting a pipe and a rumpled light brown suit, noticed Attaborough and tipped his hat. Another one looked in our direction and, as he did, his eyes narrowed. He was mildly handsome with curly dark hair.

"Oh my," whispered Attaborough as he nodded at the man who'd tipped his hat.

"What?" I asked.

Still whispering, he answered, "There's the whole of the Southern Rhodesian power structure right there in the slightly flabby flesh." He looked down at the table and seemed to be trying to make up his mind about something as he tapped his fingers.

Right then, our waiter appeared with our drinks. He set them out and then waited.

Attaborough looked at me. "I'd suggest the cottage pie for the both of you. It's hearty, truly English, and they do it right here."

"What's that?" asked Carter.

"A layer of ground Rhodesian beef with fresh vegetables in a brown gravy covered with mashed potatoes and baked in a pie. You can't miss."

Carter and I both nodded. The waiter nodded and said, "Cottage pie for the gentlemen." He looked at Attaborough. "And for sir?"

"I'll have a steak, rare, if you would."

The waiter nodded and retreated the same way he had before.

"So who were those men?" asked Carter. I glanced over to a table by the window where they were seated and talking to a waiter.

Attaborough leaned forward. "The man who tipped his hat is Sir Edgar Whitehead. He's the P.M. of Southern Rhodesia. Nice fellow, tries hard, but is completely muddled on matters of race. He giveth with one hand and taketh with the other. The curly-haired man is Ian Smith. He's an M.P. in the Federal parliament and is the Whip. He's an up-and-comer in the U.F.P. but I hear he's unhappy with Sir Edgar's work with Britain on a new constitution for Southern Rhodesia. The third man is the American Consul. He's the one in the blue suit who's all smiles. Name of Jeremy Laughton. Supposedly knew Eisenhower during the war. I understand he'll definitely be replaced after Kennedy takes office." Attaborough frowned. "I wonder what he could be here to discuss? He really has no right to interfere with local matters." Shrugging, he continued, "The fourth man, the obnoxious one in tweeds with the fatuous grin on his face, is D.C. Lilford. He owns a huge ranch and tobacco plantation and pity the African who works for him." Looking at Carter, he said, "He would do well in a place like Georgia in the States."

Carter nodded and took a sip of his coffee. "I know the type."

Looking at me, Attaborough added, "He's probably the second richest man in Salisbury at the moment." Grinning, he said, "You being the first."

I shrugged. That kind of talk always made me uncomfortable.

Carter, who was aware of how I felt, quickly changed the subject. "You mentioned a federal parliament while ago. What does that mean?"

"There are three British colonies in federation since 1954. Northern Rhodesia, Southern Rhodesia, and Nyasaland. If you look on your bank notes, you'll see they've been issued by The Bank of Rhodesia and Nyasaland." As if coming out of a daze, Attaborough looked at me. "Speaking of money, how went your visit at Barclays Bank?"

I grinned. "They called the police on us once the bank officer figured out who we were."

Attaborough sat up straight. "Did they, now?"

Carter said, "But the police inspector was nice enough. Nick got his bank account and more pounds and they'll have checks for him tomorrow morning. We did get to ride over to the police station, though."

"But no arrest?"

I shook my head. "No. Just the usual warning from an Inspector Harold Graves."

Attaborough grinned. "Ole Harry is a good 'un. He's not an out-and-out racist, which for the Salisbury police is saying a lot."

"He did say that he already knew we'd been to Madv..." I couldn't pronounce the name.

"Mabvuku," prompted Carter.

Nodding, Attaborough said, "That's hardly surprising. He doesn't miss much, our Harry."

Carter leaned forward. "Speaking of Mabvuku, what'd you find out about Freddie?"

"He's in quod, all right."

"Quod?" I asked.

"Sorry. Jail." Looking at me, the lawyer asked, "Do

you have the additional 450 pounds?"

Carter patted his coat. "I have it here."

"Good. Once we're done here, you can give it to me and I'll have a receipt for you tomorrow. I have a meeting right at half past 2 but I should be able to get over to the Magistrate Court by 4 and apply for Mr. Nyemba's release. If everything goes as usual, he'll be out of Salisbury Central by 8 tomorrow morning." He leaned forward and, in a lower tone of voice, said, "Which brings us to a problem. I don't think anyone has put two and two together and realized he's a foreign national. So we need to get him and stash him somewhere and then you'll have to smuggle him out of the country if you don't want him deported back to the Congo. Can you do that?"

I nodded. As I did, the man Attaborough had pointed out as being Sir Edgar walked up, all grins.

"Well, Attaborough. You three look thick as thieves over here. Not plotting to get one of your favorite terrorists out of quod are you, what?"

Keeping a straight face, the lawyer stood and offered his hand. "Good to see you, Sir Edgar." He looked over at the other table. "I should ask you the same thing." He grinned at the older man. "Plotting with Boss Lilford and the American Consul. Naughty, naughty, Sir Edgar. What would Her Majesty think if she knew her Prime Minister was up to something tricky?"

That obviously made Sir Edgar angry. He was holding his pipe in his right hand. He poked the bowl in Attaborough's face and said, "Now see here, you radical, you. I won't have you accusing me of any such thing. I can bring you up on charges of slander, don't you know?"

Attaborough put a hand on the man's shoulder. "Oh, Sir Edgar, I was just strutting about and making noises to entertain our friends, here." He motioned to me and I stood. "Sir Edgar Whitehead, may I present Mr. Nicholas Williams of San Francisco? Mr. Williams, this is our illustrious Prime Minister."

I offered my hand. "How do you do, sir?"

He shook but without much enthusiasm. "Pleased to meet you, Mr. Williams. What brings you to the heart of Africa?"

"We have a friend who is in the hospital."

Sir Edgar put his pipe in his mouth and frowned. "Sorry to hear that. Whereabouts is he?"

"Central Hospital," I replied.

"Fine, fine. It's a fine place. I'm sure your friend will be put to rights in no time."

I smiled as much as I could and nodded. Then I pointed to Carter who then stood. "Sir Edgar, this is my business associate, Mr. Carter Jones, also of San Francisco."

Carter offered his hand. "Sir Edgar."

The prime minister shook and said, "Mr. Jones." He then looked at Attaborough. "Well, behave yourself, sir. I know you're doing what you believe in even if not everyone agrees upon your methods."

Attaborough clapped Sir Edgar on the back and said, "I shall try. But let me walk you back to your table. I especially want to have a little chat with Mr. Lilford on a small matter."

The prime minister shook his head but didn't object. As the two of them crossed the room, Attaborough looked over his shoulder and winked at me with a quick grin.

Carter and I took our seats right as our waiter arrived with our food. Once it was all set out, he asked, "May I bring you anything, sirs?"

Carter said, "No, thank you. This looks good."

"Be cautious, sir. It just came out of the oven and is piping."

Carter smiled. "Will do. Thanks."

I smiled at the man as he retreated from the table.

I poked the potatoes on top of my pie with a fork to let out the steam. "This smells good."

Carter nodded and took a sip of his coffee. "It does." He looked over at the far table where Attaborough was grinning wildly while Mr. Lilford was going on about something and the American Consul looked mildly shocked. "He and Lettie need to get together."

I snorted. "He could move to San Francisco and become the fifth terror." Several years earlier, I'd come up with the name "Four Terrors" as a kind of joke to describe Lettie, Carter's mother, her sister, and Mrs. Geneva Watkins. They were four women to be reckoned with and even Eisenhower knew who they were. They weren't afraid to demand whatever they thought was just and fair for people who weren't able to do so themselves. I loved them all and admired them all and was a little afraid of them at the same time.

Carter said, "Speaking of Lettie, I hope she has some ideas for us when we get back to the hotel."

I took a bite of the mashed potatoes. They were still too hot so I swallowed them quickly, hoping not to burn my mouth. "I'm beginning to have an idea of my own but I'm sure Lettie has something better in mind."

...

"Now, that was some fun there." That was Attaborough as he took his seat. "I got to pull the tiger's tail and didn't get bitten." He grinned at me. "Well, not too much." He cut into his steak, took a bite, and swallowed without chewing very much. Pointing at me with his fork, he said, "You need to move."

"What?" I asked.

"When your Mr. Nyemba is released from quod, you have to hide him until you're ready to leave. Not to worry," he said as he took another bite of steak and pretty much swallowed it whole. "I've got a plan."

I waited and listened as I had a sip of coffee.

"I've a house I rent out from time to time. It's perfectly respectable. Bought it from a client who needed to leave in a rush and was willing to part with it on the cheap." He grinned as he pushed another piece of meat into his mouth. "One of us, don't you know, and so it's a deluxe arrangement. There's a swimming pool in back and, down in the lower garden, there's a brick hut for a house-boy. Nice place, as they go, with running water and electricity. It's a perfect place for Mr. Nyemba to hide out. He'll blend in perfectly. But, unless there are some nice white folks for him to care for, the neighbors will get suspicious." He leaned forward as he had more coffee. "Don't suppose you have any ladies around who could move in with you?" Without waiting for me to answer, he added, "It's a big place. Four bedrooms, matter of fact, and two baths. Having ladies in the house would give you a facade of respectability, don't you know?"

I nodded and said, "There are two gals with us. One of them is my secretary and the other works for us as a P.I."

"Perfect!" said Attaborough. "How about we say fifty pounds a week, including all utilities? The house is completely outfitted with anything you could want and there's a phone on the premises but likely it's bugged. I assume all my phones are except the one at work which I keep an eye on." He shoved another piece of meat in his mouth and grinned.

"Fine with me," I said, hoping Marnie and Mrs. Dewey would be willing to move in with us.

Carter cleared his throat and frowned at Attaborough. "Freddie is not going to live in a hut down by the pool even if it has electricity and running water. Not if I have anything to do with it."

The lawyer swallowed his latest bite, again without chewing, and looked over at Carter. He nodded. "It's all for *show*, man. When Tavvy and I were together, he made a show of living in the hut at my house but, then, when the lights were out and it was dark outside, he would come in and we certainly slept together in the same bed. Every night we were together. There's no other way to do it. Otherwise, some nosy neighbor calls the police and next thing you know, you're in quod and there's no way out." He shook his head and whispered, "Sodomy with an African? I could have been put to death, quite easily." He cut another piece of meat. "Every morning, rain or shine, he would go outside, first thing, before sunrise and do this and that. He would then return and we would sleep a bit more together before getting ready for the day."

Carter took all of that in but still wasn't happy.

"There are four bedrooms, Mr. Jones. The two of you take one, you have one for Mr. Nyemba, and the rest are for your ladies." He shrugged and sat back. "Plenty of room for everyone."

Chapter 12

Central Hospital
North Avenue and Mazoe Street
Room 311
Monday, December 12, 1960
A few minutes before 3 in the afternoon

"*Ilfakis obeyed the emir's orders, and agreed to his proposal. Young Habib was committed to his new master. They lived together in the same tent.*" That was John Murphy reading to Paul as Carter and I quietly walked in the hospital room. Captain O'Reilly was snoozing in the chair at the end of the bed while John Murphy sat on a chair right by the bed with the book on his lap and a small pair of metal-rimmed glasses perched on his nose. The windows were open and there was a nice breeze blowing through the room.

Carter whispered, "How goes it?"

The first mate stopped reading, stood, and stretched. "Boyo over there is out like a light and Master Paul hasn't moved or said a word in almost three hours. Nurse says that's a good sign that he's resting better."

Captain O'Reilly suddenly came to with a snort. He ran his hand over his face and yawned. After looking around the room, he smiled at me and asked, "Any luck today?"

I grinned. "We hired a lawyer, opened a bank account, got a stern warning from a police inspector, found out Freddie is in jail, put up the fine to get him out..." I looked at Carter and asked, "What else?"

He crossed his arms. "We scared the bank officer once he found out who we were—"

"Bringing in the police, I assume?" asked the captain.

"Yep," said Carter. "We also met the prime minister, went to the American Consulate, and had a nice lunch of cottage pie."

Captain O'Reilly patted his stomach. "We didn't fare as well. We ordered a lunch from the cafeteria. The only thing I liked was the Jell-O, to be honest."

I said, "We came by to give you a break."

John Murphy said, "Thank you, Mr. Williams. We can come back tonight."

Carter said, "Well, talk it over with Marnie and Mrs. Dewey."

The captain nodded and yawned again. "Can we bring you anything?"

"Yeah," I said. "Check to see if we have any messages."

"We can bring them for you with some dinner, if you like," offered the captain.

"Sounds good. We're moving into a house tomorrow, hopefully with Marnie and Mrs. Dewey, but would you let the hotel know you'll be needing rooms through Saturday. And let the crew know the same thing. I said they could leave, but we need them on standby."

John Murphy looked from me to Carter and then asked, "Anythin' you can tell us about?"

I quickly explained the situation with Freddie needing a place to hide out and why Attaborough thought it was a good idea to bring Marnie and Mrs. Dewey along.

The first mate shook his head with a sigh. "Don't like it here one bit."

Carter nodded. "Me, neither."

John Murphy then looked over at the bed. "Master Paul, we'll be seein' you soon."

The captain walked around the far side of the bed and kissed Paul on the forehead. "Be good and don't flirt with the nurse."

They both waved at us as they left.

Carter sat down where John Murphy had been and picked up the book. I walked over to the window and looked down at the park as Carter began to read. "*The cares of the governor found a soil so naturally happy, and so well prepared in his young pupil's mind, that it was fit to receive every degree of cultivation. Habib was soon able to tell the names of all the stars, to describe the paths of the planets, and to calculate their sizes and distances. He knew the various species of trees and plants, and could describe their properties.*"

. . .

"Knock, knock." That was Marnie at the hospital door. The sun was low in the sky but I had no idea what time it was. I knew it was close to dinner because my stomach was grumbling.

"Come in, doll," I said quietly. Carter was snoozing in the chair at the end of the bed. I had pulled down Paul's thin white sheet and was gently rubbing his arms and chest with alcohol using a set of small soft cloths. The nurse had come in a few minutes earlier to do it and I had asked her if I could. When she quietly protested, I told her I'd once been a hospital orderly in San Francisco and a medical corpsman in the Navy. Satisfied I was qualified, she'd shown me how she wanted it done and then left me to it.

Marnie walked over to the table where the radio was sitting and put a couple of brown paper bags down there. "I brought you some sandwiches and a bottle of beer to share. Mrs. Dewey will be here around 10 if you can hold on until then unless you want me to stay."

I shook my head as I rubbed Paul's chest. All the muscle was gone and it was practically bones. I tried to ignore that and focus on rubbing in circles like the nurse had showed me. "That's fine, doll."

"Well, I'll be back at 5 in the morning to take over from Mrs. Dewey. What's this I hear about you moving us into a house?"

I explained it to her.

"That's fine. I'd rather be in a house anyway. I'm sure Mrs. Dewey would too, but I'll check with her."

"Thanks, doll. I asked John Murphy to take care of the rooms for the two of them and the crew through Saturday. Do you mind double-checking on that when you get back to the hotel?"

"Sure, Nick."

I looked up and saw the dress she was wearing. It was a light purple and just perfect for her. "So you went shopping today?"

She modeled her dress for a moment. "Do you like it?"

I smiled. "Sure, doll."

"I went to a couple of places. Barbours and..." She thought for a moment. "Oh yeah, Haddon and Sly." She frowned.

"What?"

"Well, I could have imagined it, but I'd swear I saw some Negro men following white women. And always three or four steps behind. They didn't go inside the stores but waited outside with bags and boxes."

"I saw the same thing this morning too."

"Why do they do it?"

"Who? The women or the men?"

She thought for a moment. "Both, I guess."

I shrugged. "I'm the wrong person to ask. Did your mother send a telegram?"

Marnie sighed. "No, not yet. Seems strange, doncha think?"

"I do. What about Alex?" I looked up from Paul to see how she reacted to my question.

She smiled. "He sent me a long one. We're all made up now."

I smiled back. "I'm glad to hear that. How's he liking Paris?"

"He said he moved into your house and is helping Gustav and Ferdinand clean things up."

"Oh," I said and began to rub Paul's left arm.

"Nick?"

"Yeah, doll?"

"Why didn't you want us to stay there?"

I sighed. "I wanted to give Gustav and Ferdinand some time to themselves. They don't get as much of that as I think they deserve. It's also nice when they have the run of a house since I can't convince them to move up to the third floor at home. We did expand the rooms in the basement and they both say theirs is fine. But I wish they had a view of the park from the third floor."

"You really like both of them, don't you?"

I nodded as I used a cloth to rub Paul's palm. As I did, I felt him gently squeeze. I stopped and looked at his face. In the fading light, I could see his eyes rolling around under his closed eyelids. I said, "Go tell the nurse I think he's coming around."

Marnie ran out the door.

I said, "Paul?" I waited. "Paul? It's Nick. You're in the hospital."

He moaned slightly.

Right then, the nurse ran up to the other side of the bed. She felt his forehead and lifted his left eyelid. "Say his name, sir."

"Paul?"

We all waited.

"Paul, it's Nick."

"Ask him to wake up," whispered the nurse.

"Paul, wake up. Paul?"

After a long moment, he sighed and then whispered something. The nurse bent close to listen and then smiled at me. "He asked for water. I'll get some ice chips and then call doctor. Keep talking to him."

I leaned forward. "Paul? How do you feel? We're in Salisbury in Southern Rhodesia. You're in the hospital."

He opened his eyes and blinked. He closed them again.

"Paul, wake up. The nurse'll be here with water in a minute."

He ran his tongue over his lips and nodded slightly. He said something.

I stood and bent over so my left ear was right over his face. "What?"

"Carter?" he croaked.

I pulled back so I could see his face. "He's here too."

Marnie walked over and put her arm on Carter's shoulder. "Carter, wake up. Paul is awake and he's asking for you."

Carter sat up. "What?"

She repeated, "Paul's awake and he's asking for you."

Carter stood, patted Marnie's arm, and walked over to where the nurse had been standing. He took Paul's left hand and held it gently. "Hi, Paul. Good to see you awake."

Paul whispered something else.

I leaned over again. "What?"

"Freddie?"

"He's around but he's not here right now," I replied looking over at Carter.

Carter added, "But he's fine. We'll see him tomorrow."

"What day?" asked Paul, sounding a little stronger.

"Monday, the twelfth of December," I replied.

He nodded. "Water?"

I looked at Marnie who was standing at the end of the bed. She nodded and ran out the door. I said, "The nurse'll be here soon."

Paul smiled a little. "Sorry I miss *de* gym." I could hear his Dutch accent more strongly than I remembered from before.

Carter ran his hand over Paul's forehead. "It'll be there when you get better. I promise."

Paul shook his head slightly. "*Nee*. I hear *de* doctor."

Carter caressed his forehead again and said, "We don't know anything yet, Paul."

He opened his eyes and looked up at Carter. "*Het is* OK." He closed his eyes again and sighed.

Right then, a couple of doctors and the nurse rushed in. I'd never seen either doctor before. The nurse said, "Please, sirs, stand back."

Carter and I walked around to the end of the bed and watched as the doctors began to prod and probe. The nurse had a coffee cup with ice chips. As the doctors stood on one side of the bed and took Paul's pulse and temperature, the nurse gently rubbed a big ice chip on Paul's lower lip.

After a moment, one of the doctors began to speak in what I was pretty sure was Dutch. Paul replied and nodded slightly. The doctor put the back of his hand on Paul's forehead and waited for a moment. He asked another question and Paul nodded slightly.

Finally, the doctor patted Paul's arm and said a final few words in Dutch. He then walked towards us, with his colleague in tow, and motioned for us to follow them.

Once we were out in the hall, the first doctor said, "I am Dr. Visser. Your friend, did he mention if he could hear you speak when he was unconscious?"

I nodded. "He said he heard the other doctor..." I looked at Carter.

"Dr. Thomas," he said.

I nodded. "He heard Dr. Thomas tell us he would die in the next few days."

Dr. Visser and his colleague both made faces that gave me the feeling they didn't approve. "I won't detain you so you may speak with him for his fever is very high now and I think he has not much longer. Maybe a day, maybe an hour, maybe less."

"What about an ice bath?" asked Marnie.

Dr. Visser nodded. "Yes, we will prepare one for him." He gently pushed on my arm. "But now you go and speak with him. He will sleep if he tires but is more important that you talk with him while he is awake."

I nodded and led the way back in while Marnie said, "Thank you, Doctor."

. . .

"Tell me *de* truth *over* Freddie." That was Paul. He had slightly more color than before but, whenever I touched him, his skin felt as if it was on fire.

I looked at Carter who nodded. We were seated on either side of him. Carter had the cup of ice chips and was rubbing Paul's lips with them. The nurse had said not to let him swallow any because he might choke on one.

I said, "Freddie is in jail."

Paul smiled slightly as Carter ran a chip over his lips. "Poor bugger."

"Do you want us to tell him anything?" asked Carter.

Paul blinked a couple of time. I saw a tear emerge on the side of his left eye. "Tell him I love him." He sighed and shifted a little. "Bloody fool."

Carter and I both chuckled.

Paul closed his eyes and seemed to drift off to sleep. Carter kept rubbing his lips gently. After about five minutes, Paul suddenly came to. He said something in Dutch.

I asked, "What's that in English?"

Paul smiled a little and opened his eyes. "I want to see Freddie."

Carter said, "He's in jail right now."

"Will he be out?"

"Tomorrow morning at 8."

Paul nodded, swallowed with some effort, and then said, "I love..." He seemed to fall back to sleep and then came back with a start. "Your voice..." He started to turn his head back and forth as if he was struggling.

I said, "It's OK, Paul."

He relaxed and swallowed again. "Carter..."

My husband leaned forward. "Yes?"

Paul smiled and croaked in a way that I was pretty sure was a laugh. "Georgian Arab *verhalen*."

"What?" asked Carter.

From the end of the bed, Marnie said, "I think he likes the way you read those Arabian Tales with your Georgia accent."

Paul nodded with as much vigor as he could muster and then chuckled again, very hoarsely.

In a thick accent, Carter said, "Well, son, I'm mighty pleased you enjoyed them there tales."

Paul smiled as tears appeared in the corners of both of his closed eyes. "No more."

I asked, "No more what?"

He smiled faintly.

I put my hand on his forehead. It was hot, way too hot. I looked at Marnie and whispered, "Where's the ice bath?"

"I'll go check." She rushed out the door.

Paul very faintly said, "Love you, Nick."

I kissed his forehead very gently. "I love you too, Paul."

He nodded slightly.

Carter leaned over and kissed our friend's forehead. "I love you, Paul." He then looked at me and mouthed, "He's burning up."

I nodded as Paul very quietly said again, "No more."

"No more what?" I asked.

Paul sighed and then stopped breathing and never did start again.

Chapter 13

The Ambassador Hotel
Union Avenue
Room 1006
Monday, December 12, 1960
Half past 10 in the evening

"Where'd you get all this?" That was me. I was talking about the three bottles of Johnnie Walker Red Label Scotch whiskey. Carter and I were sitting on my bed. Captain O'Reilly and John Murphy were sitting on the floor next to each other. Mrs. Dewey was in the one chair and Marnie was perched on the desk with her legs crossed. I wasn't sure how we managed to squeeze into the room, but we did.

John Murphy said, "Never you mind, boyo. Just drink up."

I opened the first bottle and took a long drink. The heat of the liquor hit my stomach and felt good. I passed the bottle to Carter who took a long gulp as well. He handed it to Mrs. Dewey who took a slightly smaller drink and was about to hand it to Marnie. She stopped and said, "Hell," and had another gulp. We all laughed at that and she passed the bottle to Marnie who took the biggest gulp of us all.

Captain O'Reilly took the bottle and looked at it. "To one hell of a kid, to Paul!" He held the bottle up and we all said, "To Paul!" He took a long drink and then handed the bottle to John Murphy who drained it.

...

"How'd you meet Paul?" That was Marnie. We were down to the third bottle.

I looked at Carter who smiled. "We needed some clothes for livin' in the tropics and Paul owned a men's clothing store he'd inherited from his father."

"How'd he meet Mr. Nyemba?" asked Mrs. Dewey as she sipped whiskey out of a paper cup.

Carter sighed. "Freddie managed my gym and Paul was a regular. One thing led to another and they fell in love."

Marnie sighed. "People fall in love around you guys all the time. You go to Italy. You go to Africa." She looked out the open window and across the night sky. "If I had a dollar for every man and woman who've fallen in love after they met you..." She giggled and then hiccuped, covering her mouth as she did. "Well, I would have a few dollars, that's all I'm sayin'."

"You're drunk, my dear," said Mrs. Dewey as she swayed slightly.

"Yes, Violet..." Marnie leaned forward. "You don't mind if I call you Violet, do you?"

Mrs. Dewey waved away her question. "Not in the slightest, my dear."

John Murphy leaned forward. "Now when was the last time you was as drunk as all this, Mrs. Dewey?"

The older woman laughed. "Oh, it's been ages and ages." She put her finger to her head and said, "Let me think." She giggled. "Oh, yes, it was New Year's Eve of 1937, I believe. We went to a party. *Alone.*" She looked around the room swaying. "The rest of you have no idea how wonderful it is to have children." She burped and laughed. "And how wonderful it is to get away from them... When one wants."

We all laughed at that.

She continued, "We went to Winnipeg to a party hosted by some friends of friends. It was at a private home. I don't know why the police weren't called. We were all quite loud and rambunctious." She sighed. "Yes, that was the last time I was this soused." Swaying slightly, she looked at Marnie. "Is that the word, my dear?"

Marnie nodded earnestly. "Soused is right. Don't they say that in Manitobababa?"

Everyone laughed as Mrs. Dewey replied, "Not as a rule, my dear. *Pickled* was my late husband's favorite word for the subject. I remember, on that night in Manitobabababa..." She and Marnie started laughing at the word while the rest of us chuckled. Finally, Mrs. Dewey got hold of herself and said, "Yes, he liked that word very much. On that night in Mani—" She held up her index finger. "No! It was in Winnipegigegigeg." She fell forward and started laughing again.

Marnie reached over, put her hand on Mrs. Dewey's head, and, in a fit of laughter, said, "Winnipegigegigeg in Manitobababa..."

Mrs. Dewey took a deep breath and said, "Quite so, my dear."

Marnie replied, "Quite."

The two of them didn't stop laughing for a while.

. . .

"Did you remember to take some aspirin?" That was me.

Carter moaned. "Yes, Nick, I did. For the last time, I did."

"Good," I said. For some reason, I was wide awake. It was just about 5 in the morning and the light outside was getting brighter. Miraculously, my head didn't hurt but I was thirsty so I stood up, walked into the small bathroom, and got a glass of water.

Once I was done, I walked over to the window and looked out over the city. Marnie was right. It did look like Sacramento. Or, at least, it reminded me of that city somehow even though it didn't really look like it.

I thought about a similar morning, during the war, when I had been stationed in New Guinea and had spent a weekend in Port Moresby with two Navy pilots. We had made love through the night, the three of us, and I had sat in the window of the little hotel and watched as the sun rose and one of the pilots and I had talked about all sorts of things, but mostly nothing, which was my favorite topic.

They died later that same day when their plane crashed in the jungle. I was supposed to be on that plane but, at the last minute, I was transferred to another one. I remembered sitting in the barracks after I heard the news. I was unable to decide whether to cry, or get angry, or just slit my wrists. In the end, I had smoked several cigarettes and then went for a swim in the bay outside the hospital where I was stationed.

As I watched the African sun rise over the strange white city in the middle of the jungle, I felt the same way about Paul as I did about the two pilots. I didn't know how to react. He was gone. And I saw him leave. It was sad and strangely beautiful, both at the same time.

In the back of my mind, I kept thinking, again and again, that we had all gone through this same scenario before. Not John Murphy and Captain O'Reilly—but Carter, Marnie, Mrs. Dewey, and myself—the four of us together taking care of someone who was sick and dying. I couldn't remember when or where but it was all so eerily familiar.

. . .

"How ya doin'?" That was me. I was sitting on the desk, like Marnie the night before. It was just past 7 and the room was bright from the morning sun. Carter was sitting on the edge of the bed with his head in his hands.

He grunted and said, "I must've forgotten the aspirin last night."

"I asked you a couple of times but you told me you had."

"Fuck you, Nick."

I laughed. "Later. Right now, we need to get in the shower and get some food because we need to be at Salisbury Central jail at 8 and I have no idea where that is but we only have an hour to get there."

Carter stood, swaying slightly as he did, and made his way into the bathroom. After half a minute, I heard him throwing up so I got off the desk and walked in to hold his head until he felt better.

. . .

"OK. I think I'm going to live now." That was Carter. He'd just finished an immense English breakfast (without that terrible black sausage).

I'd had some fresh orange juice and coffee with a sweet roll. I wasn't hungry and felt almost euphoric for some reason.

Carter wiped his mouth and looked at me. "What are you so cheery about this morning?"

I shrugged. "I'm not, really. I guess I've decided to hold off on crying or getting angry. It's weird."

Carter nodded and looked at me searchingly. "This is usually where I ask you if you're OK. But you seem fine."

"What about you?"

He looked down at his empty plate. "I want to punch something or someone."

"How about after we pickup Freddie and get moved in to the house, we find you a gymnasium?"

Carter nodded and stood. "That would be good."

Chapter 14

Salisbury Central Gaol
Enterprise Road
Tuesday, December 13, 1960
A few minutes past 8

"There he is." That was me. We'd taken the station wagon when we'd left the hotel. I was pointing through the windshield at a very dark black man sitting on his haunches being watched by a much lighter-skinned African policeman. They were just outside a building made of light-gray stone with a dark slate roof that looked to be about 50 or so years old. It was two stories tall with bars over all the windows and a heavy red metal double door as an entrance. A wooden sign in front read, "Salisbury Central Gaol." I'd seen that third word before but, until that moment, hadn't realized it was a different spelling of the word, "jail."

Freddie stood when he saw us pull up and smiled. He wasn't as muscled as he'd been the last time we saw him but at 6'3" and broad, he was still impressive. And he still had the biggest mouth full of white teeth I'd ever seen. He was wearing a pair of dirty dungarees that were too short and too tight. His shirt was just a grimy white t-shirt that had been ripped at the neck. He was wearing canvas shoes without laces, but they didn't fit and his heels were sticking out at the back. I thought he could use a long, hot shower but he looked happy and relieved.

I was certainly glad to see him, alive and healthy, but I could feel a knot in my stomach as I thought about the fact we were going to have to break the bad news to him about Paul.

As Carter came to a stop in the parking lot and turned off the ignition, he said, "Wait here. Let me take care of this."

I nodded and said, "Sure, Chief."

Carter got out of the car and walked over to the policeman. All the windows in the car were rolled down so I could hear what he said.

"That's my house-boy, Freddie." He was using his thickest Georgia accent.

The policeman nodded. "You will ensure he has the proper papers, sir?"

Carter nodded brusquely. "Of course." He snapped at Freddie. "Come on, boy. Let's go."

Freddie frowned at first and then looked down at the ground as if he suddenly understood what Carter was doing.

Turning on his heels, Carter quickly strode back to the car. The pained look on his face was heartbreaking. I realized that, in that little play he'd just put on for the policeman, he'd been acting like his father who would have been right at home in Southern Rhodesia.

Carter quickly got behind the wheel while Freddie climbed in behind me. I kept my eyes on the stone building of the jail, not wanting to give anything away. As Carter started the engine, he quietly said, "No one say anything yet."

I heard Freddie whisper in reply, "Yes, boss."

...

Once we were headed back towards the center of town, I turned in my seat and looked at Freddie. "*Mbote*." That was a Lingala greeting. "How are you?"

He smiled, all teeth, and said, "*Mbote*. I am very happy to see you."

I smiled wanly and nodded. I wasn't sure how to tell him about Paul so, instead, I asked, "How was jail?"

His smile faded. "It's stinkin' in there. Not a good place at all."

I nodded. "Sorry that happened."

He frowned slightly. "It is not your fault, no? Thank you for paying the fine."

"Of course," I said. "We're going to a house we've rented and you can take a hot shower when we get there."

Freddie nodded and said, "Thank you, *monsieur*."

Carter added, "You can wear my clothes until we can get some for you later today."

"Thank you, boss."

Freddie had been right about the jail. He had brought the stench with him. Even with all the windows down, I could smell body odor, urine, and worse.

Freddie tilted his head to the side as a tear ran down his dirty left cheek. "So, my dear Paul, he is dead, no?"

I nodded, unable to speak.

Freddie looked out the window to his right. "Yes, I know this. He came to me last night in a dream. We danced and danced and talked and laughed and then he say to me, 'No more,' and he was gone."

I pulled out my handkerchief and handed it over to him. He wiped his face with it and then looked at me. "You were with him in hospital, yes?"

I nodded. "Yeah. He loved you, Freddie. He wanted us to tell you." I glanced over at Carter who was wiping his eyes with the back of his hand while driving through the traffic on Enterprise Road.

Freddie nodded. "This I know." He put his big hand on his chest. "I feel it here and I love him but now he is no more."

Suddenly, Paul's phrase from the night before made sense. When we'd lived in Léopoldville, I'd heard Congolese men and women use that phrase to say that someone was dead. "He is no more."

Chapter 15

Montreal Road
Braeside
Tuesday, December 13, 1960
Just before 9

"Where is he?" That was Carter. The three of us were sitting in the car and waiting for Attaborough to show up. He'd said he would meet us at 8:45 with the keys and to show us around.

Carter had pulled up the driveway and stopped just shy of the detached garage. From where I sat, the house looked large. It reminded me of farmhouses I'd seen around Salinas, near Monterey, more than anything else. It was painted white with green trim. The front door was painted a dark green and had a brass handle. A broad porch wrapped around the house in all directions. The backyard was surrounded by a chain-link fence. I could see a pool with a brick ribbon surrounded by palm trees in the back. And, just as Attaborough said, there was a small brick building at the bottom of a slightly sloped green lawn. That must have been the "hut."

Everything looked freshly painted and well maintained, even the gravel driveway which was even and free of weeds. As we sat there, I felt a slight breeze through the open windows. Looking up, I noticed dark clouds gathering off over downtown, which I was pretty sure was north. At sunrise, the sky had been clear but clouds had been building all morning even though it wasn't particularly warm. I wondered if it might rain before too long.

Freddie sat in the backseat and was quiet. I wondered if he was afraid or sad or angry or all three. From the outside, other than being dressed in clothes that didn't fit, dirty, and disheveled, he looked like the Freddie I remembered from Léopoldville.

There was one noticeable difference, however. He looked leaner and tougher. His muscled physique had always struck me as being almost artificial. He always looked a little puffed up. That was the best way to describe it. Now that several months had passed since he'd lifted weights, it seemed as if his body had taken on a more natural shape. Considering he'd been traveling a long distance under difficult conditions, he looked reasonably well-fed. Paul, on the other hand, had wasted away. I doubted I would ever forget the feel of skin and bones as I had rubbed him down with alcohol the night before. Now that I could see Freddie in the flesh, it was obvious that Paul had been malnourished thanks to whatever disease he had.

As I was mulling that over, a green Jaguar coupe pulled up and stopped right next to us. Attaborough, who looked ridiculously large in the small British car, grinned at me and said, "Sorry I'm late." He looked at

Freddie and said, "*Mbote*," with a smile and a nod of his head.

From the backseat, I heard Freddie softly reply, "*Mbote*."

. . .

"Well, there you have it." That was Attaborough. He'd just finished showing us the house and how everything worked. Instead of taking us out into the backyard, we stood just inside the kitchen as he described everything by pointing through the windows by the breakfast nook.

Looking at Freddie, he said, "That brick hut out there —"

"That is my house, yes?"

Carter crossed his arms and said, "No. You're staying with us. One of the bedrooms is yours."

Freddie frowned slightly and then nodded.

Attaborough continued, "But you must make a pretense of living out there in order to keep the neighbors from calling the police. Do you understand?"

Freddie nodded. "I will be the house-boy."

"You'll *pretend* to be the house-boy," added Carter emphatically.

"Yes," said Freddie without much emotion. I figured he was still dealing with the news about Paul. It was a lot to take in.

Attaborough looked at me and then pointed at the windows that ran along the side of the living room and looked out over the driveway. "All these blinds that are closed? Keep them closed. It's a must. Even now, I can promise that madame next door is already wondering what we're up to.' He looked at Freddie. "She'll be sending her house-boy and garden-boy and cook and maid over here to nose around. Be very careful, Mr. Nyemba."

Freddie nodded, crossed his arms, and drifted over to the living room. The stench wafting off him was still strong. As we'd walked around the house, Attaborough had opened some of the windows and a small breeze was moving through but it didn't do much. Only a hot shower and getting rid of the clothes Freddie was wearing would do the trick

"Madame?" I asked. I wondered why Attaborough had used that word.

"Posh name for a housewife."

Carter and I both chuckled.

Attaborough rolled his eyes. "Yes, well..." He looked at his watch. "Oh! Must dash."

I pulled an envelope out of my pocket and handed it to him. "That's a hundred pounds. I doubt we'll be here for two weeks, but just in case."

He quickly looked at the contents, smiled, and put the envelope in his inner coat pocket. "Thanks." He pulled two pieces of paper from his left outer coat pocket and handed them to me. "Receipts for the cash you gave me at lunch yesterday for the fine and for your donation. I'm going this afternoon to apply for Mr. Chuma's release thanks to that. I'll be sure to tell him who his benefactor was."

I shook my head. "I'd rather stay anonymous."

Attaborough nodded. "Many do. Feel free, of course, to send any anonymous donations my way whenever you like." He then frowned at me slightly and asked, "Why are you here, by the way? I know you're not here on holiday."

I stepped back for a moment. I realized we had never told Attaborough the full story. Glancing at Freddie, who was standing in the living room a few yards apart from us and looking out at the backyard, I said, "A friend of ours from Léopoldville was in the hospital. We came down to get him and take him to San Francisco or New York or Paris, maybe. Someplace where they could help him."

Attaborough didn't like the sound of that. He crossed his arms and his frown deepened.

Carter jumped in. "What Nick means is that the doctors here had never seen whatever disease Paul had and so we hoped he might be able to get help somewhere else."

Attaborough sniffed. "Salisbury isn't the center of the world, but the doctors here do know their way around tropical diseases." He pointed out at the palm trees around the pool. "This is the tropics, after all."

I nodded and said, "We're not doubting that. We just wanted to do whatever we could to help."

The lawyer sighed and relaxed a little. "My apologies. I love my country. I don't love what happens here or that we don't share the land, but I love this *Zimbabwe*."

"What's that?" I asked.

Out of the blue, Freddie said, "It is the name of this place."

I turned and looked at him. He was still staring out at the backyard but I had a feeling he was looking at something, or someone, I couldn't see.

Attaborough added, "Precisely. Now, you flew down here for your friend. What was his name?"

Freddie replied, "Paul Vermaut. He was a Belgian and I loved him." He walked over and joined the group.

Attaborough looked at me. "He's gone?"

I nodded, trying to hold it together. "Last night."

Walking over to Freddie, Attaborough put his hand on the man's arm. "I'm so sorry, Mr. Nyemba."

149

Freddie nodded. "*Tatenda.*"

The lawyer smiled and bowed slightly. "*Ndini* Lionel. *Munonzani?*"

Freddie looked at Carter with a question on his face.

"Don't look at me," said my husband with a grin.

Attaborough laughed. Looking at Freddie, he said, "You said 'thank you' so politely in Shona so I introduced myself and asked your name." He offered his hand. "My name is Lionel Attaborough. At your service."

Freddie shook and smiled as he did. "I am Freddie Nyemba."

Carter added, "And we're Carter and Nick."

Attaborough turned and grinned. "*Tatenda.* Call me Lionel. All my friends do." He then looked at his watch. "Crikey! I really am going to be late!" He turned, leaned forward, and gave Freddie a kiss on his dirty cheek. "Bye, love." He then walked over and did the same to Carter and me. "Really must dash. May I invite myself to dinner tonight? I want to hear the rest of why you're really here."

I nodded and put my hand on my cheek. It was such a startling and endearing move that I was left speechless.

Lionel dashed towards the front door, saying over his shoulder, "Ta, my dears." With that, he was gone.

Carter asked, "What just happened?"

I looked at him and then at Freddie. "I think we just met the real Lionel Attaborough."

Carter said, "I think you're right."

Freddie, for his part, nodded as he looked at the front door somewhat wistfully.

...

"Oh, Nick, I love this house." That was Marnie. Carter and I had left Freddie there to get cleaned up and had driven over to the Ambassador to get our luggage and pick up Marnie and Mrs. Dewey. We'd also picked up one of the Ford Anglias, which Mrs. Dewey had driven, following Carter back to the house.

While at the hotel, I'd checked on the flight crew. They were planning on taking an overnight trip to Victoria Falls on a chartered flight. I'd bought another hundred pounds at the front desk to give to the crew to cover the cost of their trip and to cover their other expenses. Carter had checked in with Captain O'Reilly and John Murphy. He invited them to join us for dinner and gave them directions to the house.

Pointing to the left, I said to Marnie, "There are three bedrooms down that hallway." We were in a short hallway. On our right stood a bathroom. A longer hallway on our left led to the bedrooms. "There's one for Freddie, one for you, and one for Mrs. Dewey. Carter and I are going to take the master bedroom which is on the other side of the house."

Marnie and I were by ourselves. When we'd walk in the front door, I'd seen Freddie standing in the living room and looking out the back windows just like he'd been doing earlier. Obviously, he'd taken a shower because I saw that he was wearing the clothes Carter had loaned him and his hair was wet.

For his part, Carter had taken Mrs. Dewey around to the back. She'd wanted to see the pool and the palm trees.

Marnie frowned at me and opened her mouth to say something but then didn't.

"What, doll?" I asked.

"I guess I shoulda told you this before we left the hotel, but..." She looked in her purse for a moment and then pulled out a folded-over telegram. She handed it to me.

```
MARNIE LEBEAU HOTEL AMBASSADOR
SALISBURY SO RHODESIA. ARR TUES DEC 12.
BOAC FLT 115 1205 PM. MEETING ALEX ROME
MON NIGHT. FLYING DOWN TOGETHER. LOVE
MOTHER.
```

I looked up. "You're fucking kidding me."

Marnie shook her head. "No. You know Mother."

"When did you get this?"

"It came yesterday while we were at the hospital but I only got it this morning. With the way everything was, I didn't check messages when we got back to the hotel."

I nodded. After Paul had passed away, I'd had to do some paperwork with an official from the hospital to authorize them to release the body to a funeral home. I'd left Lionel's office as a point of contact. Carter, Marnie, and I had then wordlessly loaded into the car and driven back to the hotel. Once we got there, we'd gone straight to my room and proceeded to get drunk. None of us had stopped to check for messages. Getting drunk was more important.

I asked, "Did you have any idea she was coming?"

Marnie shook her head.

"Did your mother know about your fight with Alex?"

Marnie shook her head again. "She didn't know I was down here. I can't figure out how she found out."

I blushed. "Actually, I told her in a telegram Sunday night."

She hit me on the arm. "Nick!"

I shrugged. "You know she would have killed me if I hadn't told her."

Marnie sighed. "You're right."

"She must have called Alex in Paris after he sent you the telegram yesterday."

"That's what I think."

I actually felt relieved. I had a vague idea about how to smuggle the Congolese refugees out of Rhodesia but hadn't come up with anything concrete. I looked at my watch. It was a few minutes before 10.

Right then, I heard Mrs. Dewey and Carter walk in the house through the back door. Freddie introduced himself to Mrs. Dewey. Carter called out, "Nick?"

I took a deep breath, looked at Marnie, and said, "Let me handle this."

She nodded and followed me around the corner and into the kitchen where we found Mrs. Dewey opening and closing cabinet doors and drawers. Carter and Freddie were watching her, looking amused as they did.

Before I could say anything, Mrs. Dewey declared, "First things, first, I say. We have an excellent kitchen here and I propose to take the big estate wagon to the local supermarket and stock up." She looked Freddie over. "After we've done that, our next job is to find you some new clothes, young man."

He blushed slightly under his very dark skin and looked at Carter who nodded encouragingly.

Mrs. Dewey asked, "Marnie? Will you join me?"

Marnie nodded as Carter asked, "Where is the supermarket?"

Mrs. Dewey replied, "There's a Bon Marché in Eastlea. The nice man at the front desk gave me directions from here. He said it's new and would have everything we want."

I said, "I'm out of pounds but about to go the bank. Can you wait until then?"

Mrs. Dewey waved me away. "I have plenty from the money you gave me earlier and I'm sure Marnie has plenty as well."

Nodding again, Marnie didn't reply.

Carter looked at her and then at me. He narrowed his eyes. "What's wrong?"

I handed over the telegram and let him read it. When he was done, his eyes widened as he said, "Damn, son."

I nodded. "I know."

"Problem?" asked Mrs. Dewey.

Carter wordlessly handed the telegram over. After she read it, she smiled and said, "I don't know what you're worried about. I say thank goodness. From what I know of her, there's no problem Mrs. Williams hasn't been able to solve." She passed the telegram back to Marnie. "If your mother can wrangle"—I grinned as she used that word—"the Governor of California and the President of the United States, some Prime Minister of a middling British colony in Central Africa doesn't stand a chance."

We all laughed at that.

Chapter 16

Salisbury Airport
Viewing balcony
Monday, December 12, 1960
Half past noon

"To be honest, I'm looking forward to seeing her." That was Carter. We were standing outside on the second floor above the main waiting area. The flight, coming in from Nairobi, Kenya, was only ten minutes late.

"Me too."

"I wish Marnie was with us, though."

I nodded.

. . .

We'd left the bank with a new checkbook in hand, a slip showing something just south of eight thousand pounds on deposit, and another couple of hundred pounds in Carter's inner coat pocket.

After that, we'd stopped by the house since it was

south of downtown and on the way to the airport. We'd waited as long as we could for Mrs. Dewey and Marnie to get back from the supermarket. But they didn't return in time.

Freddie had wanted to go with them. He'd said it would look right for madame (Marnie) and her mother-in-law (Mrs. Dewey) to have a house-boy along with them who would help carry their groceries. Mrs. Dewey had then pointed out that Carter's shoes were too big and mine were too small, so he'd decided to work out in the backyard.

While we were waiting for Marnie and Mrs. Dewey, he'd told us that Anna, the maid who worked at the house to the right of ours, had stopped by while we'd been at the bank. She'd told him her madame was Mrs. Watson and she was a fine employer. There was a garden-boy (John) and a house-boy (Nelson). They lived in the brown hut back behind the fence while Anna lived in the green hut near the pool. Madame did her own cooking but sometimes, Margaret (Anna's sister) would come in from Tafara to cook when madame had a big party. All in all, the work wasn't too hard.

Sir worked for an insurance company downtown and drove a very big car that Nelson kept sparkling. Sir and madame had two grown sons. One was in the army down by Bulawayo and the other was in England and worked for a bank and lived in a big house and had very many servants. Madame often talked about the size of the house and the number of servants. Madame had once explained how servants in England were all European, which Anna didn't believe. Freddie had told her it was likely true. He had seen many European servants in San Francisco. Anna had shrugged and said the large house with all the servants was in a place called Mayfair. The son was very rich and had a very wicked and very spoiled English wife that madame didn't like at all.

Anna had asked Freddie if he was Shona, although she thought he might be Karanga, and where his people were from. He'd replied that he was from the Congo and that his people were Mongo. They lived along the river, north of Léopoldville. His madame (Marnie) and his sir (me) had lived in the Congo before coming to Southern Rhodesia because of all the violence. He'd also explained we were American and that we were from San Francisco and how he'd been there with us since the rebellion began in Léopoldville in July. When asked, he'd told Anna that he didn't know the name of my company because sir didn't speak of such things before the servants.

Anna had gone on to quiz him about whether his madame had a maid. He'd said madame had a maid in Léopoldville but, after the rebellion began, she'd returned to her people in Kikwit, in the interior. Madame's mother-in-law (Mrs. Dewey) was helping out until a proper maid could be found. He'd also added that madame's mother (Lettie) and madame's brother (Alex) were arriving from America that very day to help everyone settle in.

He'd then told Anna that madame would very much like if she could recommend a maid. Maybe a relative? At that point, however, Mrs. Watson had called out for her maid and the girl (Freddie thought she was about 25) had quickly headed over to her employer's house.

I was really impressed with how quickly Freddie had come up with a plausible backstory that was close enough to the truth to make it easy to use but that also covered all the bases. I'd told him so and how I thought he would make a great private investigator. He'd blushed, looked at Carter, and mumbled something in Lingala.

Carter pointed over to a plane that was parked next to a hangar. "There's our Comet."

I nodded. "It sure is pretty."

"I still prefer the look of the Super Connie although I'd rather fly in the jet."

I thought for a moment. "Maybe the way we start all this is to have Robert send all our planes this direction. I bet we could have the whole fleet here by Thursday. We could have our version of the Berlin airlift."

Carter cleared his throat. "Son, some of our planes can't cross the Atlantic. Besides, you don't think someone, somewhere isn't gonna get the teensiest bit suspicious when all your planes started heading in the same direction?"

"You're right."

He put his hand on the back of my neck for a moment. "One of the things you always tell me is to let the experts do their jobs. Lettie is the expert here. I'd bet she has a plan already."

I nodded and sighed. "I feel better that's she's on her way."

Carter pointed off in the distance. A white Comet was descending through the dark clouds over the city. "There she is. Ready?"

I laughed. "Is anyone ever ready for Lettie?"

...

"Hello, dear Nicholas." That was Lettie, my stepmother and Marnie's mother. She was wearing a very simple dark brown dress with a black leather belt and a dark green hat. Considering how far she'd flown in the last couple of days, she looked fresh as a daisy. She kissed me on the cheek and then did the same with

Carter. She'd emerged from the customs area first. Alex was next. He was talking with a short official in a khaki uniform. "Where is Marnie?" she asked.

"She and Mrs. Dewey went to the supermarket. They weren't back by the time we had to leave for the airport. But I'm sure they'll be there when we get to the house."

Lettie looked at me and then at Carter. "Supermarket? House? What about the Ambassador Hotel?"

"We rented a house for a reason I'll explain in the car."

She took the hint and nodded. "Very good." Looking around at the small crowd, she added, "I suppose we should wait to talk about *everything* until we get to the car?"

I nodded. "How's Father?"

She smiled. "Back in Seattle again. He sends his love." Turning to Carter, she added, "As does your mother. And Velma." That was Carter's aunt.

"How is Geneva?" She was the fourth of the Four Terrors.

"Oh, Geneva is splendid. She's been doing some wonderful work with prisoners' aid up at Folsom."

"How was the event at the Ambassador on Friday?" asked Carter. "The one in L.A., I mean."

Lettie smiled. "Roz did her usual thing and raised more money than anyone thought possible." Roz was our friend, the actress Rosalind Russell. She was great at raising money for charitable causes.

"That's wonderful," said Carter.

Lettie nodded and looked at me. "Of course, your contribution was the biggest and Roz made sure to mention your foundation. Before she left, Marnie made sure to switch the funds from your personal account to your foundation. You really must be more cautious, Nicholas."

I shrugged as Carter said, "You know people have been saying that to Nick since he got his inheritance and he hasn't paid attention yet."

I rolled my eyes and said, "Oh, brother."

. . .

"Where's Marnie? I was hoping she would be here." That was Alex. Unlike Lettie, he looked rumpled and tired. There were bags under his eyes. I wondered if that was from his fight with Marnie or from lack of sleep on the way down or both.

Lettie put her arm under his and said, "Now, Alex, we'll explain it all in the car." She looked at Carter. "In the meantime, could you lead us and these fine gentlemen"—she was referring to the two men carrying Lettie and Alex's bags who were the African equivalents of skycaps—"to the car. We need to get on our way."

Carter nodded and did just that. Lettie and Alex followed. I fell in line behind them with the skycaps following me while I fished for two five-pound notes in my wallet.

. . .

"I am so very sorry about your friend, Paul," said Lettie. "How are you both feeling today? You've had quite a succession of awful adventures since you arrived here." She was in the backseat with Alex. We were headed up the Queensway road and back into town.

I turned and looked over the backseat. "I feel fine, somehow."

Lettie nodded. "The shock of it all, I imagine."

I shrugged and looked over at Carter. He just said, "I'm not ready to talk about it. I just want to get a plan and get these people out of here."

"Remind you of Georgia, does it?" asked Lettie.

Carter sighed heavily and nodded. "It does. Only it's worse."

I added, "Marnie and I both saw housewives yesterday walking through downtown with black men following them three steps behind."

"Thieves?" asked Lettie with a frown.

I shook my head. "No, house-boys. That's what they're called here. They were carrying madame's packages." I gave a shot at mimicking a Rhodesian accent but didn't get it right.

"*Madame's packages*?" asked Lettie incredulously. She looked out the window at the passing town. "I see." She sighed and said, "It really is just as I was led to believe."

"Led to believe?" I asked.

She nodded. "After I received your telegram, I realized there was nothing to do but fly over and as fast as possible." She glanced over at Alex who was looking out his window and wasn't really paying attention to the conversation. "I left San Francisco on Sunday, late morning, and, somehow, managed to catch a flight to London that night where I connected to the jet we just flew in on. On all three flights, I button-holed anyone I could find who knew anything about this part of the world. Fortunately, on the flight from New York to London, I found an Episcopal priest who lived here up until the end of last year. He gave me a very clear and unbiased picture of the political situation. I learned a lot from our conversation." She sighed. "He said that he knew the Rhodesian government was welcoming Europeans—he said that's how things break down here: *European* and *African*." She looked at me with her head tilted, as if she was asking me a question.

I nodded. "That's what we've noticed."

She nodded and moved her purse from her lap to the space between her and Alex. "In any event, he said that the although government has been freely welcoming European refugees from the Congo, they've done nothing for the small number of Africans who've made their way here." She shook her head. "Did you know it is more than two thousand miles from Léopoldville to Salisbury? And that part of that trip is right through the middle of the worst part of the civil war in the Congo? Can you imagine that kind of journey on the back of a truck, bouncing from one village to another?" She looked out the window again. "I'm very much looking forward to meeting your Mr. Nyemba. He must be quite remarkable."

Carter nodded. "He is."

Chapter 17

Montreal Road
Braeside
Tuesday, December 13, 1960
Half past 1 in the afternoon

"Well, that's a good sign." That was Lettie. We'd all just walked in the door and, without saying anything, Marnie had walked up to Alex, taken his hand, and led him down the long hallway to one of the bedrooms.

Carter said, "Lettie, do you remember Mrs. Violet Dewey? She was at Mama's wedding."

With a welcoming smile, Lettie walked forward and offered her hand. "Yes. It's so good to see you again, Violet."

Mrs. Dewey smiled in reply. "As soon as I heard you were on your way, I knew the cavalry was at hand. How are you, Leticia?"

"Very well, all things considered." Lettie looked over at Freddie. who was standing by the living room windows again. "Will you introduce me to Mr. Nyemba?"

"With pleasure," said Mrs. Dewey. The two walked over to where Freddie was standing. Mrs. Dewey put her hand on his arm. "Mr. Nyemba, may I introduce Marnie's mother, Mrs. Leticia Williams?"

Freddie, coming out of his daze, turned and gave Lettie a big smile, all teeth.

She offered her hand. "Such a pleasure to meet you, Mr. Nyemba."

He gently shook and said, "*Mbote, Madame* Williams."

She nodded and replied, "*Mbote*." She got it right in one. It had taken me a few days to get the pronunciation down. "What does that mean?"

"It is Lingala, the language of the Congolese in Léopoldville, and it is a polite greeting."

Lettie nodded and said, "May I offer you my deepest condolences? I am so sorry to hear about your dear Paul."

Freddie nodded. "Thank you, *Madame* Williams." He looked out at the backyard. "He is no more but I feel him very close. I watch those deep grasses in the distance." Mrs. Dewey and Lettie both turned and looked to where he was pointing. "I think Paul will come through them but he has not and will not. He is no more."

Carter put his arm around me and squeezed me tight as Mrs. Dewey took a small plain handkerchief from her dress pocket and dabbed her eyes.

Lettie patted Freddie's big arm and said, "He is here, with you, in your heart."

He nodded without turning and replied, "Yes, I know you are right, *Madame* Williams."

. . .

"I was thinking some quick sandwiches, if that is agreeable to all?" That was Mrs. Dewey. She and Lettie were in the kitchen. Carter and I were sitting at the small table in the breakfast nook. I was watching Freddie skim the pool with a net on a long pole. It was perfectly clean because he'd done it earlier. I suspected it was something he was doing to stay busy and not look at the big grass behind the brick hut. Marnie and Alex were still in one of the bedrooms.

Lettie nodded. "That sounds sensible. Allow me to help."

Mrs. Dewey said, "Of course. There are aprons in the cupboard over there." She pointed to a pantry with a full-size door. Lettie walked over in that direction. "And there are packages of sliced meats in the refrigerator. At the supermarket, they had ham, bologna, liverwurst, and something called olive loaf. Marnie said you would like that."

Lettie laughed. "I'm addicted to olive loaf, to tell the truth."

With a chuckle, Mrs. Dewey said, "We all have our secrets, don't we?" She paused for a moment as she began to slice a loaf of bread. "There are also a variety of pickles. Oh my, and I found some beautiful tomatoes. I just love a good sliced tomato with a bit of salt, don't you?"

Lettie, who was tying the back of her apron, nodded. "I do. I always say they taste like summer."

"These are really marvelous. My husband and I tried to grow them on the farm but I'm afraid Manitoba is just a bit too far north. We finally gave in and built a greenhouse, as our neighbors did a few miles down the road."

As she began to take jars out of the refrigerator and put them on the counter, Lettie said, "You must have been able to grow all sorts of things with a greenhouse."

I looked at Carter who was leaning back in his chair with his arms crossed. His chin was on his chest, his eyes were closed, and a little trail of drool was visible on the left side of his mouth.

I sighed contentedly. Considering everything that had happened over the last few days, I felt very much at home and very grateful for Lettie's presence. When she'd married my father back in '54, he'd suddenly come back to life. Before, he'd been a mean old man who was impossible to get along with. Because of that, I hadn't talked to him after the summer of '39, when he'd kicked me out the house, unless I'd absolutely had to. Lettie had done her magic, whatever that was, and he'd changed. He was happy and alive and doing well, which made me happy.

When I thought about how far we'd come, I felt like I had to pinch myself. Things were far from perfect, but so many things had gotten better.

Sitting there, in that kitchen, thousands of miles from my physical home and in the middle of Africa, I felt more at home than I had in a while. And watching Carter drool on himself while he lightly snored was one of the most wonderful things I'd seen in a long time.

. . .

"Should I knock on their door, do you think, Leticia?" That was Mrs. Dewey. We were all seated around the dining table and having sandwiches, potato chips (called "crisps" on the bags), pickles, and sliced tomatoes for lunch. Freddie, Carter, and I each had a bottle of Castle, a local beer, while the others were each drinking a Pepsi. Marnie and Alex were still in one of the bedrooms.

Lettie wiped the side of her mouth with her napkin. "I don't think Alex has slept a wink since Marnie abandoned him in Paris. We should let them sleep."

I looked over at her. I didn't like how she'd said that. "I think this was a long time coming."

She raised her left eyebrow at me. "Are you saying, Nicholas, that you approve of her running off the moment they had a disagreement?"

I shook my head. "No, because they've been fighting about this for months."

"Fighting about what?" asked Lettie as she sprinkled some salt on a tomato slice. "I couldn't get one word out of Alex."

Carter said, "About how he won't spend any of *her* money." I was glad he spoke up. He knew more about the way Alex felt than anyone.

"*Her* money, Carter?"

He nodded. "Yes, ma'am. Dr. Williams settled it on *her*."

"Marnie has talked to me about his cheapness and I certainly don't approve of that, but surely Alex knows about the community property laws in California."

Carter nodded. "Yes, ma'am. I'm sure he does. But that doesn't change the fact that he doesn't feel entitled to it. That's why he hasn't wanted to spend any of it. He considers it hers not theirs."

Lettie looked at Carter a long moment. "You probably know more about this than anyone I know. How have you handled it?" She carefully cut the tomato slice in half, speared it with her fork, and then popped it in her mouth.

"Well, it was hardest for me in the beginning, back in 1948 when Nick first told me about the money."

Mrs. Dewey looked at me with surprise on her face. "You didn't tell him when you first met?"

I shook my head. I didn't want to interrupt what he had to say.

Carter turned to her and explained. "When we met, Nick was an orderly in a hospital. He told me about his childhood and how his father threw him out when he was just 16."

Freddie's eyes widened. He asked me, "So young for an American, no?"

I nodded.

Carter continued, "I assumed he had a little money from his father but, then, after a few months, I began to think he probably didn't. He lived on his own pay, or so I thought." He looked at me with a grin. "Of course, he moved into an apartment not long after we met. I didn't know at the time that he'd bought the building because he didn't have anywhere to stay. His previous lover had thrown him out—"

"I left him," I said with a grin.

"And moved in with me and Henry," Carter said. "But then moved into his own place and I followed."

To move the story along, I said, "But then Carter was picked by his captain to go to an arson training class in Sacramento—"

Lettie exclaimed, "Sacramento! That's what this town reminds me of. I've been wracking my brain about it since we first flew over downtown."

Carter and I laughed. I said, "Marnie said the same thing."

Lettie nodded. "Of course she did since we have a history there. But, do go on. My apologies for the interruption."

Freddie leaned forward. "Arson? What is this?"

Carter smiled. "When someone deliberately sets fire to a building. That's arson."

Freddie nodded. "Oh, yes. I forget you were *pompier*." He frowned.

"Fireman," prompted Mrs. Dewey.

"Yes, *merci, madame*," said Freddie with a smile. "Fireman."

Lettie sat up. "I beg your pardon for my further interruption, but we do have to get on with the business at hand, dear boys, and don't have time for a lengthy explanation."

Carter and I grinned at each other.

"Have you talked with Alex about this?" asked Lettie, getting right to the point.

Carter shook his head. "I have talked to Marnie—"

"And," I added, "that's why she sent Alex a telegram, apologizing—"

"And that's why he's here," finished Carter.

Lettie looked directly at Carter. "He's *here*, dear boy, because, when I got to London, I called him in Paris and told him to get on a plane for Rome and meet me there last night so he could fly down with me." She softened a bit. "But I take your point." She sighed. "And I owe my daughter an apology."

"Maybe," I said. "But maybe, she'll be thanking *you*. Of course, it may be a while before they come up for air—"

Scandalized, Lettie said, "Really, Nicholas!"

Mrs. Dewey, for her part, started to giggle.

Looking over at her, Lettie grinned a little. "Oh, it's just awful to imagine your own child that way, don't you agree, Violet?"

Mrs. Dewey nodded and giggled a little more. "When I first saw my Susan, after she got pregnant, I would blush every time I saw her Pete. It took me several days before I could look him in the face."

Lettie put her hand to her mouth, looked around the table, and then burst out laughing. The rest of us joined in.

Chapter 18

Donnybrook Road
Mabvuku
Tuesday, December 13, 1960
Half past 3 in the afternoon

"It would start raining, wouldn't it?" That was Lettie. She was in the backseat behind me. We were on our way to the river near Tafara where the Congolese refugees were camped out. After lunch, Carter and I had made a quick run to a men's clothing store downtown and picked up a few things for Freddie, including two pairs of shoes that would fit him. He was sitting in the backseat next to Lettie and behind Carter, who was driving.

"This is the rainy season, *madame*," said Freddie.

Lettie said, "Of course, how stupid of me." She sighed. "Nicholas, did you bring any cash with you?"

Carter answered, "I put another hundred pounds in ones and fives in an envelope before we left the house."

"Good," said Lettie.

"Do you have a plan?" I asked as Carter slowed down. We were coming into the village and the holes in the road were increasing and getting bigger.

"I'm still thinking on it, Nicholas. I want to see how many people we're talking about." She added, "Mr. Nyemba?"

"Yes, *madame*?"

She sighed. "You can call me Lettie, or Leticia, if you like."

"Thank you, *madame*, but it is not respectful."

"Well, I keep thinking about what you told me about Anna, the maid next door. You said she called her employer, 'madame'."

"Yes, but she use the word in the English way. 'Madame'." I could hear the difference. He said the word in a way that sounded flat and almost nasal. "But, in French, the word is truly, '*madame*'. That is a word of respect in the Congo."

Lettie sighed. "Very well. Now I have a question for you."

"Yes, *madame*?" I was still facing forward, looking through the windshield wipers, and watching Carter dodge the potholes, but I was pretty sure I heard some amusement in his voice.

"My friend said that there are a number of languages in the Congo other than French, is that true?"

"Yes, *madame*. There are many. I have heard some say the number is 40 or more. I speak Lingala. That is the language of the people of Léopoldville. But I also speak Kituba, which is the language of my people upriver."

Carter said, "Nick and I completely forgot to ask. How is your mother doing? Did she go upriver?"

Freddie was quiet. I turned around in my seat. He

was looking out the window. I could see a tear running down his left cheek.

Lettie patted his left arm. He put his enormous right paw over her small hand and left it there.

"I'm sorry," said Carter in a small voice.

"Thank you, boss," croaked Freddie.

I looked at Lettie who was frowning. Her eyes were red. She glanced at me. "War is hell, isn't it Nicholas?"

I nodded and could feel the tears trying to get out. I took a deep breath and held them in. For the time being, at least.

. . .

Carter pulled over at the same place where we'd parked the last time. The same group of tents and tarpaper shacks were still in place. The rain was steadily falling. I noticed, however, that there was no smoke coming out of the makeshift chimneys. But, it was warmer than it had been on Sunday and dinner time was a couple of hours away.

I led the way down the side of the bank. As we approached, Freddie called out, "*Mbote*," and followed that with a string of words in Lingala.

No one replied.

As Freddie and Carter walked down around the tents and shacks, I took a look at the wet ground. Since it had only started raining a short time earlier, I figured the dirt and grass would still have some good signs showing what might have happened.

As I examined the area, I could see that a group of people had climbed up the side of the short bank. Over a space ten feet wide, or so, all the grass had been flattened. As I walked back towards the car where Lettie was standing, I could see a couple of sets of what appeared to be wide tires. I called out, "They're gone."

Carter replied, "Looks like it. There's no one down here."

I turned and looked at where he and Freddie were standing. "Any clothes or personal belongings?"

Carter nodded. "Some. But they all look like trash that's been left behind." He put his hands on his hips. "What do you see up there?"

"Looks like a couple of trucks, or maybe buses, were here."

Freddie saw something in a tent and bent over. When he stood up, I could see a piece of blue paper in his hand.

"What is it?" I asked.

Carter walked over and gaped at what Freddie was holding. He bent over and reached for something for a long moment. When he stood up, he said, "There's fifty or sixty pounds here."

"What?" I asked as I clambered down the bank towards him.

Carter waved the money in the air. "What does this mean?"

I walked up to where he and Freddie were standing. I counted the blue five-pound notes. There were eleven of them. "Why would anyone leave all this money here?" I looked into the tent. There was a flat rock near a small pile of blankets. Standing up, I asked Freddie, "Were they under that rock?"

He nodded. "I see a small piece of paper."

I sighed. "I don't know what this means, Carter."

Suddenly, I heard a voice. "Hello there."

Looking up, I saw a tall African man standing on the bridge that crossed the river. He was dressed in a what looked like a black gown and was holding a black umbrella over his head. He had short-cut black hair and reminded me of a friend of ours from Kenya, Dr. Harvey Thuku. I asked, "Do you know what happened here?"

The man nodded and walked over the bridge in our direction. "I do, indeed. One moment, if you please. I'd like to have a word with you." His accent was British and precise.

The three of us walked up the side of the bank and met him and Lettie by the car. He courteously offered his umbrella to Lettie and said, "Please, madame, I insist."

Lettie took the umbrella and held it up high. "Thank you, young man."

He smiled. "Perhaps you do not know many Africans, madame, but I am 60 this very year."

Lettie smiled in return. "You're still a young man, as far as I'm concerned."

"Surely not," he countered.

I stuck out my hand. "My name is Nick Williams."

The man nodded and shook. "Yes, Mr. Williams. It is a great honor to make your acquaintance. I am Dr. Albert Kimani."

"Are you from Kenya?"

He frowned slightly. "Yes, indeed I am. Perhaps you have known others of my country?"

I nodded. "We have a friend, Dr. Harvey Thuku, who's from there."

"How very nice," replied Dr. Kimani.

Carter offered, "Dr. Thuku grew up in Nairobi and went to school in England at Winchester and then King's College at Cambridge."

Dr. Kimani smiled. "I, too, am from Nairobi. I was blessed to attend Rugby and King's College at Cambridge, during and right after the Great War. But, I suspect my compatriot was at Cambridge after my time." He looked around, a little disappointed. "And now I am here, in Southern Rhodesia. I am the Master of Bedford Secondary School here in Tafara. In England, it is what is known as a day school. The students do not board with us. But, sadly, a fee is required for attendance, since secondary education for Africans is not mandatory or provided by the government. That limits the scope of our student body."

Carter offered his hand. "Very nice to meet you, Dr. Kimani. I'm Carter Jones."

"Yes, I am quite honored to know you, as well, Mr. Jones."

"How do you know who we are?" I asked.

"I have been aware of you since your adventures, shall we call them, in Hong Kong in 1955. But, more to the point, there is a small item in today's *Rhodesia Herald* mentioning that you are in the colony. It reported how you were greeted by our Prime Minister, Sir Edgar Whitehead, yesterday at Meikels Hotel."

I snorted. "That's what it said, huh?"

"Indeed," replied Dr. Kimani, "Is that not true?"

Carter said, "It's partially true." He motioned toward Lettie. "May I introduce Nick's stepmother, Mrs. Leticia Williams?"

Dr. Kimani waited for her to offer her hand and then gently shook it. "A pleasure to meet you, madame."

Lettie smiled and said, "Very nice to meet you, Dr. Kimani. May I ask a small favor?"

"Indeed."

"Please don't call me, 'madame'. I don't like the way that word is used around here."

Dr. Kimani looked at her for a moment before saying, "Perhaps I am not mistaken, then, when I say you must have a keen awareness of how the races divide themselves in Southern Rhodesia."

"I do. And I don't like it one bit."

He nodded earnestly. "Nor do I, Mrs. Williams. Nor do I."

She smiled. "Thank you for that, Dr. Kimani." She looked at Freddie. "May I introduce Mr. Nyemba of Léopoldville?"

Dr. Kimani's eyes widened slightly. "A pleasure, Mr. Nyemba."

"Thank you, *docteur*."

Dr. Kimani said something in French and Freddie replied with a big smile.

Lettie asked, "Now that we know one another, how about we get in the car and away from the rain and the awful smell of sewage?"

Carter nodded. "Dr. Kimani, would you like to take the front passenger seat?"

The man nodded after a slight hesitation.

We all piled in. I squeezed in the middle of the back seat, leaning against Freddie as much as I could. After a moment, he put his big left arm around my shoulders.

Dr. Kimani turned and looked at me. "May I ask why you are here, Mr. Williams?"

"We found out about this camp on Sunday. We came back today to check on everyone but they'd all left. Do you know what happened?"

"They were taken away, I'm afraid," said Dr. Kimani. "The father of one of my pupils witnessed the whole thing and came to let me know as soon as it happened. I had to wait until the end of the school day before I could inspect the situation on my own." He hesitated and then asked, "Did you, perhaps, find any money?"

I nodded and showed him the stack of fives. "This was left under a rock in one of the tents. How'd you know?"

"Mr. Kabeya, he was the one man in the group who spoke English, he told me you had stopped by looking for Mr. Nyemba on Sunday. He also said you left ninety-five pounds with him. He was afraid the police would finally come to take them to the airport to send them back to Léopoldville. And he promised that, in that event, he would leave what pounds he had left for the school." Dr. Kimani sighed. "You see, we have a small fund for our students whose families cannot afford the fees. Without the fees, I cannot pay the teachers and without the fund, we do not have enough students."

I nodded and handed over the money. He graciously took it and said, "God bless you, Mr. Williams."

In the front seat, Carter pulled out the envelope from his pocket and handed it over. "Here's another hundred. And, as soon as we can, we'll set up an endowment you can use going forward."

Dr. Kimani nodded wordlessly as he looked at the envelope in his hand. Lettie offered her handkerchief. He shook his head as he stuffed all the money under his black gown. "Thank you, Mrs. Williams. I am not crying. I am offering up a prayer of thanksgiving for this abundant generosity."

After a moment, I asked, "Do you think the police took them to the airport?"

He shrugged. "I do not know. The local constables have threatened such action for weeks now."

Lettie asked, "Did you organize the blankets and tents down there?"

Dr. Kimani blushed slightly. "Yes, Mrs. Williams. But the entire township came together. We managed to feed them and keep them in as much comfort as possible. I wished to place families and individuals in private homes but was forbidden to do this by the police. The district commander, a European, paid me a visit and warned that anyone who did such a thing would be subject to penalties, although he did not specify which and I can find no law that forbids such a thing."

Freddie said, "If they have been taken to airport, maybe we go?"

I nodded.

Dr. Kimani said, "May I suggest we stop at the police station in Mabvuku? I am friendly with Constable Gwelo."

Carter said, "We met him on Sunday," as he started the ignition.

Dr. Kimani nodded. "Yes, and Mr. Kabeya reported how kind the constable was in allowing you to give him the money."

...

"I am afraid I cannot say." That was Constable Gwelo. Lettie, Dr. Kimani, and I were standing in front of his desk inside the police station, which was mostly empty.

Lettie said, "My good man, are you aware that my son here"—she pointed to me—"is a personal friend of Sir Edgar Whitehead?"

Unperturbed, the constable stood and said, "Yes, I read this in the newspaper today."

"Well, then, don't you think Sir Edgar would want my son to receive equitable treatment in your police station?"

"I am sorry, madame, but I have instructions, specific instructions, to say nothing about the Congolese who have been transported to Salisbury airport." He offered up the smallest smile.

A voice from the lieutenant's office barked out, "Gwelo!"

The constable tipped his cap at Lettie and said, "Pardon me, madame." He then slowly walked towards the office door.

I pushed Lettie and Dr. Kimani towards the door and

whispered, "Go, go, go." The three of us jogged out of the police station and quickly piled into the car.

Carter asked, "How'd it go?"

Lettie said, "Let's burn rubber and get the hell out of here, right now, Carter."

As we all laughed, Carter did just that.

. . .

"Make a left at this road, Mr. Jones." That was Dr. Kimani. We were about a mile down the Umtali Road from the police station. "We can take a shortcut I know through Epworth and Hatfield."

Carter nodded and made a left turn. As we moved down the road, Carter asked, "What happened in there?"

After I told him, Dr. Kimani added, "Constable Gwelo has always been very kind. I do hope he does not suffer as a result of his actions today."

I said, "Let us know if there's anything we can do to help the man if something does happen."

Dr. Kimani nodded. "Yes, indeed, Mr. Williams. Thank you, again, for your generosity."

Carter looked in the rear-view mirror at Lettie. "What's next?"

"We can always drive out onto the runway and block the plane," I said.

Lettie, who was looking out the window, said, "Now is not the time for levity, Nicholas. Allow me to think in peace."

"Yes, ma'am," I replied.

I caught Carter's eye in the rear-view mirror. He winked. I smiled in reply.

Chapter 19

Salisbury Airport
Tuesday, December 13, 1960
Just before 5 in the afternoon

The rain was falling hard as Carter pulled up in front of the terminal. Lettie said, "Nicholas, you come with me. Everyone else, wait here in the car. Carter?"

"Ma'am?"

"Keep the engine running."

"Yes, ma'am."

With that, the two of us piled out of the backseat. I followed Lettie as she briskly walked through the rain and into the terminal building. Almost immediately, I realized the place was nearly deserted. I guessed the B.O.A.C. plane had headed back north already. As we passed the three or four ticket counters, I noticed they were all closed up with little signs posted announcing when they would re-open.

Lettie said, "I hope we're not too late."

"Me too."

We picked up the pace and began to jog towards the one gate that was open. As we walked outside and back into the rain, I could see a DC-7 on the runway. I didn't recognize the markings, but it looked like a military plane and it was in position to take off. Leaving Lettie behind, I took off running as fast as I could, not worrying about the puddles that I was splashing through or the fact that my socks and feet were getting soaked.

However, I only got about a hundred feet before the plane started moving forward. The propellers began to rev up, creating a large curtain of water as they did, and the DC-7 gained speed. I stopped and, as I did, I thought I heard a voice yelling at me, but I didn't care. I couldn't turn away from the plane. I stood right where I was and, feeling helpless, watched the aircraft as it moved down the wet runway and began to lift off into the clouds.

After a moment, I heard someone behind me ask, "Mr. Williams?"

I turned and saw Inspector Graves in his trench coat and holding a large umbrella over his head. He smiled. "Come with me, if you please."

I walked over towards him. He lifted his umbrella up to let us both walk under it. Neither of us said anything until we were inside the deserted terminal. Lettie was nowhere to be seen. I hoped she'd had the sense to go back and get in the car and get the hell out. If the police caught us with Freddie, he'd be on the next plane to Léopoldville.

"Now, what is this all about?" asked the inspector as he shook his umbrella over by the gate door.

"I don't know what you mean."

"I was sitting in a police car on the tarmac and saw you and an older woman run out through this very door. You ran towards the airplane that just took off as if you were hoping it would stop. Why?" By that time, he'd closed up his umbrella and leaned it against the wall.

I shrugged and didn't reply.

He reached inside his trench coat and pulled out a pack of Pall Mall cigarettes. He tapped one out and offered it. "Smoke?"

"No, thanks," I replied.

He nodded and took one for himself.

Out of habit, I reached into my trouser pocket and pulled out my old Zippo. I held it out and he leaned forward to light his cigarette.

As he puffed, he looked at the lighter. "Mind if I take a look?"

I shook my head and handed it over.

He held it up and looked at it. "How'd it get bent? Never seen anything like that." He gave it back.

I dropped it into my pocket and said, "Happened when I was in the Navy."

He nodded and exhaled to the side. "So, why are you here?"

"In Salisbury?"

"Sure," he said with a grin. "Let's start there."

"My friend, Paul Vermaut, was in the hospital and needed some help."

"Which hospital?"

"Central."

The inspector took a deep drag. "I see. And have you been able to help him?"

"He died last night."

Frowning slightly, the inspector said, "I'm sorry to hear that."

"Thanks."

"I don't mean to be crass, Mr. Williams, but does this

mean you'll be leaving the colony soon?"

"We have to bury him first."

"Why not take him home?"

"He's from Léopoldville."

The inspector looked at me for a long moment. "I see." He exhaled to the side again. "So, you're planning on burying him here in Salisbury?"

"Something like that." I looked around the empty building. "Where is everyone?"

"Terminal closes at 5 in the afternoon. No more flights."

I nodded. "What about cabs?"

The inspector grinned. "They're all gone too. How'd you get here?"

"In a cab."

He shook his head. "No, Mr. Williams, you didn't. I believe you arrived in a blue Ford Anglia. Maybe that car is still out front?"

I shrugged.

"Well, I assume your Mr. Jones and whoever he was with, two kafirs included, have fled the scene, leaving you holding the bag."

I looked at the inspector. "What bag?"

"Why were you running after that plane?"

I kept staring and didn't answer.

"Who were the two kafirs with you?"

"I hate that word."

He chuckled. "To be honest, so do I." He took a long, last inhale of his cigarette, dropped it on the tile floor, and then stubbed it out with the toe of his shoe. He looked back at me and added, "I guess since all the boys at the station use it, I've gotten in the habit." He sighed and looked out the window. "Bad habit," he said to himself in a near whisper. After a moment, he turned back to me. "I'm not a Rhodesia for Rhodesians man, myself. I love this country and believe we should share it. But the government doesn't agree, nor do my fellow Europeans. But what can I do? I'm just a cop."

I nodded. I wanted to say something like, "You're just a good German," but decided not to press my luck. I couldn't tell if he was playing good cop to get me to open up or if he was being sincere. I suspected it was probably both.

"So, I take it you thought you could keep that plane from taking off for Léopoldville?"

I didn't reply.

"You know what I think?" He didn't wait for me to answer. "I think you thought you could load up your jet over there with 30 or so Congolese and maybe smuggle them into the U.S. I know you know your country doesn't want them anymore than mine does. They're just a lot more polite about it." He frowned. "Although I understand that's not the case in Alabama and Mississippi, am I right?"

I didn't reply.

"Well, that's not possible now. I just hope you're not thinking of doing anything else like that." He grinned at me. "My suggestion would be that you bury your friend and then leave Southern Rhodesia. Maybe you should go back to San Francisco and stay there."

. . .

"Pull over here, Constable." That was Inspector Graves. He and I were sitting in the backseat of his police car. We had driven in silence from the airport, past the turn-off for the neighborhood where the house was located, and back to the spot in front of Barclays Bank. It was still raining and my wet feet were cold.

Turning to me, the inspector said, "I hope you can stay out of trouble before you leave town, Mr.

Williams." He reached across me and opened my door. As he pulled back, his arm and hand brushed my crotch. It took me by surprise but I didn't react. I just stepped out of the car and onto the sidewalk. We were in front of a department store called Barbours, right across the street from the bank. It was still open and I had the idea to go in and buy a new pair of socks and a new pair of shoes.

But, before I did, I looked back inside the car. "Thanks for the lift, Inspector."

He winked at me and said, "Any time, my boy."

I closed the door and made my way inside the department store. I checked my watch. It was a quarter until 6 and the sign on the door said they closed at 6:30.

Chapter 20

Barbours Department Store
Corner of Stanley Avenue and First Street
Tuesday, December 13, 1960
A few minutes before 6 in the evening

"May I help you, sir?" That was a clerk just inside the men's store section, which didn't seem to have a lot of customers at that time of day. He was about my height, had dark hair and brown eyes, and was dressed in a well-tailored blue three-piece suit with a red tie. He sported a pinkie ring with a ruby on his right hand, something I hadn't seen in a while.

"Hi, I got soaked in the rain and was wondering if I could buy some new socks and shoes?"

The man looked at me for a long moment and then nodded. "Of course, follow me." He had a British accent similar to Dr. Kimani's. Leading me into the shoe section of the men's store, he asked, "Are you wearing garters?"

"Yeah."

"Well, let's get you dry, into a new pair of socks, and then we can fit you with new shoes." He turned and looked at me again, his eyes narrowing. "Wait here." He paused. "Mr. Williams."

I grinned. "You saw the paper."

He nodded but didn't smile. Turning on his heel, he walked over behind a counter and opened a drawer. Pulling out a thin beige box, he put it on the counter and removed a pair of socks. He walked around the counter and pointed to a comfortable green leather chair. "Have a seat, sir."

I did just that.

He walked over to another counter, reached underneath, and brought out a small towel. Returning to where I was sitting, he sat on a stool in front of me, grabbed a familiar piece of furniture, and put it in front of my chair. "Put your left foot on the fitting stool, please."

I followed his instructions.

He began to untie my shoe. He then lifted my foot up and pulled the shoe off. He looked at it for a moment and then dropped it on the floor. "I'm afraid the leather won't recover for this pair. Were you running in a fast-moving stream?"

I chuckled. "Something like that."

He moved my trouser leg up and then unfastened the sock from the garter. He pulled off the sock and dropped it on the shoe. Using the towel, he vigorously dried my foot for about half a minute. He then grabbed the new sock and pulled it on my leg and fastened it to the garter. He pulled the trouser leg down and patted the top of my foot.

"Switch, if you would."

I did so and, as he began to untie my right shoe, he asked, "What brings you to Salisbury, Mr. Williams?"

"I'm here to help a friend."

"I see." He pulled the shoe off and put it down next to the other one. "Did you buy this pair in Paris?"

"Léopoldville, actually."

"They have that unique French style, particularly in the way the uppers are shaped. I suppose the Belgians do the same. Shame about the Congo."

"Yeah," was my only reply as he unfastened the right sock from the garter.

He pulled the sock down, discarded it, and dried off my right foot. He pulled out the new sock, slipped it on, and fastened it to the garter. He pulled down the trouser leg and then stood. As he picked up my shoes and socks, he asked, "Shall I discard these?"

"Sure."

He walked over behind the counter where he got the towel and dropped them in a garbage pail. He looked at me. "I think I have a pair that is similar. Shall I bring it out."

I nodded. "Sure."

He walked back towards a curtain and disappeared. While he was gone, I looked around. The store was as empty as the terminal building at the airport had been. After a minute or so, he returned with two boxes. "I found another pair you might like as well."

I nodded. "Where is everyone?"

He stood where he was and looked around. "The store management believes staying open thirty minutes later than normal will bring in more traffic in the summer. I hope they see how wrong they are and soon." He sighed.

I grinned up at him. "Well, I'm glad you're open. What's your name?"

"Giles, sir."

"Nice to meet you, Giles." As he sat down on the

stool, he put the two boxes on the floor, and began to take a shoe out of the top box. "How long have you been here?"

"At Barbours, sir?"

"In Salisbury."

He worked the leather of the shoe by squeezing it and moving it in different directions. "I arrived in Salisbury in 1950, sir. I came from Manchester in England." He then began to insert the shoe strings.

"How do you like it?"

He replied, "Fine, sir," as he pulled the string through the eyes of the shoe.

"What made you move here?"

"It was either here or Australia, sir. I chose Rhodesia because I can easily go back to England once a year. My dad and mum live in Manchester and I visit during summer there, winter here." He finished the string and put the shoe on the floor. Picking up the second shoe, he asked, "How do you like Salisbury?"

"It reminds me of Sacramento," I replied, thinking of Marnie.

"That's in California, is it not?"

"Yeah. It's the state capital."

"Is it? I would have thought the capital would be Los Angeles."

I snorted. "Hardly."

Giles looked up from his work. "Not a fan?"

"Not really."

"And, yet, you own a movie studio."

"I do, but I bought it because one of my friends is a great producer."

"That would be Mr. White, correct?"

I nodded.

"Give me your foot, if you would." I lifted my left foot. He slipped the shoe on and put it down on the fitting stool. As he began to tie the shoe, he said, "I'm quite the fan of those Monumental westerns."

"Really?"

"Switch feet, if you would."

I did that. "Why do you like them?"

As he took my foot and slipped the right shoe on it, he grinned at me all of a sudden. "Well, the two cowboys are always in love, aren't they?"

I smiled and nodded. "Most people don't see it."

He blushed slightly. "Oh, I saw it in the very first film."

"Who's your favorite?" I asked as he tied the shoe.

"Rudy Belmont. But I hear he has a girlfriend." He stood up and said, "Have a go at it, Mr. Williams."

I stood and walked around. "These feel great. I'll take 'em. And Rudy has a boyfriend. It's Pete. The other cowboy."

Giles blinked for a moment and then asked, "Would you like to try the other pair?"

I shook my head. "I'm late already."

"Of course," said Giles. "If you'll step this way, I'll write out your ticket. The cashier at the front will take your payment."

I nodded as I followed him to the counter. "Do you take American Express?"

"I'm afraid not yet. You can always open an account with us." He took out a receipt book and began to write in it. "Barbours would be more than happy to have your trade."

"I don't think we'll be here very long." I thought for a moment and then asked, "Is this store segregated?"

Giles looked up. "In what way?"

"If I brought an African friend here, would you serve him?"

Giles pursed his lips. "To buy clothes for himself?"

I nodded.

He sighed and tapped his pen on the receipt book. "I would, without question, but then I would be dismissed. The same would happen in any of the major stores in Salisbury. Africans are encouraged to shop here for their employers but are required to purchase their own personal items, such as clothing, in the settlement areas."

"I see."

Giles looked back down at his book. "May I have your address?"

Chapter 21

Montreal Road
Braeside
Tuesday, December 13, 1960
A few minutes before 7 in the evening

"Keep the change." I handed the cab driver five pounds as I opened the door. We were in the driveway of the house on Montreal Road. I noticed all our rental cars were in the driveway along with Lionel's Jaguar. The rain had stopped.

He looked at it and then asked, "Are you sure, sir?"

"Yeah. Have a good night." I stepped out and closed the door behind me.

"Same to you, sir."

I walked up towards the front door as I heard him put the cab in reverse, back out of the driveway, and make his way back towards Canada Drive. I pushed open the front door and found everyone in the kitchen.

"Nick!" That was Marnie.

Everyone stopped talking as Carter asked, "Where've you been, son? We were about to go out to look for you." He sounded irritated. I couldn't blame him.

"Inspector Graves picked me up at the airport, we had a little talk, and then he dropped me off downtown in front of Barclays Bank."

"Did he hold you for questioning?" asked Lionel.

I shook my head. "He was real friendly. I didn't tell him anything but he knew why I was at the airport." I looked over at Lettie. "I'm glad you left."

She nodded. "I saw his car and dashed back through the terminal. We felt it was wise to leave before the police could spot us."

"Well, someone saw us because Inspector Graves asked me who the two Africans were." I looked around. "Where is Dr. Kimani?"

Carter said, "We took him to a friend's house. He thought it was too dangerous to drive him back to Tafara."

I nodded. I could see that Carter was still upset. I said, "The reason I took so long is I really needed some new socks and shoes. When I was running across the tarmac, my old ones got soaked. So I stopped at the department store across the street from the bank and got some."

Lionel asked, "Barbours?"

I nodded as I watched Carter whose frown deepened.

To explain, I added, "They were the only pair I brought."

He nodded and then slipped out the door and headed towards the pool.

Marnie said, "He was real upset when you didn't come back, Nick."

I nodded and walked past Captain O'Reilly and John Murphy to get to the back door. As I stepped outside, I closed the door behind me.

Carter, who was standing by the pool, heard me and said, "You really scared me, Nick."

I walked up and stood next to him. "I know and I'm sorry, Chief."

He stood there and looked at the pool for a long time. Finally, he sighed and said, "I want to go home and stay home."

"Me too."

He put his hand in mine and squeezed it. He quietly said, "We need to be alone."

"I know." I started to list some of the specific reasons why but thought better of it. I was thinking of the sex but I knew he was talking about something deeper.

I looked out at the grassy field behind the brick hut. It was where Freddie had been staring all day. I thought about Paul and suddenly wondered how they had ended up in Salisbury and why. There was a reason he and Paul had traveled two thousand miles to get away from Léopoldville. But, for the life of me, I had no idea what it was.

Why not Kenya? I didn't know my geography but I had a sense Kenya was closer. Or why not just go across the river to Brazzaville and call us? They both knew we would help them. Or I thought they did.

I looked around the yard and then up at Carter as he, too, stared out at the grassy field behind the brick hut. Maybe he was looking out at the grass and wondering if his father, a horrible man, would suddenly appear. His father had been a terrible husband, an indifferent parent, and a tyrannical white man when it came to the Negroes unfortunate enough to come into contact with him.

Once again, I thought about how Mr. Wilson Jones would have fit in perfectly in Salisbury. He would have smirked every time an African called him, 'sir'. He would have thought they needed to and that he deserved to get all the bending and scraping they would give him.

I remembered the man we'd seen the day before at lunch—the one Lionel had called Boss Lilford. That was the Rhodesian version of Wilson Jones. Only richer and with a bigger piece of the pie than Mr. Jones could have ever dreamed of.

"What are you thinking about there, son?" asked Carter. "Your mind seems to be racing a mile a minute."

"Your father would have loved it here."

He looked down at me in surprise. "That's what I was thinking about. I felt like him this morning at the jail or goal or whatever it was called. That little dance I had to do to keep the policeman from asking to see Freddie's papers just about broke me."

I looked up at him. He looked upset in a way I'd rarely seen before. "We need to get out of here," I said.

He nodded and sighed deeply. "We do."

Neither of us, however, moved.

"And then we need some time, just the two of us," I added.

"We could take a long drive somewhere and stay in roadside motels."

The thought of that made me laugh. "I was thinking more of spending a couple of days in my grandfather's bed. We could leave Gustav and Ferdinand in Paris and unplug the phone."

Carter pulled me in close. "Now you're talkin', son."

I leaned against him and said, "I love you, Carter."

"I love you too."

He looked down for a moment. "I do have to admit those are nice shoes."

I laughed as I showed them off. "It wouldn't matter to me if they were red with pink polka-dots. They're warm and they're dry."

We stood there for another long time until it started raining again.

. . .

"I wasn't sure if there would be an outdoor grille here, so I passed on all the steaks, although I've never seen such big ones and so cheap." That was Mrs. Dewey. She and Lettie were setting the dining table.

Marnie, who was tossing a big green salad in the kitchen, added, "I told her about Mother's famous stuffed pork chops." She looked over at Freddie. "I hope you like pork, Mr. Nyemba."

He was sitting on the sofa in the living room next to Lionel. He smiled and replied, "Yes, *madame*. I am sure it will be very delicious."

Marnie smiled and said, "It's my favorite dish. Mother made it all the time when I was growing up."

Lettie walked back into the kitchen and opened the top oven door. There were two built into the wall and both were on. Fortunately, we had several windows open and a nice breeze was moving through the house. She took a look and said, "I'd say about ten more minutes before we're ready to eat." She closed the oven door and looked around. "Has everyone washed up?"

At that, Lionel stood and asked Freddie, "Have you seen the bathroom with the walk-in shower?" He was talking about the one off of our bedroom on the back side of the dining room.

Freddie shook his head and stood. "No, I have not *Monsieur* Lionel."

"Just Lionel is fine, Freddie. Follow me."

The two disappeared down the hall that led in that direction. I glanced over at John Murphy who was nodding at Captain O'Reilly. They were both sitting at the table in the breakfast nook.

Mrs. Dewey said, "It's none of my affair, but I do hope that Mr. Attaborough remembers that Mr. Nyemba is, in effect, a recent widower."

John Murphy jumped up and said, "You're right about that, Mrs. Dewey. I think I'll have a quick chat with his nibs. There's nothing quite like a son of Ireland to bring a good dose of what's good for 'im right down on the head of a Limey who's ridin' a bit too high."

Both Mrs. Dewey and Captain O'Reilly laughed as John Murphy headed down the hallway himself.

Alex looked up at Mrs. Dewey from a magazine he was reading in the corner. "I didn't catch all that."

She smiled in reply, "He was just saying that Mr. Attaborough needs a reminder to take things more slowly. And I heartily agree."

I grinned at Carter as Alex said, "Thank you, ma'am," and looked back at his magazine, blushing a bright red.

...

"This is indeed very delicious, *Madame LeBeau*." That was Freddie as he helped himself to a third pork chop. He was eating steadily without saying much of anything and was way ahead of the rest of us.

Marnie smiled. I was pretty sure she loved the way he said her last name with his deep French accent. "I'm so glad you like it." Looking at Lettie, she added, "Of course, it's Mother's recipe."

"And I think you've improved on it, Marnie. I don't remember mine tasting quite this good."

Marnie blushed slightly. "Well, they had fresh sage at the supermarket. I'd never seen that before."

Mrs. Dewey nodded. "There was a wide variety of fruits and vegetables and herbs I'd never seen before."

Captain O'Reilly looked up and asked, "How long have you been in America, Mrs. Dewey?"

She smiled. "Five years, but if you're referring to *herbs*"—she used the "h" instead of keeping it silent—"I'm afraid that's from living in Canada."

Alex looked around. "I don't get it."

Mrs. Dewey explained, "In Great Britain and Ireland—"

"And Rhodesia," interrupted Lionel.

"Yes," nodded Mrs. Dewey, "And Australia, New Zealand, and South Africa, no doubt, the word h, e, r, b is pronounced with the h aspirated. *Herb*. In America and parts of Canada, you know it as 'erb."

Alex nodded. "I didn't know that."

Freddie looked up from his stuffed pork chop and said, "In America is like in France, no?"

Mrs. Dewey nodded. "Indeed it is."

He looked at Alex. "I did not know that, either."

John Murphy stood up. "I'm up for another beer. Any takers?"

Carter said, "I'll take one. I had a Lion this last time. I think I'll switch back to Castle."

Lionel stood and followed John Murphy into the kitchen. "It's always Lion versus Castle."

"But what's that you're drinking?" asked Alex.

"A shandy. Beer and lemonade."

"Where on Earth did you get the lemonade?" asked Lettie.

"I snuck some in when I arrived, Mrs. Williams," replied Lionel with a big grin.

"You brought your own lemonade?" asked Marnie.

"Sure did. It isn't summer without a shandy and I supposed you wouldn't think of it so I put some in a Coke bottle." He pulled one out of the refrigerator and showed it off. Sure enough, it was a Coke bottle with a light yellow liquid in it.

"Do you keep lemonade handy?" asked Mrs. Dewey.

"I do at that," he replied as he poured some in his glass and then replaced the bottle in the refrigerator. "I start making lemonade when the rain starts. I've a lemon tree in my back garden." He poured some Lion beer into the glass. It foamed up a little more than normal. I'll bring some around if you'd like a bag or two."

"That would be very nice," replied Mrs. Dewey.

"Anyone care for a sip?"

Most everyone shook their heads except for Alex. "I'm game," he said.

Lionel walked back into the dining room and offered his glass.

Alex took a sip and then shook his head. "Not my style at all."

"What'd it taste like?" asked Marnie.

"What else? Beer and lemonade," replied Alex.

We all laughed at that.

. . .

"Now then," said Lettie with a deep breath as Carter and Captain O'Reilly began to clear the table. I was at the sink in the kitchen with John Murphy. Alex had volunteered to help but Carter had suggested he take Marnie outside to the backyard so they could enjoy the evening. Through the window over the sink, I could see the two of them sitting close to each other by the pool and holding hands.

"Yes?" asked Lionel, teasingly.

I glanced over at the living room and saw Carter do the same.

Lettie squared her shoulders and said, "Mr. Attaborough, I am grateful for all the help you have given my son and Mr. Nyemba but please do let me collect my thoughts, if you don't mind. This is an important and difficult conversation and I prefer not to be interrupted."

Lionel looked embarrassed and replied, "My apologies, Mrs. Williams."

I turned back to the sink so Lettie wouldn't see my big grin.

"That's quite alright. Now," she said again. "Since I arrived this afternoon, I've been listening to each of you talk about the situation here in Salisbury. I've had the great fortune to make the acquaintance of Mr. Nyemba and you and, of course, dear Dr. Kimani. And, I must say that, although the landscape is quite beautiful, life here is unappealing." She looked at Lionel. "Do you have anything to say about that, young man?"

Lionel looked down at the floor. "I can't disagree with you, Mrs. Williams. Rhodesia, this *Zimbabwe*, gets in your blood. I love the landscape, as you say, but I find life here to be appalling. That is why I do what I do."

Lettie nodded. "Yes." She turned to Freddie. "That brings me to my next question. And, I apologize for being direct but, Mr. Nyemba, what in the hell were you and Mr. Vermaut thinking by coming here?"

Everyone got quiet and waited. After a long moment, Freddie said, "I ask this all these days. Not to Paul but to God and I only know this." He shifted in his seat and ran his left hand over his head. "Paul say that he has family here. That is why we come."

We all looked at Freddie.

Carter and I both asked, "What?" at the same time.

Freddie nodded. "These are his father's people. They are cousins and leave from Léopoldville in 1954, I think."

Before I could help myself, I asked, "Why didn't you cross the river and contact us from Brazzaville?"

201

Freddie nodded. "Yes, I ask God this question often. I think this is why you are here."

Carter walked over and sat next to Freddie. "You know you can always call us."

Freddie took Carter's left hand and held it. "I know, boss. Paul, we argue about this. He say he didn't want to bother you. He say you had left Africa and you had your life to manage."

No one said anything. I swallowed hard and tried very hard not to cry. I was mostly successful.

Finally, Carter said, "Well, we're here and we're going to do whatever you want us to do."

Freddie nodded but didn't say anything. Carter reached over and kissed him on the cheek.

With a small smile, Freddie said, "Thanks, boss."

Lettie cleared her throat. "You can't stay here, Mr. Nyemba, nor would I think you would wish to. Would you like to come home with us?"

Captain O'Reilly, who was carrying a handful of silverware said, "Johnny and I can fly back to Marseilles and get you a birth certificate and an American passport. It'll take about three days, tops."

I said, "That's a great idea."

Freddie didn't say anything.

Leaning forward, Lettie asked, "Would you like that, Mr. Nyemba? Or would you like to go home?"

Two big tears rolled down Freddie's face.

Carter reached into his pocket and handed over his handkerchief.

Freddie nodded silently and took it. After a moment, he said, "I cannot return. My mother is dead. My people upriver have found out about Paul. I have no home. I have no family."

Carter put his arm around Freddie. "Yes, you do, Freddie."

Mrs. Dewey moved over and sat on the arm of the sofa on the other side of Freddie. She put her hand on his cheek. "Yes, dear Mr. Nyemba, I promise you have a family here. These are some of the most loving friends I've been blessed to know." She sniffed a little as Freddie nodded.

I looked over at Lionel. I could see how much he wanted to say something but whatever John Murphy had said to him earlier seemed to have made an impression. He was quietly watching Freddie but keeping to himself.

Lettie who, in all the time I'd known her, had never been patient with sentimentality (that was one of the reasons she and my father were perfect for each other), shifted in her chair and asked, "What do you think, Mr. Nyemba?"

Freddie sighed and looked down at the floor. "What will I do in America?"

"Work for me, if you want," said Carter.

"At a gym?" Freddie looked over at Carter as Mrs. Dewey stood and walked over to the kitchen. She grabbed the spare towel off John Murphy's shoulder and began to help Captain O'Reilly dry the dishes.

Carter nodded. "Sure."

Freddie looked at Lettie. "Then I go to America."

From the kitchen, Captain O'Reilly asked, "Under what name?"

Freddie frowned. "Frederick Nyemba."

Lettie shook her head. "No. Not Nyemba." She looked at Lionel. "What is a nondescript African surname?"

Lionel frowned and looked at Captain O'Reilly. "Since Freddie has a mostly French accent, I would suggest you get a French passport with an American permit to live and work in the States."

The captain grinned. "And a French birth certificate?"

Lionel shook his head. "Have him born in Brazzaville close to, but not on, the date of his actual birth." He looked over at Lettie. "Brazzaville is across the river in what was the French Congo."

She nodded thoughtfully.

John Murphy offered, "That's easy enough. Pierre can take care of that."

The captain nodded as he dried a plate. "Aye, he can."

Lettie asked, "Is there a common surname in Brazzaville, Mr. Nyemba?"

Freddie thought for a moment. "I know some. Makala." He frowned. "Goma, Mpaka, Loendo." He looked at Lettie.

She said, "Keep it simple. Frederick Goma. How's that?"

He smiled, all teeth. "This I like."

Captain O'Reilly said, "Then it's set. What's your date of birth?"

"Nineteenth of February, 1930."

John Murphy said, "We'll make it the first of February in 1931." He laughed. "You don't mind havin' another thirtieth birthday, do you?"

Freddie shook his head. "No."

Carter said, "Then it's all set. And we'll have a big birthday party for you in a couple of months."

"Thanks, boss," said Freddie.

"Now," said Captain O'Reilly with a handful of forks he was drying, "do we take the jet back?"

Before I could answer, Lettie said, "I think not. Better to travel commercial, would you agree, Mr. Attaborough?"

Lionel grinned. "Now, why would you ask me, Mrs. Williams?"

She rolled her eyes. "I'm pretty sure you've done something like this before. Flying commercial is a little less suspicious than flying in the only jet of its kind, is it not?"

I turned off the water over the sink and asked, "Lettie, how do you know that?" She was right. It was one of two Comet 1 jets in service. The other one was flying for the British Royal Air Force. And ours had the new Rolls-Royce engines that were being used on the Comet 4, the jet that B.O.A.C. was using to fly back and forth to London.

She smiled at me. "Never you mind, Nicholas. Let's stay on topic here." She turned back to Lionel. "Now, when is the next commercial flight to Marseilles?"

"There's only one way to get to Europe tomorrow. There's a South African flight that leaves at half past 2. It arrives in Rome around 8 in the morning, if I remember rightly. I'm sure there's some flight from Rome to Marseilles from there."

Captain O'Reilly nodded. "Leave that to me. We'll get there."

"When will you be back?" asked Carter.

The captain looked at John Murphy who said, "Let me think for a moment."

"Wouldn't it be easier for all of us to go to Europe?" asked Mrs. Dewey.

I said, "We have to get Freddie to the airport and on the plane without him being arrested. And we can't go direct from here to Europe. We have to stop in Khartoum."

"Or Kano, Nigeria," added Lionel.

Lettie asked Lionel, "What if we were to get Mr. Nyemba on the jet? Where could we go from here? Providing bribes could be paid, of course."

Lionel nodded. He thought for a moment and then said, "I seem to remember hearing about someone making it to Brazil from here. I can't quite remember how they got there." He looked down at the floor.

John Murphy snapped his fingers. "Of course! Luanda!"

"Where's that?" asked Lettie.

Freddie, Carter, and I chimed in. "Angola."

I continued, "It's not far from Léopoldville."

John Murphy said, "Fly from here to Luanda and then on to Recife. It's on the northeast corner of Brazil. You could go up to Mexico City from there and we could meet you there when we have everything."

I nodded. "Then Carter and I fly with Freddie over to Ensenada and do our usual trick of flying from there to San Diego or L.A."

Carter shook his head. "You and I have to fly right into San Francisco. We can't risk landing anywhere else in California."

I nodded as Lettie asked, "Why is that?"

Carter replied, "We barely got out of L.A. County after we were down there earlier this month. There's an open warrant for our arrest."

Lettie sat back. "For what?"

"Sodomy," I replied.

She shook her head. "Well, for goodness sake. That charge never sticks and it does get old, does it not?"

...

"So this is what we have." That was me. We were all in the living room. Marnie and Alex had wandered back into the house as we were going over the details. Captain O'Reilly had called the hotel near Victoria Falls where Captain Clement and his crew were staying to confirm that the Comet could fly to Brazil. He said that Carter and I had suddenly decided we wanted to spend Christmas in Rio with some friends. The pilot had confirmed it was easily done and had said we'd probably go via Luanda. He'd also said they would be back late

Wednesday afternoon and were ready to leave whenever we were. Before making the call, Lionel had told Captain O'Reilly that the phone might be bugged which was why the captain had come up with the story about Rio.

I leaned forward. "Captain O'Reilly and John Murphy will fly to Marseilles tomorrow. They'll get there on Thursday evening, most likely, after stopping at the Beau in Nice to get some cash." That was one of the two hotels we owned there. I looked at Captain O'Reilly. "I'll tell Hortense"—she was the manager of the hotel—"to have the Credit Suisse wire enough to the hotel account for you to get half a million French francs." The captain nodded. I continued, "Then, hopefully, you'll have everything needed by Sunday night and can fly from Marseilles to Paris and then on to Mexico City. We'll wire the Beau once we know where you should meet us."

John Murphy said, "I'd suggest you make a very big deal out of the whole thing. Get the biggest suite in the best hotel in the city."

I nodded. "Good idea." I thought for a moment and then looked at Carter. "To protect the captain and his crew, we'll tell them over the Atlantic that we want to go to Mexico City instead of Rio."

Lettie said, "I don't think it wise to keep your captain in the dark."

Captain O'Reilly nodded. "Captain Clement knows who he's working for. So do the rest."

I looked over at Freddie who was listening intently. "I don't want any of them to give away what we're doing."

"Well, there's not going to be a lot of time for that," said Marnie. "You said we're gonna leave here first thing on Thursday morning, right?"

I nodded.

"So you tell them after Freddie is on board and then there's no chance of anyone backing out."

Captain O'Reilly frowned slightly. "I still think you're underestimating the crew. Again, I say, they know who they're working for."

Alex raised his hand.

I chuckled and said, "Alex? Have a question?"

He nodded. "You do realize how illegal all of this is, right?"

Before I could say anything, John Murphy said, "My lad, every day the six of us"—he pointed to Freddie, Lionel, Captain O'Reilly, and me—"break the law several times a day." He looked at the captain. "Every time I kiss boyo here, I'm breaking the law." He reached over and planted a big kiss on the captain to prove his point.

Alex sat back, blushing slightly, and said, "I hadn't thought about that."

Marnie patted him on the leg. "Now you know why I love working for Nick."

He frowned at her for a moment. "I don't get it."

We all laughed as Mrs. Dewey said, "These laws are patently unfair and frankly ridiculous. The same reasoning that keeps Mr. Nyemba trapped here as second-class citizen—"

"Who is required to have papers just to go walk down the street," added Lionel.

"Well, it's the same thinking that makes it illegal for these men to love each other," finished Mrs. Dewey

Marnie added with a grin, "And it's the reason I can't get an American Express card in my own name."

Alex smiled a little at that. "I just don't want any of you to get in trouble."

I shrugged. "We're all in trouble right now." I hooked my thumb at Freddie. "We're harboring an undocumented alien."

"And you're in trouble under Rhodesian law right now, Mr. LeBeau," added Lionel, "because you're not on the phone reporting Freddie for being here. It's called failure to report a crime." He looked at John Murphy with a grin. "And there should be a law about harboring attractively roguish Irishmen, but I believe that was repealed by Parliament after the establishment of the Irish Free State."

John Murphy and Captain O'Reilly both laughed at that.

I looked at Alex. "Does that help explain why we're doing what we're doing?"

He nodded and looked around. Taking Marnie by the hand, he said, "Now I get it, hon."

She smiled and reached over to kiss him on the lips.

I glanced over at Lettie who was beaming and dabbing her left eye with a small lace handkerchief as Mrs. Dewey patted her arm.

. . .

Lionel stood and stretched. "I believe we all have our assignments for tomorrow." He grinned at Lettie who stood and nodded.

"My only question is this," said Lionel as he took his glass to the kitchen.

"And what is that, Mr. Attaborough?" asked Lettie.

"I count nine adults and there's certainly plenty of room for your party, but I somehow doubt everyone wants to share a bed."

Marnie said, "We figured that out before you got here, Mr. Attaborough. Alex and I are going back to the Ambassador with Captain O'Reilly and Mr. Murphy. Our bags are loaded in their car."

Lionel, who had been looking at Freddie out of the corner of his eye, appeared to be disappointed for a moment but then nodded agreeably and said, "Very good. I hate to be a meddlesome landlord."

John Murphy said, "Meddlesome being the key word." He looked right at Lionel and grinned. "Am I right, boyo?"

Alex glanced at Marnie. "I don't get it."

The rest of us, including Freddie, laughed. Marnie smiled and tilted her head to the side. "I'll explain it in the car."

Captain O'Reilly put his hand on John Murphy's next and said, "His nibs will do all the explainin'."

As everyone made their way to the front door, Lionel stopped. "What about Mr. Vermaut's family here in Salisbury?"

We all looked at each other. I asked, "And what about a funeral? Can we do that before Thursday morning?"

Lionel sighed and put his left hand on his forehead. "My word, I completely forgot. The health authorities are insisting on an autopsy since the disease was unknown." He looked up at the ceiling. "This is a difficult conversation, but they are suggesting a cremation following the autopsy as they plan on extraction of various organs and tissues and an open casket will not be possible."

I said, "He didn't look like himself at the end, so I think that makes sense." I turned to Freddie. "But it's your decision."

"What is cremation?"

Lionel replied in French.

Freddie nodded. "Yes, this is right." He looked at Carter. "The soul has risen to heaven, no? It is no longer with the body, I do not think."

Carter nodded and quietly said, "I think you're right, Freddie."

Lionel sighed. He looked at Freddie. "Was Mr. Vermaut a Catholic?"

Freddie nodded but didn't say anything.

After thinking for a moment, Lionel said, "I think it's best to find a priest of the Church of England. He couldn't get a Catholic service since cremation isn't permitted. May I arrange that tomorrow, Freddie?

"Yes and I thank you."

"What about Paul's family?" I asked.

Lionel sighed again and nodded. "Vermaut is an unusual name for Salisbury. I'll see if I can find them tomorrow."

Lettie said, "Thank you, Mr. Attaborough. You have been more than helpful."

He grinned at her. "And hopefully not too much of a pain in the arse."

We all laughed at that, even Lettie.

. . .

"What a day." That was me. Carter and I were in bed and my head was on his chest. He was running his hand over my belly.

"It sure was."

"I'm so glad we found Freddie and that he's here and safe."

"Yes," said Carter.

I sat up and looked down at him in the dark. All the blinds were drawn but my eyes had become accustomed to the light. I could see what looked like a worried crease on his forehead. "What?"

He sighed. "Lionel Attaborough, that's what."

I was sure I knew what had him worried but I asked anyway, "What about Lionel?"

"Ever since he walked in tonight, he looked like he wanted to take Freddie home with him."

"I think John Murphy nipped that in the bud."

"Maybe." He turned on his side. "Did you see that car? And what about this house? His fee was only fifty pounds, which I guess is normal, but where is all his money coming from?"

I ran my hand along his arm. "Why are you so suspicious?"

"I don't know. And another thing. I think that whole, you know, whatever it was at lunch yesterday with the Prime Minister and that bigwig was a set-up and staged for your benefit."

I laughed. "You sound like me."

"I don't trust him, Nick."

"I can tell."

Carter sighed. "You don't feel the same way?"

"Not really. He's probably rich from family money. And my guess is that there aren't that many white people here. They probably know each other, particularly people like that."

"Like what?" asked Carter.

"Lawyers, politicians, bigwigs."

Carter looked up at me. "This ain't funny, Nick."

I nodded. "I know." I stood and walked over to one of the windows that faced the backyard. I opened the blinds and looked outside. "Can you believe we were standing in that cemetery on Capri just four days ago?"

Carter stood and walked over. He put his right hand on the back of my neck. "It seems like a lifetime ago."

"Sometimes, when we get tied up in things like this, it feels like everything rushes by."

"I know."

I watched the blackness of the water in the pool. "Every time we were with Paul, I had a feeling we'd all been there before."

"What do you mean?"

"I mean I have a memory of the four of us. You, me, Marnie, and Mrs. Dewey all standing around Paul, or someone like him, as he's dying. And there's nothing we can do." I could feel the tears coming up and I knew I wouldn't be able to hold them back.

Carter said, "But we've barely spent any time with Mrs. Dewey since we hired her."

I turned and put my arms around Carter's waist. "I know. It's crazy and doesn't make any sense." The tears were coming hard.

"You're just tired, Nick." Carter reached over and pulled the string on the blinds to close them. "We both are."

"You're right," I said as he led me back to bed.

"This has been one hell of a month so far."

We crawled into bed together. As the tears kept coming, Carter gently kissed me all over my face and, while that didn't make them stop right then, at least I knew they would at some point.

Chapter 22

Montreal Road
Wednesday, December 14, 1960
Just past 8 in the morning

Someone was frying up bacon so I thought I would open my eyes. When I did, I realized it was dark in the bedroom. I sat up and looked down at Carter who was lightly snoring. He'd kicked off all the covers on his side and, I had to admit, I spent a minute or two just admiring the sight of my husband stretched out and uncovered.

Finally, I got out of bed and walked over to one of the windows that looked out at the backyard. I peered out through the blinds. The day was cloudy and it looked like it might rain at any moment.

Down by the brick hut, I could see Freddie talking to a man and a woman, both African. I figured the woman was Anna from next door and the man was probably one of the men who worked with her. I wondered what they were talking about. I started to worry about what Freddie was saying until I remembered how he'd handled his encounter with Anna the day before. There was nothing to worry about.

Right then, I heard a sharp knock on the door.

"Time to get up." That was Lettie. "Breakfast is almost ready."

I replied, "Thanks. We'll be there in five."

She said, "Good," and then walked away.

...

"This is really tasty." That was Carter. He was smearing some red jam on a piece of buttered toast. He looked at the unlabeled glass jar and asked, "Where'd it come from?" We were sitting at the breakfast table with Lettie and Mrs. Dewey. Freddie was still out back talking to Anna and the other man.

Lettie said, "It's early strawberry jam, courtesy of madame next door." She made a face. "That's so..."

"Creepy?" I asked.

She nodded. "That's as good a word for it as any." Looking at Carter, she asked, "Is this how it was in Georgia?"

He shook his head as he put down his piece of toast. "Not exactly. Mama never had any help in the house, which was just as well, because my father was always mean to any colored folks he ever came across. Aunt Velma and Uncle Roscoe had a maid named Mattie who cooked for them. She didn't live in. When they lived in their first house, Mattie and Velma did all the housework while Mattie also did all the cooking. After they moved to the big house, I think Velma hired someone to come in a couple of times a week to clean."

"Is the big house where they were living when we were there in '53?" I asked.

Carter nodded. "That was the only time I saw it. They were still living in their first house when Henry and I left in 1939."

"Did you ever go to Mattie's house?" asked Mrs. Dewey.

Carter nodded. "Once or twice. It was small but nice." He looked out the window. "It certainly wasn't a brick hut."

Lettie leaned forward. "But Velma told me some of the women she knew had live-in help."

"Sure," said Carter. "But that was like what we have at our house. A room or two connected to the kitchen with its own entrance through the back door."

I looked up from my eggs. "I really want Gustav and Ferdinand to move up to the third floor or get their own place but Gustav says he prefers the basement rooms they have."

Carter chuckled. "*Ferdinand* likes the basement. I think Gustav would rather live out."

Mrs. Dewey looked over at Carter. "But could the live-in help in Georgia come and go as they pleased?"

Carter thought for a moment. "Up to a point. If a colored man was walking through a white part of Albany at night, the cops would stop him. He could get arrested for loitering but, more likely, they'd tell him to get back over to dark town."

"Dark town?" asked Mrs. Dewey.

"The colored side of town," replied Carter with a slight frown.

"Oh, of course, I see." She looked out the window again. "But there were no passes?"

"No, nothing like that," said Carter. "But there are some towns, and not just in the South, where they have sundown laws." He thought for a moment. "Or, at least, they did."

"What are those?" asked Mrs. Dewey.

"If any colored person is caught in town after sundown, they can get in a lot of trouble, including being lynched." Carter looked out the window right then and added, "Looks like the pow-wow is over. Here comes Freddie."

Lettie got up with her plate and silverware. "Good. I can't help but want to feed him."

Mrs. Dewey stood with her own plate and added, "So do I, Leticia."

Freddie walked in the back door. He looked at Carter and grinned. "Good morning, boss. Did you sleep well?"

Lettie, who was standing in front of the open refrigerator, interrupted. "First things, first, young man. How many eggs do you want?"

Freddie asked, "Eggs?"

"Fried eggs," prompted Carter.

"Oh," replied Freddie, appearing unsure.

"You don't like fried eggs?" asked Carter.

Freddie shook his head. "No, I am sorry."

"Don't be sorry, young man," said Lettie. "We have all sorts of things. What would you like?"

"Please, *madame*, do not busy yourself for me."

I grinned because I knew what was coming.

Lettie put both her hands on her hips and said, "Mr. Nyemba, I want you to sit right down and tell me what you want for breakfast. And no back talking."

Freddie looked startled but sat down in the chair next to Carter, which was where Lettie had been earlier. "Back talking?"

Carter laughed. "Don't argue."

Nodding, Freddie smiled a little. "Yes, I see." He thought for a moment. "*Madame*, may I have some fried meats and some fried bread? If you have any potatoes, I would like some that are sliced and fried as well."

Lettie nodded. "How about bacon?" She held up a thin piece from her plate.

Freddie nodded doubtfully.

Mrs. Dewey said, "We have a lot of bacon, Mr. Nyemba."

Looking relieved, Freddie said, "That is good. I am very hungry."

Lettie said, "That's all I need to know." Turning to Mrs. Dewey, she asked, "Violet? Could you bring me a couple of potatoes from the pantry."

"Of course, I'll slice them nice and thin just like my husband liked."

Looking at Freddie, Lettie asked, "Do you like fried tomatoes?"

"Oh, Leticia," said Mrs. Dewey from the pantry, "those are too good to fry."

Freddie said, "*Madame* Dewey is correct. I would like those tomatoes without the frying." He quickly added. "If I may."

Lettie walked over to the breakfast table and kissed Freddie on the forehead. "You may have anything you like, dear boy."

Carter and I looked at each other. We were both shocked. I'd never seen Lettie do anything like that before.

Lettie caught us and gave me a kiss on the forehead and then gave Carter the same. "There. Are all my boys happy?"

I grinned. "Yes, ma'am."

She nodded and made her way back to the stove. "Good. Now, Mr. Nyemba, please tell us all the local gossip."

Freddie nodded. "Yes and there is much important to tell."

"Before you begin, would you like some coffee?" asked Mrs. Dewey.

"Yes," replied Freddie. "You are very kind."

"Not at all. Do go ahead." Mrs. Dewey walked over and reached for a cup from one of the cabinets.

"Well," said Freddie as he looked at Carter. "It seems that sir is very concerned about things in this house."

"Really?" I asked, feeling a knot forming in my stomach.

"Yes. Nelson, he is the house-boy, he say that sir and madame speak much about this. Nelson and Anna say they cleaned the kitchen after the dinner was served and they moved very slowly, listening carefully."

"Why?" asked Mrs. Dewey as she put down a cup of coffee in front of Freddie.

Freddie smiled, all teeth. "Because Anna is very smart." He looked at Mrs. Dewey. "Thank you, *madame*." He grabbed the cup by the rim, took a quick sip, and then continued, "Anna know Mr. Attaborough and that he own this house and that he is a great help to the people and her cousin who lives in Mufakose, that is a nearby town, was helped by Mr. Attaborough. She say she hear my lies yesterday." He laughed and then looked at me as he took another sip of coffee. "I do not think I will make very good private dick."

I grinned and said, "Well, we'll see."

Carter asked me, "Should we be worried?"

Lettie, who was frying bacon, said, "Hush, Carter, let the man speak."

Carter winked at me and sat back in his chair.

Freddie said, "Anna say that madame disagree with sir. That she see madame of this house and mother of sir and they seem very nice. Sir say that he know Mr. Attaborough too and that he do not like the man and that is all very..." Freddie paused. "What was the word?" He thought for a moment and then nodded. "Suspicious. That is what he say."

"Did Anna say what he was going to do?" I asked.

"Yes, Anna say that he will call police service and report this afternoon after big meeting." He looked at me and frowned. "I must go, no?"

I thought for a moment. "Maybe Dr. Kimani could help us."

"How?" asked Lettie as she took a slice of bread and put it in the skillet.

"Maybe he knows somewhere Freddie could hide in one of the African areas."

Lettie shook her head. "That's too much to ask. He'd get in a lot of trouble if he were caught."

I nodded. "You're right."

"The problem is that this is a small town, when it comes right down to it." That was Mrs. Dewey.

I nodded. "Agreed."

We were all quiet for a long moment.

Finally, Carter said, "Why don't Freddie and I just get in one of the cars and go driving around?"

"What if you get stopped by the police?" asked Lettie.

Carter nodded. "Good point."

I started to say something when there was a knock on the front door. We all froze. After a moment, Lettie nodded at Mrs. Dewey and made a motion towards the front door with her hand.

As Mrs. Dewey scooted around the kitchen and down the hallway, Freddie stood and quietly slipped out the back door. I watched him pick up the net on the long pole and skim the pool.

For his part, Carter dashed over to our bedroom and softly closed the door.

Lettie put Freddie's plate of bacon and fried bread in front of me and whispered, "Eat."

I picked up the fork and just held it in my hand as if I had been eating. I wasn't hungry and, regardless of the consequences, the bacon was all crispy.

At the front door, I could hear Mrs. Dewey talking to someone female. After a moment, she said, "Oh, of course, do come in and meet everyone. My daughter-in-law, Marnie, and her brother are off shopping, but my son is here along with Marnie's mother, Mrs. Keller."

I looked at Lettie who was whispering to herself, "Keller, Keller, Keller." As the women made their way towards the kitchen, I stood and walked over to the counter. Without thinking about it, I slouched and leaned against it.

Lettie caught me out of the corner of her eye and started to say something but didn't.

The woman following Mrs. Dewey had dark hair out of a bottle and wore cat-eye glasses. She was in her 50s, probably close to 60. She was wearing a lemon-yellow patterned summer dress and the hem was a little too high, showing her knees. Her shoes were wooden and clacked on the floor as she followed Mrs. Dewey into the kitchen.

"Nicholas, may I introduce Mrs. Helen Watson? She lives next door and sent us some of the excellent strawberry jam."

I kept my eyes on Mrs. Watson while I tried to remember if the jam was still on the table or not and said, "Nice to meet you, Mrs. Watson." I didn't offer to shake her hand. I had decided to be the oafish husband.

Lettie looked at me and shook her head. Walking over to Mrs. Watson, she said, "My name is Leticia Keller. So nice to meet you."

Mrs. Watson shook and smiled. "Now, I understand you are Mrs. Williams's mother, is that right?"

I looked over at Mrs. Dewey, whose eyes bugged out a bit for just a moment.

Lettie nodded. "Yes, that's my daughter Marnie. She and her brother, Alex, are out doing some shopping."

Mrs. Watson nodded sympathetically. "There's so much to do when one moves, particularly from America." She ran her hand over her neck. "When does their ship arrive?"

Lettie asked, "Ship?"

"She means when does the ship from San Francisco get here." I tried to make myself as rude as I thought I could get away with. "That's how it works here in Africa. Most of our stuff is on a ship. And I don't know when the heck it's getting here, to be honest. When we moved to the Belgian Congo, it took those sumbitches nearly three months and a month of that was sitting on the goddam train." I ran the back of my left hand over my face and yawned.

"Now, Nicholas," said Mrs. Dewey. "Let's watch our language around company." She looked at Mrs. Watson apologetically. "Even though he's a Vice-President at Anglo-American, you'd think he was still in the mines."

Mrs. Watson chuckled. "My husband is the same way. We're both from Britain and he's still got a bit o' the Welsh in him." She sighed. "But that's life in Rhodesia." She grinned slightly. "Ain't none of us too fancy here." She then looked at me. "However, I am surprised, Mr. Williams, that you're leasing this house from a known communist."

"What's that?" asked Lettie, looking shocked and alarmed.

"Certainly," confirmed Mrs. Watson with a smug expression. "Mr. Lionel Attaborough owns this house. He's a solicitor but he's also a communist. Or that's what we hear. He usually leases it out to more unsuitable folks. My husband, in fact, was frettin' about just that thing last night. He was plannin' on callin' the police service this afternoon." She smiled at Lettie and then at Mrs. Dewey. "But I'm glad I dropped in. Obviously, you're just plain folks." She leaned over and looked out the window. "I do love the garden here and I see your boy is doing good work keeping it nice and clean." Turning to Lettie, she added, "Now, you tell your daughter to come to me when she's ready to add a maid and a cook."

"Oh, I will," said Lettie, enthusiastically. "It's so nice to know that when Violet and I leave in a few weeks, there will be such nice people as yourself, Mrs. Watson, who'll be keeping an eye on things for us."

"Oh, yes, I'll be more than pleased to." She looked over at the breakfast table. "Oh! I see you've sampled some of my early strawberry jam." She laughed. "We've been in Salisbury since just after the Great War and I still can't quite believe that strawberries are ready in November or that it can be quite warm at Christmas."

Mrs. Dewey laughed. "We'll be leaving right after Christmas and, although I do love a nice wintry holiday, it will make a nice change for once."

"And where do you live, Mrs. Williams?"

Mrs. Dewey walked up to me, her eyes bugging out slightly, stopped just in front of where I was standing, and put her right hand on her right hip. "Now, Nicholas Williams, I've had just about enough of your slouching and unshaven ways in front of our guest." She pointed to the bedroom. "You march right in there and clean yourself up. What Mrs. Watson must be thinking, I really don't know." As she talked, her accent moved around from Canadian to English and back again.

I stomped off towards the bedroom, muttering, "One of these days, I'm gonna give it to you..." I opened the bedroom door. Carter was nowhere to be seen. I slammed the door behind me.

Carter had been hiding behind the door. We grinned at each other and then both leaned against it and listened.

"I am so sorry, Mrs. Watson." That was Mrs. Dewey.

"Men can be so difficult, my dear," replied Mrs. Watson, "I completely understand. Think nothing of it." She sighed. "I am so glad you liked my jam. I'll send my girl over with another jar later today. She said your daughter's boy came with them from the Congo. Is that right?"

"Oh, yes," replied Mrs. Dewey. "He's practically one of the family."

"Well, this isn't the States," said Mrs. Watson with a note of concern in her voice. "Of course, having lived in the Belgian Congo, I'm sure your daughter is aware of how things work here in Africa. We don't let them have too many liberties."

"May we drop in tomorrow, Mrs. Watson? I would really like for Marnie to meet you."

"Oh, please do. And don't worry about my husband. Now that I've met you both, I know you have nothing whatsoever to do with that awful Mr. Attaborough."

"Of course, not," said Mrs. Dewey. "Why I don't think Nicholas even knew the man's name."

Lettie added, "This was all arranged by a real estate agent Nicholas knew from his work. I'm sure that if we knew a communist was involved, Nicholas and Marnie would never have taken this house."

"Oh, but I'm so glad they did," gushed Mrs. Watson. "Otherwise I wouldn't have had the pleasure of meeting you two." She sighed. "And it is a lovely house with a beautiful garden. I'm so glad you're here."

"Thank you, Mrs. Watson." That was Mrs. Dewey.

As her shoes clacked on the floor and her voice faded away, I heard Mrs. Watson ask, "Are you, by any chance, British? I do hear a bit..." And, with that I heard the sound of the front door open and close with the muffled voices of the three women chatting on the front porch.

. . .

"I am so sorry, Mr. Williams." That was Mrs. Dewey. Once Mrs. Watson was gone, we all gathered back in the kitchen. Carter knocked on the window and Freddie came back inside. He then sat down and began to wolf down his breakfast.

I smiled and said, "You did great, Mrs. Dewey."

She shook her head with a slight frown. "But, where oh where, did that accent come from? She was quite right. I could hear London and then Winnipeg and then San Francisco and they kept changing." She looked over at Lettie, who was smiling. "Sometimes even in the same sentence."

Carter said, "Y'all did a great job."

Lettie looked at me. "As for you, young man..."

I held up my hands. "What can I say? Once a miner, always a miner."

Lettie looked over at Mrs. Dewey. "That was really brilliant, Violet. Anglo-American? Of course!"

Mrs. Dewey gave a small smile. "I saw the name on a billboard somewhere."

Carter leaned against the counter and crossed his arms. "The best part is that *sir* won't be putting in a call to the police."

Lettie and I both shook our heads. I said, "I wouldn't count on it. We've still gotta figure out what to do."

Carter nodded. "I think the three of us—you, Freddie, and me—should head over to Lionel's office. He'll probably have a good idea."

I grinned at him and said, "The two of us need to get cleaned up and dressed first."

"You most certainly do," said Lettie. "And, when you get downtown, would you call the hotel? Your wife and brother-in-law need to put in an appearance over here and it needs to be sooner rather than later, I think."

I nodded. "Good idea."

Chapter 23

Office of Lionel Attaborough, Solicitor
Cheltenham House
Wednesday, December 14, 1960
Half past 10 in the morning

Miss Harroway looked up from her typing and smiled. "Good morning, Mr. Williams. How may I help you?"

I was standing there with Carter and Freddie. "Is Mr. Attaborough available?"

"He's with a client at the moment but I know he'll want to see you. Please, have a seat." She smiled at Carter and at Freddie as she stood and slipped in through the door to Lionel's inner office.

Carter said, "Look at these, Freddie. Lionel's a great photographer." The two of them walked over to see Henry the Hippo from the Zambezi while I had a quick upside-down glance at what Miss Harroway was typing. It had caught my eye when I walked up to her desk and I wanted to see more.

```
A BENEFICIAL TRUST TO BE ESTABLISHED BY:

NICHOLAS WILLIAMS
SAN FRANCISCO
U.S.A.

TRUST TO BENEFIT:

SOUTHERN RHODESIAN EDUCATIONAL AND
CULTURAL INSTITUTIONS AS DETERMINED BY
TRUST MANAGER.

TRUST TO BE MANAGED BY:

LIONEL ATTABOROUGH, SOLICITOR
CHELTENHAM HOUSE
SALISBURY
SOUTHERN RHODESIA
FEDERATION OF RHODESIA AND NYASALAND

TRUST TO BE HELD ON DEPOSIT AT:

BARCLAYS BANK
SALISBURY
SOUTHERN RHODESIA
FEDERATION OF RHODESIA AND NYASALAND

TRUST INITIAL FUND:

R£ 100,000.00

TRUST MANAGEMENT FEE:

R£ 1,200.00 per annum
```

"Nick!" That was Carter, whispering.

I ambled over to where he and Freddie were looking at a group of photographs of giraffes.

"What were you doing?" asked Carter, still whispering.

In a normal tone of voice, I replied, "Beginning to agree with you about what we talked about last night."

Carter snorted. "And I was just beginning to agree with you."

I shrugged as Miss Harroway slipped back out of Lionel's inner office.

She smiled at me. "He'll be with you shortly."

I nodded and tried to smile but didn't manage to do so. I was trying to figure out what Lionel was up to. He didn't know we were coming to his office so I knew that memo, or whatever it was, wasn't for me to look at. The fee seemed really high and that made me suspicious. On the one hand, I had wanted to do something like that. And a hundred thousand pounds (I assumed the R meant Rhodesian pounds) was about right. But it would need to be invested. I knew that was how my other two foundations worked. They didn't spend the main amount—they spent out of the interest and dividends from investments. I was hazy about most of all that since I never paid much attention to it. But what amounted to something like thirty-five hundred dollars per year seemed way off.

Right then, the door to the inner office opened. An African man in a set of dark green trousers and matching short-sleeve shirt walked out. He nodded at Miss Harroway and then quickly made his way out the front door.

Lionel followed him and looked over at me. "Well, this is a nice surprise, Mr. Williams. Won't the three of you come in?"

We walked in as he was pulling a third chair over in front of his desk.

"Have a seat." He grinned. "How is everyone this morning?"

I nodded but didn't smile. "We have a problem."

"Yes?"

"The neighbors are on to us." I looked over at Freddie. "The husband thinks there's something fishy and mentioned that he was gonna call the police today."

Lionel's face paled a little under his tan. He leaned back. "I see."

Carter added, "But, we got a visit from the wife, Mrs. Watson. And she got along with Lettie and Mrs. Dewey so well that she said she was going to call her husband and tell him he didn't need to call the cops."

Lionel nodded. "Interesting." He sighed and looked up at the ceiling. After a moment, and still looking at the ceiling, he asked, "Do you think she'll do just that?"

Carter said, "I don't think we can count on it."

Lionel nodded. "And, the more I think about it, the more I'm worried about your flying through Luanda. Maybe you could fly through Léopoldville or Brazzaville?"

Freddie said, "No. I cannot go close to these places."

"But, why?" asked Lionel.

Looking down at the floor, Freddie said, "They kill my mother because of Paul. And they will kill me."

None of us said anything for a moment. I could hear the traffic outside and the sound of Miss Harroway typing but, otherwise, the office was quiet.

Finally, Carter asked, "Who?"

Freddie shrugged. "I do not know."

Lionel leaned forward. "So, some unknown group killed your mother and has threatened to kill you?"

Freddie slowly nodded. I couldn't read his expression. He wasn't crying but he was obviously upset.

"And you don't know who it is or don't want to tell us."

Through gritted teeth, Freddie replied, "I do not know."

Lionel narrowed his eyes. "And they made these threats because you're a homosexual?"

Freddie jumped up out of his chair and began to throw punches in the air as he muttered in what I thought was Lingala. It was an odd thing to watch. He was being careful not to hit anyone or anything. More than anything, he looked like a boxer who was training.

Carter stood and made sure Freddie could see him but stayed far enough away to keep out of harm's way.

After a minute or two, Freddie began to cry. He dropped to the floor, his legs crossed, and bent over. As he cried, he rocked back and forth and made a wailing sound that was heartbreaking to hear.

Carter dropped to the floor and sat next to Freddie on his left. He put his right arm over the man's broad back and held him.

Without thinking about it, I got out of my chair and sat on the other side of Freddie. I leaned against him just to let him know I was there. We sat that way for a while. I had no idea how long.

. . .

After the storm passed, and Carter, Freddie, and I were back in our seats, I noticed a change in the way Lionel interacted with us. I had a feeling he wasn't used to sudden outbursts of emotion and had become uncomfortable. In particular, I wondered if he saw Freddie as a quiet, suffering type and he was no longer attracted to him since he had seen some intense grief. That was probably for the best, but it made me agree even more with Carter about not being able to trust Lionel.

"There has to be a way for us to get out of here," said Carter impatiently.

Lionel shrugged. "If anyone has been able to successfully bribe a European policeman in this country, I've yet to hear of it."

"What about the Africans?" asked Freddie.

"There are no African police who work at the airport," replied Lionel. "So that wouldn't help us there."

"Can you tell us what the problem is?" asked Carter.

"The problem, Mr. Jones, is that an African seen boarding a plane better be in a uniform and there to do a job and be seen getting off. It's not just the police. There would be plenty of airport workers and passengers coming and going who would find it odd to see an African getting on a plane." He leaned forward and looked at me. "Particularly your plane. It won't be long —"

Right then, I heard the door open behind us.

Miss Harroway said, "A Mrs. Williams is here to see you and she's rather insistent."

Lionel nodded. "Bring her right in."

The four of us stood as Lettie marched in. "Mr. Attaborough, I've had a brainstorm and know *exactly* how we're going to take care of this intolerable situation."

Lionel smiled. "Won't you have a—"

"No time for that."

I looked around for Mrs. Dewey. "Lettie, how'd you get here?"

"I drove. How else?"

Carter asked, "You drove? On the other side of the road?"

Lettie waved him away with a gloved hand. "Please, Carter." She looked at Lionel. "Did you or did you not tell us last evening that you know the Prime Minister?"

Lionel, who had been grinning up to that point, cautiously answered, "Yes."

"Take me to him at once."

Lionel's eyes widened. "I beg your pardon?"

"Take me to him at once. I know exactly how to take care of this whole thing." She looked at her watch. "It's a quarter past 11. He should be in his office, wherever that is."

Lionel shook his head. "But, Mrs. Williams—"

Carter said, "Forget it, Lionel. Just do what she says."

Lettie looked over at Carter with a small smile. "Thank you, dear boy. Now, the two of you"—she was pointing at Carter and Freddie—"need to make yourselves scarce."

Carter looked at Lionel, who was frowning in confusion. "Where can we go?"

Lionel sputtered. "Well, uh, I guess." He looked up at the ceiling. "Yes, I guess, the best thing to do is get on the highway to Bulawayo, drive out for a couple of hours, and then turn back. Make sure Mr. Nyemba is in the back seat."

Lettie nodded. "Good." She turned to me. "Nicholas, you will go with Mr. Attaborough and myself. Do you have your checkbook with you?"

I nodded, beginning to have a glimpse into her plan and feeling better by the second. "The Rhodesian one. I also have some American checks. And a French one."

"Excellent." Lettie then marched over to the door. "Young lady!"

Miss Harroway suddenly appeared, her eyes as wide as saucers. "Yes, madame?"

Lettie snorted. "Please do not use that term in my presence. Mrs. Williams will do just fine."

Miss Harroway looked at Lionel and then back at Lettie. "Yes, Mrs. Williams?"

"Thank you. Now, my dear friend, Mrs. Violet Dewey, is likely on her way in a taxi. When she arrives, will you tell her just to go home and wait." Lettie held up her gloved hand. "No, better yet..." She paused and looked at Lionel. "Are *these* phones tapped?"

He shook his head wordlessly.

"Good." Turning back to Miss Harroway, Lettie continued, "Would you call the Ambassador Hotel and ask for Mrs. LeBeau? Simply tell her to go back to the house with Alex and wait for us there. You can tell her I told you to call her."

"Yes, Mrs. Williams."

"And do ask Mrs. Dewey to go back there as well. Tell her Marnie, that's Mrs. LeBeau, my daughter, and Alex will meet her there. They're to stay put until we get this all taken care of. Do you understand?"

"Yes, Mrs. Williams."

"Could you repeat my instructions? This is very important, my dear."

Miss Harroway did just that.

Lettie put her hand on the younger woman's arm. "Thank you, my dear. Mr. Attaborough is lucky to have you working for him."

Miss Harroway nodded mutely and then fled to her desk.

Lionel, who appeared to be in shock, asked me, "Is she always like this?"

I nodded with a grin. "You're damn right she is."

In an exasperated voice, Lettie said, "Nicholas! Please watch your language."

Chapter 24

Prime Minister's Residence
Fifth Street
Belgravia
Wednesday, December 14, 1960
Just before noon

"How may I help you, madame?" That was a blond kid of about 25 or so who was almost as tall as Carter but as skinny as a rail. He was tan, had sharp blue eyes, and thin lips.

"I'd like to see Sir Edgar." We were standing just inside a rambling house that looked like it dated to the 20s or so. We were in a kind of receiving room. We'd waited only ten minutes after talking to the middle-aged woman who was seated at a small desk next to a staircase. There had been a man in uniform outside but he'd just tipped his hat at Lettie as we'd walked through the front door.

"I see." The young man looked at me and then at Lionel. "Who may I say is calling?"

"Mrs. Leticia Williams of San Francisco."

The man, who had been stooping a little, suddenly straightened up. He looked at me again and then back at Lettie.

"I'm sorry, but the Prime Minister is in conference. Would you care to make an appointment?"

"No, I would not, young man. I want you to go tell Sir Edgar that I'm here with my son, Nicholas Williams, and he is prepared to bequeath a hundred-thousand pound gift for the benefit of the charity hospitals of Salisbury." That was news to me. I quickly did the numbers in my head. It came out to just under three hundred thousand dollars which wasn't bad. "We're leaving town this evening and don't have time for any dilly-dallying."

The man looked at Lionel and asked, "Is this true, Mr. Attaborough?"

Lionel nodded without smiling. "It is, Cecil."

I wasn't surprised. Lionel seemed to know everyone.

Cecil nodded and said, "One moment, madame, if you please." Turning on his heel, he quickly made his way to the door just behind the desk where the middle-aged woman was sitting. She was paging through a binder and trying to look like she was ignoring us and not doing a good job.

Lionel walked over to a group of leather chairs next to a window that looked out over a big green lawn. He extended his hand. "Mrs. Williams? Would you like to take a seat?"

Lettie didn't move. "I would not, Mr. Attaborough, thank you."

Right then, the outside door opened and Inspector Graves walked in, still in his trench coat. He looked at me, shook his head with a grin, and then walked over to where we were standing. "Mr. Williams. How are you today?"

"Fine, Inspector. What brings you here?"

"Keeping tabs on you. Or trying to." He looked at Lettie. "Allow me to introduce myself—"

Lettie waved him away. "Oh, I know who you are Inspector Graves. And you know who I am. What seems to be the problem?"

The inspector glanced over at Lionel who had moved over to stand next to me. "I'm afraid I'm going to have to ask your son to come in for questioning. It seems he is harboring a fugitive."

"Is that so?" asked Lettie with a frosty tone.

"It is, madame."

Lettie looked around. "I see no fugitives here, Inspector."

I heard the woman at the desk cough suddenly.

The inspector grinned at Lettie. "Quite right." He looked up at Lionel. "The fugitive is currently residing on Montreal Road and is in the colony without permission and traveling without proper pass papers."

"Inspector?" That was the woman at the desk.

Graves turned. "Yes, Mrs. Ingles?"

"Mr. Williams is here to bequeath a hundred thousand pounds to the charity hospitals and then he is departing Salisbury tonight. Perhaps you'd like to return tomorrow?"

I looked over at the woman behind the desk. She was still paging through the binder and didn't look up.

"I see," said the inspector. He turned to me and asked, "Is this true?"

"All of it," I replied with a smile.

He nodded and then asked, "Will your friend be leaving with you?"

I replied, "Yes," not sure who he was talking about but figuring that was the best answer.

The inspector looked around the room and said,

"Perhaps I will return tomorrow."

"Good," said Mrs. Ingles. "You can take me to lunch at the Royal Golf Club. I do love their roast beef. They do it so well."

The inspector laughed and tipped his hat. "I'll look forward to that." He grinned at me. "Mr. Williams." He then bowed slightly. "Mrs. Williams."

"Inspector," was Lettie's mildly triumphant reply.

. . .

Lionel, who was sitting in the front seat, said, "Well, that's that, then." It was half past noon and we'd just piled into the cab which had been waiting for us out front. We never saw Sir Edgar or Cecil. Mrs. Ingles had arranged everything for us. I got the impression she unofficially ran the Prime Minister's office behind the scenes. She took the check I wrote, shook my hand, and wished us a pleasant journey. And, as Lionel had said, that was that.

Lettie, who was looking out the window on her side said, "It's so much easier when women run things. We're so much more logical than men. Don't you agree, Nicholas?"

I grinned at the cab driver who was watching me in the rear-view mirror and said, "You're absolutely right."

"You need to set up a trust here in Rhodesia, Nicholas."

I nodded as I saw Lionel turn around. "That's a good idea. Lionel, could you take care of that?"

He nodded.

To head him off, I added, "I want you to run it by my lawyer at home so he can approve it. And, of course, I'm pretty sure my trustee at Bank of America will want to do annual audits." I had no idea if that was true and was quoting a line from a movie. But it sounded good. "Will you manage it for me here?"

Lionel, looking slightly disappointed, replied, "Of course."

Right then, we drove past the grounds of Central Hospital and I suddenly remembered the Vermauts. "Have you had a chance to find Paul's cousin?"

Lionel sighed and gave me a grim expression. "It's not good. His cousin's wife told me off. She said Paul got what he deserved and they didn't want to hear any more about him or that friend of his." Lionel quickly glanced over at the cab driver. "Apparently, Paul talked to them a couple of weeks ago when they got into town and it went just as badly."

I nodded and looked out my own window. "I still don't understand why he never tried to get in touch with us."

Lettie patted my hand. "Not everyone is willing to ask for help, Nicholas. He must have been made of some tough stuff. That was a long and difficult trip to make, just the two of them and all on their own."

I turned and looked at Lettie. She was an amazing woman. I said, "I'm so glad you're my mother."

She reached into her purse and pulled out her lace handkerchief. After dabbing her eyes with it, she said, "And I'm so proud you're my son."

Epilogue

1198 Sacramento Street
San Francisco, Cal.
U.S.A.
Friday, December 23, 1960
A little before 7 in the evening

"I made three pans of lasagna. They're cooling in the kitchen." That was me. I was sitting at my end of the redwood dining table at our house. Carter was on the other end. Freddie, Henry Winters, and Robert Evans were on my right. Mike Robertson and Greg Holland were on my left. We were all eating green salads and bowls of an Italian soup Greg had brought over. There was a big jug of red wine sitting on the bar behind Carter. Robert had bought it up in Sonoma County the previous weekend. And we were all drinking glasses of the stuff.

"What's this soup called?" asked Carter.

"I call it Italian soup," replied Greg. "It's a recipe I found in a magazine a couple of years ago. Mike likes it."

After slurping loudly, Mike said, "Yes, I do. Can't get enough of this stuff."

"It has escarole. That's the green stuff. And some rice and herbs."

Carter winked at me when Greg said, "herbs."

Robert said, "Oh, by the way, Nick. Gustav and Ferdinand will be arriving tomorrow evening."

"Have they been in Paris this whole time?" asked Greg.

I nodded as I helped myself to some bread from the basket in front of Freddie. He'd devoured most of it already but I managed to grab one last slice. "Yeah."

"Were they cleaning up your house?"

"That and they were getting some good alone time."

Mike said, "Speaking of that, since we have a couple of guest rooms in our new house, I already invited Freddie to stay with us tonight and tomorrow night. Since you're not putting up a tree here this year, I asked him if he wanted to help us decorate ours."

I smiled at Freddie. "I hope you don't mind."

He grinned at me and said, "No, *Nicholas*." As he'd started doing the day we left Salisbury, he was pronouncing my name the French way, without the final "s." Glancing at Carter he added, "I think it will be very noisy in this empty house here tonight."

Carter and I both blushed while everyone else laughed.

Greg asked, "What time are we having Christmas dinner on Sunday?"

Carter said, "Mama and Aunt Velma are arranging all that. They said to tell you to be at the Mark Hopkins at half past 11."

"Are we eating at the Top of the Mark?" asked Henry.

I shook my head. "No. We'll be in the Room of the Dons."

"Isn't that a little large?" asked Henry.

"No. Carter's mother is setting up one long table. I think there's 26 of us."

"29," corrected Carter.

I shrugged. "But be there by 11:30. We'll have champagne to start and then eat around noon."

Robert looked at me. "I wish you would let us get a tree for here and have a Christmas potluck."

Mike took a swig of wine and then snorted. "Dr. Parnell Williams doesn't attend Christmas potlucks."

I grinned. "Yeah. And, besides, everyone working that day is getting triple time plus a Christmas bonus."

"Well, they deserve it," said Greg.

I nodded. "Definitely. Carter and I have been invited to join them for dinner that night in the kitchen. We stop serving at 6 and the staff have their own party after that."

"That sounds like fun," said Robert.

Carter said, "We're just putting in an appearance."

Greg asked, "Why?"

"Because we're taking the week off starting Monday. Nick and I are gonna fly down to Phoenix for a few days."

Mike said, "Good. I'm glad you're definitely gonna go. You both need the break."

"But what about New Year's?" asked Henry. He looked at Carter. "I thought you were going to have a party here." He looked around the table. "Just for people like us."

Carter nodded. "We're coming back Saturday morning. Gustav is in charge of the party. When I sent y'all the telegram from Brazil about it, I sent him one too. He said he'd like to organize it."

Henry stood with his wine glass and walked over to the bar. As he poured himself another glass, he said,

"I'm glad you're both back. I miss you when you're not in town."

Mike, Greg, and Robert all nodded.

Greg said, "I know it's selfish of me, but I don't want you to go anywhere out of the country for a while. I want you both to stay put."

Henry took his seat and raised his glass, saying, "Hear, hear!"

...

"Now, there's plenty of lasagna. I used three of the biggest pans I could find."

Everyone had a plate and Freddie was about halfway through his already. He didn't seem to gain any weight, no matter how much he ate. And, having spent the last ten days with him, I'd seen him put away a lot of food. And he wasn't picky.

Mike picked up his wine glass and said, "Nick."

"What?"

"It's time for you to tell us what the hell happened in Africa."

I shrugged. "Marnie will submit my report by January 15th."

"And mine," added Carter.

Mike shook his head. "Nope." He took a drink of his wine. "I want to hear you and Carter and Freddie tell the story."

Henry leaned forward and looked at me. "And I want to know how your stepmother was involved."

Greg grinned at me. "I heard she yelled at some cop."

I laughed. "She didn't yell. But she wasn't taking any guff."

"Start from the beginning," said Mike right as he swallowed a big bite of lasagna.

So, I did.

. . .

"What the hell? Twelve hundred pounds a year to manage the trust?" That was Mike.

Carter looked at him. "That's the most important thing you got from Nick's story?"

Mike shrugged with a grin. "I just hope you told him not just no but hell, no."

I nodded. "More or less. I gave him a cock and bull story about my trustees wanting to audit the trust."

Robert, Carter, and Mike all started talking at once. They all laughed and Carter said, "But they do audit everything. There's a whole group of accountants who work for Arthur Anderson who audit every one of your companies."

I took a sip of wine and shrugged. "I guess that's good. I've never heard anything about it."

"For pity's sake." That was Henry.

"The point is," I said, "that I'm pretty sure Lionel might settle for something more like twenty pounds a month to manage the trust."

"How much is that?" asked Greg.

"It's a little less than sixty dollars," answered Robert. He took a quick bite of his lasagna and then asked me, "What about Paul's body?"

"Last I heard, the health department, or whoever it is, was still doing an autopsy or research or something."

Greg asked Freddie, "How do you feel about that?"

Freddie shrugged. "The soul is not in the body so I think it does not matter."

Carter nodded over his glass of wine.

I added, "When they're done, the body will be cremated and Lionel promised to have the ashes sent here."

Freddie nodded. "That, I think, is right."

Henry looked around Robert and asked, "I hope it's OK if I ask about this, Freddie, but I still don't understand why the two of you went to Rhodesia of all places."

Freddie nodded and leaned back in his chair. "Paul, he was very stubborn. He believe his cousin would help us."

"But why didn't you call Nick?" insisted Henry.

Freddie looked at me. "Because Paul did not want to bother such a great man."

Henry, Greg, and Mike all laughed at that. Robert, on the other hand, looked down at his plate. When I glanced at Carter, he was smiling at me.

I put my hand on Freddie's arm and asked, "You know that's bullshit, right?"

"What is this?" asked Freddie.

Mike said, "What Nick means is that he's just a nice guy who got lucky and has a lot of money. He's not a great man."

Robert quietly said, "Yes, he is. You don't know everything, Mike."

No one said anything for a moment. Freddie put his hand on mine and began to rub it. "I think you are a great man, *Nicholas*. And I am honored to sit at your table. I owe my life to you."

I turned red and tried to clear my throat. With my left hand, I lifted my glass and drank from it to hide my embarrassment.

Carter, my ever-loving husband, said, "We're glad you're here, Freddie."

Mike added, "And I'm sorry that I'm such an ass." He took Greg's hand in his. "We're glad you're here, too."

Robert put his hand on Freddie's shoulder. "So are we."

Nodding, Freddie said, "Thank you, men."

. . .

"The other part I don't get is why that cop just let you go." That was Henry. Most everyone was done eating but Freddie was still at it.

Carter said, "It's the power of Lettie."

I nodded. "And that other gal sitting at the desk. What was her name?"

"Mrs. Ingles," replied Carter.

I smiled. "I think she probably runs the whole show."

Mike looked at me. "If that's the case, then why did you still have to be careful even when Freddie, more or less, had permission?"

I sat up. "You're right, Mike. What I mean is that she ran the Prime Minister's office. That's not the whole country, obviously, but it's significant. For us, at least."

Greg looked at me. "Do you know what happened to all the Congolese who were in that plane?"

I sighed. Before I could say anything, Carter replied, "We'll probably never know."

Freddie said, "They have gone back to hell."

I nodded and looked at my empty plate.

"Is there anything we can do?" asked Robert.

Greg said, "If the U.N. can't manage it..." He added, "Nick's not a *billionaire*."

"Not yet," replied Robert under his breath.

Freddie said, "There is nothing any of you can do. We must leave my country in the hands of God and pray. These problems, many of them existed before King Leopold came and made them worse." He sighed. "Someday I will return. When they forget who I am and who I have loved. Maybe it will be better by then."

We all sat in silence for a long moment. Carter stood and helped himself to more wine. Greg jumped up and joined him.

Mike asked, "OK, so you got us to the airport in Salisbury. What happened after that?"

"Well, I haven't told you what we did before going to the airport." I took a quick sip of wine. "Once we were done at the Prime Minister's house, we had to wait for the crew to get back from Victoria Falls at around 6 and for Carter and Freddie to get back from their drive. So, Lettie and I dropped off Lionel at his office. Then we walked over to the bank and I had them wire in more money from Switzerland to cover the hospital bequest and the Rhodesian trust."

"So what is that trust for, exactly?" asked Henry.

Carter said, "It's primarily to cover school fees for African kids. They have to pay to go to high school and most of them can't afford it."

I nodded. "And, hopefully, Lionel won't skim off it and we can expand it."

Henry frowned at me. "You really don't trust him?"

Carter said, "I don't trust him."

"Why?"

"If you could see him, I think you'd agree."

"But doesn't he do a lot of good work?" asked Robert.

I nodded. "He does and I'm on the fence."

"Maybe that twelve hundred pounds you saw was a typo," suggested Henry.

Greg and Mike, both being cops, snorted. Greg said, "Not likely. I think Carter is right. And an audit should be done sooner rather than later."

Robert looked doubtful but nodded.

"Anyway," I said, "Lettie and I then went to the hotel and settled up all the bills. I got all the luggage for the crew while Lettie took care of Marnie and Alex's things." I stood and walked over to get more wine.

"Speaking of Marnie and Alex," said Carter over his shoulder. "What did they decide?"

"That they wanted to wait until after New Years to make any decisions about what to do next."

"What to do next about what?" asked Robert.

As I poured my wine, I tried to decide how to reply. Carter, of course, was asking about whether Alex was going to start his own P.R. business and whether I would be involved or not. I knew Robert was good friends with Marnie but I didn't think it was any of my business to talk about it, so I replied, "You'll have to ask Marnie."

Robert quietly said, "Sure."

I continued, "Anyway, turns out we missed Captain O'Reilly at the hotel. They had left for the airport right before we got there. But, while we were there, I managed to get an international line pretty fast and was able to call the Beau Rivage in Nice and explain to Hortense, the manager, what we needed." I walked over and sat back down in my chair. "She took care of all the money and—"

Greg said, "I just need to get this off my chest." He glanced at Freddie and then looked at me.

"What?"

"You do realize how many laws you broke during this trip, right?"

I grinned at him. Before I could answer, Freddie reached over, took my chin in his left hand, and kissed me on the lips. As everyone else chuckled, Freddie sat back in his chair and asked, "And there is another law that is broken, no?"

Greg nodded with a big smile and lifted his wine glass in Freddie's direction. "You're absolutely right."

Once everyone had finished laughing, I continued, "We left the hotel after we got everything settled and, when we got back to the house on Montreal Road, we found Mrs. Dewey, Marnie, and Alex there waiting for us. We explained everything that had happened and then I packed our stuff." I grinned at Freddie. "While we were waiting for Carter and Freddie to get back, Anna came by with another jar of strawberry jam from Mrs. Watson. Marnie, Lettie, and Mrs. Dewey sat with her outside by the pool—she wouldn't come inside—and the four of them had a long talk."

"Did they ever tell you what they talked about?" asked Robert.

I shook my head. "Nothing other than it turned out the strawberry jam was made by Anna so Lettie kept it and, apparently, it's somehow going to be part of Christmas dinner. We left the opened jar in the icebox for Lionel, along with the rest of the beer and a few other assorted things."

Carter shook his head. "I didn't like Castle or Lion." He looked over at Henry. "Those were two local beers."

Henry, who I didn't think liked beer, simply shrugged and had a drink of wine.

"OK, so you got to the plane," said Mike. "Then what happened?"

"We got to the plane and no one said anything to us."

"That was lucky," said Greg.

"No," replied Carter. "That was Lettie."

Everyone chuckled at that.

Mike looked at his watch. "The way this story is going, we'll be here until midnight. It would help if some people would stop interrupting."

Greg drank some wine and rolled his eyes.

I grinned and said, "So, we took off for Luanda, which is in Angola. The flight took about three hours. While we were in the air, Carter, Lettie, and I talked to Captain Clement about what we were really up to and how we wanted to head north to Mexico City from Recife to meet up with Captain O'Reilly and John Murphy instead of south to Rio for a vacation."

"Going to Rio isn't a bad idea," said Robert.

Henry said, "You heard Mike. Hush up."

"Anyway, he was on board with the plan and said he was sure the rest of his crew would be too. We landed in Luanda around 9 local time. We couldn't leave until the next morning because the company selling jet fuel wouldn't sell us any until the manager came on duty the next day. Freddie, Carter, and I slept on the plane. Everyone else went to a hotel in the middle of town."

"The Hotel Angola," said Carter.

"Why did the three of you sleep on the plane?" asked Greg.

"Because no one knew for sure if there were pass laws in Angola," replied Carter. "And we didn't want to have to deal with the hotel asking for a passport."

Greg nodded.

I said, "So we left the next morning around 9. We flew over the Atlantic and landed in Brazil around half past 11 in the morning local time. We didn't have any trouble there at all—"

"Thanks to more bribes, no doubt," said Mike sarcastically.

I shrugged. "Yeah." I took a sip of wine. "Anyway, we stayed three nights, including spending all of last Friday at the beach and taking a tour of the old town on Saturday."

"Did Carter wear his Speedo?" asked Greg with a grin.

I nodded. "None of us had swimming trunks and all we could easily find were Speedos."

"They weren't really Speedos," said Carter. "They were a Brazilian brand and a little looser."

I looked around the table. "Is everyone finished?"

Even Freddie nodded so I stood to clear the table. Robert helped, as did Freddie, and we were done in no time. Henry had gone to North Beach earlier in the day and bought a coconut cake at an Italian bakery. So, we had that for dessert with coffee. While Henry, Robert, and I were getting that ready in the kitchen, Carter and Freddie worked at building a fire in the fireplace while Mike and Greg took a stroll in the back garden.

. . .

"You can tell Ferdinand hasn't been here," said Greg as we all sat down in the great room in front of the fireplace.

"How so?" I asked as I took a bite of cake.

"There are a lot of weeds back there. It rained a lot these last couple of weeks."

Carter, licking his fork, said, "They'll be gone by early next week. Ferdinand rules that garden with an iron fist."

We all laughed at that.

Robert, who was sitting on the sofa in between Freddie and Henry asked me, "Did you like Brazil?"

I nodded. "The city we were in..." I looked over at Carter.

But it was Freddie who said the name. "*Recife*." And he said it the way they did there which, to me, sounded nothing like the way it was spelled.

Henry turned to Freddie. "Do you speak Portuguese?"

Freddie nodded. "Some."

Henry looked duly impressed and went back to his cake.

I said, "The town is not as modern as Rio. Apparently it's a lot older and it looked that way." I smiled. "But I could have stayed at the beach for a month."

Carter nodded. "Me too. And I was talking to an American guy and his Brazilian girlfriend. They told me we were just a few miles away from the best surfing in the country. I definitely want to go back."

"But not anytime soon, I hope," said Henry.

"Yeah," added Mike. "I'm seriously considering hiding your passports." He grinned at me. "All of them."

I laughed. "Don't worry. We don't wanna go anywhere further than Arizona."

Carter added, "We promised ourselves that when we get a little chilly here—"

"Living in Africa definitely warmed my blood," I added.

Laughing, Carter continued, "Yeah, mine too, but not as much as Nick. Anyway," he said as he cut into his piece of cake, "we promised each other we would go to the house in Scottsdale anytime we want to get warm."

"Good," said Greg. "Because I think we're all in agreement. "He looked around the room. "None of us want you to leave for a long time."

Everyone else nodded. Even Freddie.

Robert put his hand on Freddie's big thigh. "Do you have a passport now?"

Freddie nodded. "Yes. French."

Mike said, "I think you're getting ahead of the story there, Robert." He looked at me. "Nick?"

"So we left Brazil on Sunday morning, early. I got a telegram on Saturday from Captain O'Reilly in Marseilles that they had all the papers we wanted. They were flying up to Paris that night and would leave on Monday afternoon to fly into Mexico City and get there at the end of the day on Monday."

"We got to Mexico City on Sunday at around 3 in the afternoon," said Carter. "We had to stop in Caracas, in Venezuela, to refuel." He looked at me significantly.

I sighed. "And we stayed at the Hotel Geneva in Mexico City. It's a beautiful place. Like something out of the turn of the century."

Mike frowned. "Why do I recognize the name?"

"It's where my mother stayed for a few days in 1930."

Mike nodded. "Right. She wrote one of her letters to your father from there."

"Yeah."

"Did anyone recognize you?" asked Greg.

Carter snorted. "It'd been 30 years, Greg."

He shrugged. "You told us about the clerk at the Waldorf-Astoria who recognized you and who knew Nick's mother back when you went to New York to see *Auntie Mame*."

I nodded. "If anyone put two and two together, they never said anything. And we weren't laying low. We got there on Sunday afternoon and rented pretty much half of the top floor and almost all of the suites."

Freddie said, "It was very beautiful." He sighed. "I very much like that city."

"What about San Francisco?" asked Henry.

Freddie smiled. "It is very beautiful here but very cold, I think."

Robert said, "This is about as cold as it gets."

"Until July," added Mike with a grin.

Freddie frowned and tilted his head to the side. "But July is the summer here, no?"

Henry laughed. "But the coldest winter you'll ever spend will be a summer in San Francisco."

Everyone chuckled at that.

Carter said, "The weather here is different than the rest of the country."

"It is the ocean, no?"

Carter nodded. "How'd you know that?"

"I read," was Freddie's answer.

I grinned at Carter as Mike impatiently snapped his fingers. "Come on, Nick."

"Fine," I said. "So, we had a nice time in Mexico City. Captain O'Reilly and John Murphy flew to L.A. on Tuesday. They're looking at a new boat down there."

"Sailboat?" asked Robert.

"No, it's a yacht."

He looked disappointed. "I loved that sailboat you had in France."

Carter said, "The Pacific is different than the Mediterranean. We need a big engine to go up and down the coast. And Mike is about to shove a sock in your mouth."

Robert blushed slightly and said, "Sorry," as Mike shook his fist in the air with a grin.

"Anyway," I said with a smile, "Carter, Mrs. Dewey, Lettie, and I flew straight home yesterday morning on the Comet. We were here by noon. Robert arranged the rest. Marnie and Alex flew with Freddie on a Mexican airline—"

"*Aeronaves*," said Robert.

I nodded. "That took them to Tijuana where they were picked up by one of our usual puddle-jumper friends. He dropped them off at Burbank. They flew home on the DC-3 and got here around 7 last night. After he got cleaned up, we took Freddie to dinner at the Top of the Mark."

He grinned. "Very high in the air. And very beautiful."

Mike stood and walked over to the bar. "Damn, Nick. That story took so long, I need some brandy."

"Help yourself," I said.

Greg said, "I'll take one."

"I'm on it," replied Mike. "Any other takers?"

"Not me," said Henry.

Robert asked Freddie, "Would you like some brandy?"

"Is it French?"

Mike laughed. "Damn right it is. This is from Nick's personal brandy supplier in Paris."

I rolled my eyes and said, "Oh, brother."

Freddie said, "May I have, please?"

Mike replied, "Coming right up."

Carter stood and walked over to the hi-fi. "How about some dancing?"

"Just no Elvis, if you don't mind," said Henry.

Mike laughed. "There's no rock-and-roll in this house, Henry. You know it makes Nick break out in hives."

I stood as Jo Stafford began to sing about autumn in New York. "Cut it out, Mike."

He walked over and handed a glass to Greg and then to Freddie by the sofa. They both sipped and, after a moment, Mike put down his glass on the coffee table. "May I have this dance, Mr. Nyemba?"

Freddie grinned and, as he put down his glass as well, replied, "Yes, but I can only..." He paused. "How is it? I walk backwards? That is how Paul taught me."

"That means you follow," said Mike, as he led Freddie by the arm to the large open area on the floor and by the garden door where we all usually danced. "And that's perfect since I don't know how to."

Henry walked up to me. "May I?"

I smiled and let him take me into his arms. It was always nice to dance with him and to be standing cheek-to-cheek for a change.

Robert and Greg paired up while Carter leaned against the wall by the garden door with his arms crossed, and watched me with a smile as I followed Henry around the floor.

...

"Well, son, are you glad we're all alone?"

I sighed and said, "Yeah." We were in our big bed, the one my grandfather had built. Everyone was gone and Freddie had left with Mike and Greg. The fire was blazing and Carter was holding me in his arms with my head on his chest.

He said, "I've been thinking for days and days and days about what I wanted to do to you once I got you alone, really alone." There was an unmistakable huskiness in his voice. "Like tonight."

I looked up, feeling a nice warmth inside, and said, "Oh, yeah? Like what?"

He listed a few things which had a very obvious effect on me, particularly below the waist. "But," he said as he wrapped up his list, "We'll have all day tomorrow to fool around and, to be honest, I'd much rather kiss you until we both fall asleep."

Looking into his shining emerald green eyes, I asked, "So whatcha waitin' for, Chief?"

He grinned and got right to work.

Author's Note

Thank you for buying and reading this book!

This story, like all the others involving Nick & Carter, came to me out of thin air.

Many thanks, as always, to everyone who has read, reviewed, and emailed me about the Nick & Carter books. It is deeply gratifying in ways that words will never be able to fully express. Thank you.

...

Books about Nick, Carter, Marnie, Mike, and the gang are usually available around the 30th of each month. If you would like to be notified when the next volume will be available, you can subscribe to the Nick & Carter newsletter here:

http://frankwbutterfield.com/subscribe

Acknowledgments

Right off the bat, I want to thank a fabulous group of beta readers: Justene Adamec, Ann Attwood, L.R. Bombard, Art Foley, John Johnson, Jr., David M., Mody, and Teresa Price along with several other wonderful folks. These books really would not be possible without you.

Thanks to Justene Adamec for many things, including her reminders about all things Czechoslovakian and her keen insight into the metaphysics of these stories. I very much appreciate her lawyer-like attention to consistency from book to book and to how the characters develop.

Ann Attwood helps out with all things British (and a lot more—she's a great editor). I want to thank her, in particular, for help with the scene in Khartoum where Mrs. Dewey is digging into her pocketbook for £10 in assorted notes and coins. That was a lot of fun to write and I'm glad I asked her about it since she set me straight on a couple of important points. If Mrs. Dewey and the Sudanese official don't quite know how to count in £/s/d, the fault is entirely mine.

Thanks to Art Foley for helping me with all things aviation. I suspect he doesn't really approve of Nick's unicorn-like de Havilland Comet 1 jet (with all-new Rolls-Royce engines!), but he tolerates it. He's been very helpful on a number of fronts when it comes to aviation (and in lots of other ways) but, of course, any mistakes about flying or planes in this book (or any other) are completely my own.

John Johnson, Jr., has done a terrific job helping me with language and grammar and to more deeply understand what is going on in these stories that I don't often see because of the way the words come to me. He has also helped me relax when I have thought the stories were getting too soapy. When I think about my basic inspiration for *how* to write these books, it all goes back to my understanding of how soaps have been written since the beginning of radio (as described, in particular, by Garrison Keillor in *WLT: A Radio Romance*).

David M. has kept me on my toes about cars for quite some time, specifically Buicks. My apologies to him for the three Fords in this story.

Thanks to Mody for the Canadian perspective on things and for the very important work you do when you're not reading a Nick & Carter book.

Teresa Price and L.R. Bombard give me some of the best feedback on these books that I get. I'll leave it at that with deep appreciation.

I am delighted to thank the members of the Nick & Carter Fan Club on Facebook who helped track down a supermarket not too far from the Braeside area for Mrs. Dewey and Marnie to shop at. Many thanks to Leigh Ann Wallace who helped pinpoint the Bon Marché Supermarket in the Eastlea neighborhood as seen in a British Pathé video on YouTube titled "Salisbury And Suburbs - Rhodesia (1960-1969)" at the 8:20 mark.

I have the habit of linking to websites where I find a lot of juicy details. And there are a couple which were very helpful in offering up details about life in Southern Rhodesia in the 50s and early 60s. But, before I mention them, I want to offer a disclaimer. These two sites are nostalgic for the "good ole days" of white minority rule in Rhodesia before the creation of Zimbabwe in 1980 and the long rule of Robert Mugabe. I have followed the history of Zimbabwe since it began (I was a nerdy 13-year-old with my own personal subscription to TIME magazine in 1980) and have no respect for the legacy of Mugabe or ZANU-PF, the ruling political party (as of this writing). Nor do I think the days before 1980 were better than now. That being said, I did use two websites for researching Southern Rhodesia: Window on Rhodesia – the Jewel of Africa and Rhodesia Remembered. Should you choose to click on these links, please be advised there is content on both websites that I would describe as advocating for white supremacy, something I can't abide but reluctantly waded through for the purposes of this book.

The first website mentioned above contains a link to a map of Salisbury printed by the Rhodesian government in 1975. I used that map extensively as it was the only street map I could find from any time close to 1960. As a result, I may have made mistakes about street names, locations, and the existence of various stores and institutions named in this story. I did refer to Google Maps to compare what exists now with what existed in 1975, which helped quite a bit. But I had no good reference for 1960. So, any mistakes I made with directions, locations, or the existence of buildings, stores, and institutions are entirely my own.

Historical Notes

The events in this book take place between Thursday, December 8, 1960, and Friday, December 23, 1960.

Every person named and described in Salisbury is fictional with three exceptions.

Sir Edgar Whitehead was born in 1905 in the British Embassy in Berlin. He attended University College at Oxford and moved to Southern Rhodesia in 1928. His political career began when he was elected to the Southern Rhodesian Legislative Assembly in 1939. He resigned to join the Royal Air Force at the beginning of the war. After the war, and before 1958, he held a number of governmental positions including Minister for Rhodesia & Nyasaland Affairs at the British Embassy in Washington, D.C., in 1957 and 1958. After the previous Southern Rhodesian Prime Minister, Garfield Todd, resigned, he was called back to Salisbury where he became the new Prime Minister as a member of the liberal United Federal Party. He helped negotiate the Constitution of 1961 which gave Africans the right to vote (to an extent). The U.F.P. lost its majority in the Assembly in 1962 when the newly-formed conservative Rhodesian Front won a majority of seats. He remained Leader of the Opposition until 1965 when the Rhodesian Front won all the white seats in the Assembly. After retirement, he returned to the U.K. where he died in 1971.

Douglas Collard (D.C.) "Boss" Lilford was born in 1908 in South Africa. His family moved to a farm in Southern Rhodesia when he was five. He was a self-made millionaire who provided the necessary financial backing during the founding of the Rhodesian Front party in 1962. In 1968, he was acquitted of assault when a court ruled that the complainant, an African herdsman who claimed to have been beaten with a leather thong after being set upon by dogs, could not give satisfactory evidence. He retired from politics in 1982 to work his farm where he grew tobacco and corn, raised cattle, and bred racehorses. In 1985, he was found beaten and shot to death at his farm.

Ian Smith was born in 1919 in Southern Rhodesia. During the Second World War, he served as a fighter pilot in the Royal Air Force where he received disfiguring facial wounds as the result of a crash. He required four months of surgical reconstruction after his injury. In 1948, he was first elected to the Assembly as a member of the Liberal Party. He switched to the U.F.P. in 1953 after resigning his seat in the Assembly and being elected to a seat in the parliament of the newly-formed Federation of Rhodesia and Nyasaland. Starting at the end of 1958, he served as Chief Whip for the U.F.P. in the federation parliament. After the implementation of the 1961 Constitution, he helped form the Rhodesian Front party. He became Deputy Prime Minister of the Assembly in 1962. He was made Prime Minister in 1964. In 1965, he led his cabinet to declare independence from the United Kingdom. He remained leader of Rhodesia until 1979 and became Leader of the Opposition after the formation of Zimbabwe. In 1987, he retired from political office. He lived in Zimbabwe until 2005. He died in South Africa in 2007.

Southern Rhodesia was formed as a protectorate of the United Kingdom under a patent issued by Queen Victoria in 1889. The original name was *Southern Zambezia* (referring to the Zambezi River which formed the northern border). The British government agreed that the British South African Company (BSAC), founded and run by Cecil Rhodes, would govern the protectorate. *Rhodesia* (in honor of Rhodes) came into use in 1895. *Southern* was added in 1898. White settlers mostly came north from South Africa and established farms, villages, and towns (including Salisbury) on land owned, managed, or claimed by BSAC.

As BSAC rule continued and the number of white settlers expanded, the consensus in the U.K. and South Africa was that Southern Rhodesia would be annexed by South Africa. However, a self-rule referendum was held in 1922 and, as a result, the protectorate was annexed by the U.K. in 1923 and the Colony of Southern Rhodesia was created.

The economy of the new colony was centered on agriculture, primarily tobacco. After the Depression and the Second World War, an economic boom began and continued into the early 1970s. During that time, the white population more than doubled to over 300,000. Most of the immigrants arrived from the U.K. while others were from the Belgian Congo, Kenya, and other former African colonies following their independence. By 1976, the black population was over 6 million. During most of the existence of Southern Rhodesia, pass laws and restrictive land-use laws (similar to those of South Africa) were in effect and used to varying degrees to forcibly maintain the political fact of white minority rule.

After the war, the U.K. shifted policy away from maintaining a colonial presence in Africa and towards promoting independence. As a result, the Federation of Rhodesia and Nyasaland was formed in 1953. It united Northern Rhodesia (later Zambia), Southern Rhodesia, and Nyasaland (later Malawi). In 1963, the federation was dissolved as Northern Rhodesia and Nyasaland were granted independence.

In Southern Rhodesia, however, the white minority strongly resisted any handover to majority black rule and, following the formation of the Rhodesian Front government in 1962 and the election of Ian Smith as Prime Minister in 1964, negotiations began towards the eventual independence of Rhodesia. The U.K. government, however, did not want to grant independence to a white minority government. So, in November of 1965, Ian Smith unilaterally declared independence from the U.K. That made Rhodesia one of two countries to ever do so, the other being the United States.

Rhodesia, as an independent nation, was only recognized by a handful of countries, including South Africa and Portugal (who held two large white minority-rule colonies in Africa: Angola and Mozambique, one on either side of Rhodesia).

In the 1970s, the so-called Bush War began after Portugal granted independence to its former colonies. Both Angola and Mozambique began to funnel weapons and money, most of which was funded by the Soviet Union, to black nationalists in Rhodesia. South Africa became the primary supporter of the white minority-rule government while, at the same time, urging Ian Smith to negotiate a transfer of power.

That finally happened in 1979 and led to the formation of the Republic of Zimbabwe in 1980. The new country was led by Robert Mugabe and his ZANU-PF party until November of 2017 when he was deposed in a military coup. An election was held in late July of 2018 and, as of this writing, the governing ZANU-PF party has been declared the winner with the opposition MDC party contesting the result amid violent repression of protests by the government.

...

It is likely, according to a 2014 report from a team of scientists at the universities of Oxford in the U.K. and Leuven in Belgium, that the strain of the HIV virus that became pandemic may have originated in 1920s Léopoldville in the Belgian Congo. During that time, the city was booming and new laborers were coming into the area from different parts of Central Africa.

HIV most likely passed from chimpanzees to humans many years earlier in what is now Cameroon. It was a regional virus that began to evolve into different strains and infect more and more people as Léopoldville grew. From the 1930s through the 1950s, HIV moved into different parts of the Belgian Congo, most likely spread as the railway network was expanded to support the growing mining operations around the colony.

By 1960, the one strain that became pandemic, known as HIV-1 group M, was established and making its way from the newly independent Congo to other parts of the world.

...

For more information about the gold fuss, see page 15 of the December 12, 1960, issue of *LIFE* magazine. Their clever writers explain it much better than I can.

Credits

Yesteryear Font (headings) used with permission under SIL Open Font License, Version 1.1. Copyright © 2011 by Brian J. Bonislawsky DBA Astigmatic (AOETI). All rights reserved.

Gentium Book Basic Font (body text) used with permission under the SIL Open Font License, Version 1.1. Copyright © 2002 by J. Victor Gaultney. All rights reserved.

Gladifilthefte Font (cover) by Tup Wanders used under a Creative Commons license by attribution.

Langdon Font (cover) provided freely by XLN Telecom.

My Underwood Font (telegrams) used with permission. Copyright © 2009 by Tension Type. All rights reserved.

. . .

Episcopalian burial rites recited in Chapter 4 are from "The Order for The Burial of the Dead." Excerpted from The Book of Common Prayer. The Church Pension Fund. New York. 1928.

Bedside reading in Chapter 12 is from The Thousand and One Nights, Or The Arabian Nights' Entertainments. Published by Phillips, Sampson, and Company of Boston. 1858. Text excerpted from pages 408-9.

More Information

Be the first to know about new releases:

frankwbutterfield.com